UNFORGIVEN

BRIDGET E. BAKER

For Emmy
Because villains aren't always bad
and heroes aren't always good
and you see the good in everyone
and you're more full of good than anyone
stay that way forever and ever
my little heart.

THE PRESENT

I've never believed in God. Mother mentioned that my father bought into all that nonsense, but I've always been far too practical. On top of that, the Bible is a human record, which means it isn't very reliable. Which is why, when I slam the door to my room shut and one book falls off the edge of my bookcase, I don't read anything into the fact that it's the Bible. It could just as easily have been *The Art of War*, the *Quran,* or *Quantum Physics.*

I stoop to pick it up so I can slide it back into the empty slot, but my hand freezes over the page. It's open to Genesis chapter 25, which is nowhere near the middle of the book where I'd expect it to fall open.

31. And Jacob said, Sell me this day thy birthright.

32. And Esau said, Behold I am at the point to die; and what profit shall this birthright do to me?

33. And Jacob said, Swear to me this day; and he sware unto him: and he sold his birthright unto Jacob.

34. Then Jacob gave Esau bread and pottage of lentils; and he did eat and drink, and rose up and went his way. Thus Esau despised his birthright.

A chill runs up my spine. I've read the entire Bible as part of my human studies coursework. This isn't a new passage to me. Jacob and Esau aren't even the only twins in the Bible. But in their tradition, Esau had the birthright, which meant he'd inherit all his father had as the older twin.

And he sold it to Jacob for a bowl of mush.

I don't pick up the book. I walk across the room to my bed instead, sinking down into the covers with a stifled cry of anguish, one hand clutching the figure eight necklace hiding under my tattered shirt.

My mother is dead. I fought my twin and lost, and what's worse, all of Alamecha witnessed my failure. First they saw me snatch victory from the jaws of defeat, and then they saw me hand it right back to her.

Why did I do it?

Why did Esau do it? He couldn't have needed a bowl of stew that badly. There has to be more to the story. But that line at the end is strange. I don't recall paying any attention to it before. Esau *despised* his birthright. What does that mean? I close my eyes and try to recall my human studies class.

In Ancient Near East tradition, all sons received a birthright, a share of the father's wealth, but the oldest received a double share, or something like that. בָּזָה in Hebrew means to regard lightly I believe. My tutor told me it meant that he cared more about his physical well-being in the moment than for the spiritual blessings the birthright from God would promise him.

But now I wonder whether perhaps he hated the idea of being the head of the household. Did he realize he would agonize over every single decision, rationing the seconds of every single day like a miser, eaten alive constantly by the stress of perfection? Perhaps forgoing his birthright for that bowl of stew felt inevitable to him, if he hated it so much.

Was relinquishing his birthright the best thing Esau ever did?

If so, maybe humans and evians aren't as different as I've always been taught. Because my hands begin to shake, and for the first time in my life, I take a breath, a deep, unconcerned breath. I don't care whether my heart races, or my expression wobbles, or my enemies are hatching plots based on the information they gained from the wobbles and the racing.

I'm still Chancery's heir for a while, but ultimately she will move along, and the burden of Alamecha will shift off of me.

My life will be my own.

For the first time in eighteen years, I have no idea what I'll be doing ten years from now, or even six months from now. I flop back on my bed and close my eyes. What is it Chancy's always doing? Listening to music or watching stupid stories play out about fake people on a television screen? Reading even more insipid tales about the lives of humans? Pah.

I can't waste my time like that.

A tap at my door rescues me from tipping head first into a black hole. I sit up and brush off my blood-stained pants. I really should have spent the past few minutes showering instead of lying on my formerly clean bed. At least my covers are black and unlikely to show blood stains.

"Come in."

The door cracks and Roman's head peeks around the corner. His tawny golden eyes assess the room like he's looking for a bomb or a landmine. I suppose dealing with me may have scarred him permanently.

I flop back on my bed with a groan. "What do you want?"

"Just making sure you're alive." He grins, his big white teeth bright against the dark brown skin of his face, and the mahogany bristle of his beard.

I flinch. "I'm alive. Now leave."

Roman walks inside anyway and closes the door.

I bolt upright, my shoulders too stiff. I force them to relax. "You still have to obey my commands. I'm still Heir."

Roman grins. "Yes, Your Highness. Of course, Your Highness." He crosses the room and sits down next to me. "I thought you might want to hear the news."

"What news?" I arch one eyebrow.

"Your sister has left, no one was told where, and Edam has been made Prince Regent in her absence. He doesn't appear to be handling things very smoothly."

She still hasn't named him Consort, which is bizarre. What is she waiting for? Is it possible she's holding off to try and spare my feelings? If so, she's an even bigger idiot than I thought. "Is that all?"

"That's all."

"Then you can go."

"I think I'll stay for a while." He shifts on the bed so he can see my face while sitting next to me.

"I lost." I throw the words up like a shield. Back off, Roman. I'm not in the mood to deal with you right now.

"I saw."

"I know you saw," I practically growl at him. "What I want to know is what you're doing in here right now. I don't want to talk to anyone. Was I unclear on that?"

"Sometimes what you want and what you need aren't the same," he says.

I roll my eyes. "Thanks, Gandhi. Appreciate you dropping pearls of wisdom, but I don't need or want you in my room."

Roman puts an arm around my shoulders and pulls me against his chest. I consider stabbing him with the knife I keep on my bedside table. Or a good jab to his solar plexus would remind him that I'm still his commander, even now, even after I lost to my pathetic sister. But I don't do either of those. Instead, it's like the inside of my chest splinters and I collapse against him, sobbing.

How much must he hate me, to force me to cry on his beautifully sculpted chest? Am I to have no shreds of pride left intact? No matter how much I want to pull away, I can't. Not for a long time. My tears mix with the dried blood on my face, my neck, and my shirt, and stain the collar of his polo. The sight of fat, red drops of bloody tears splattering against the fabric of his shirt pulls me out of my temporary despair. I fist my hands in the fabric covering his chest and drag in deep breaths.

I finally stop crying and wipe my face on my own shoulder.

"I'm sorry about that," I say.

Roman's face closes off. "I protect and serve, now and always."

He has always been my most devoted guard. I shouldn't be so hard on him. "I know today was embarrassing for you," I say. "I'm sorry for that, and for breaking down in front of you just now."

Roman leaps to his feet. "You were real out there, Judica, for three seconds. You let your guard down. You looked at Chancery like a person, you eased up. I thought maybe—"

I was real? I want to shred something. "I *eased up?*"

"Yes, you could have killed her, more than once, but you didn't. You let her win out there. I thought. . ." Roman spins around and stares at the wall, hands clenched, back muscles straining.

"You thought I had, what? Completely changed in every single way?" I stand up. "And that made you hopeful. Does everyone despise me that much?" But I want to ask whether he despises me that much. I know Edam does, but Roman has been my closest friend for a decade. If he hates me, too, I don't know what that even means.

"You know I don't despise you," Roman says. But he doesn't turn around. He doesn't meet my eye.

"Are you disappointed?" I ask. "That you're head of the guard for the Heir, still?"

Roman flips around to face me so quickly that I stumble back, bumping into the bed and nearly sitting back down. "Nothing about you ever disappoints me. How can you not know that?"

I lift one eyebrow. "I know you support me. You always have, and I appreciate it. I don't tell you that often enough."

"You've literally never told me that."

I lift my chin. "Well, I'm telling you now. Thank you for always being there for me."

"I don't want to be here as your guard." Roman makes a choking sound.

My heart skips a beat. "You're quitting? Why? Because I lost?" He just said he'll always support me.

He shakes his head, his jaw working. "You're probably the most gifted strategist I've ever met. Half the time I don't even understand what you're saying until I've spent some time analyzing it. You're three steps ahead of everyone else, and you show no mercy. How can you be so obtuse about this?"

"About what?"

"I'm in love with you, Judica. I've loved you for years

and years. I'm not quitting. I'll never quit, but it's time you know, because I'm sick of watching you flirting with Edam, or Havel, or Xander or anyone else."

I knew Roman wanted to be my Consort. I knew he wanted to rule. Of course he did. They all do. I even knew he respected me, and he's always been unfailingly loyal. But no one loves me, not really. I'm cruel, merciless, and intense. Edam fled the second he saw an opening.

I don't even blame him.

No one wants to kiss a copperhead. No one dreams of snuggling up next to a tiger.

"You have nothing to say?" Roman asks.

I open my mouth, but no words come out.

"I expected that, but it still hurts more than I thought it would." He swallows and nods at me. "Well, don't let me keep you any longer, Your Highness. I'll be outside if you need anything."

I walk to my bathroom like a robot after he closes the door. I toss my bloody rags into a pile and shower all the blood and gore away, watching the red water circle the drain and then disappear. I wish sometimes that my doubt, my anger, and my sorrow could be washed away so easily.

Every time I close my eyes, Roman's face swims in front of mine. His golden eyes sad, his heart in his face, plain to read.

I'm lying to myself. I've known Roman was in love with me for a very long time. And maybe for a while I thought. . . Maybe. . . But he's never been a real option. Not for me.

Because I'm a better strategist. I'm a better fighter. I destroy him in linguistics. He doesn't bring enough to the table to be my Consort, and he never will. Thinking about it makes it hard to breathe, but it doesn't change the facts, not in the slightest.

I wipe away another round of unwelcome tears and

dress quickly. I can't cower in my room. I'm not sure what I should be doing, but something. Anything but hiding.

A tap at the door sends my heart hammering up to my throat. I breathe in and out once, then twice. I can't let him know that his declaration had any impact on me at all. Once I'm in control again, I say, "Come in."

When Angel steps through the doorway with a tray, I'm strangely deflated. I didn't want to see Roman. I can never be with him, and now that he said what he said, well, some space is a good idea. Even so, I'm not so deluded I can't admit to myself that I'm disappointed.

I wanted to see him again. I want to see him all the time.

"I'm assuming you're starving, Your Highness," Angel says.

She doesn't typically bring food herself. "You're a delivery girl now?"

Angel ducks her head. "I wanted to make sure you're okay. After today, but really, after the last week and a half."

Things have been strange between Angel and me since her release, but I had to know whether she killed Mother. I doubt she'll ever forgive me for my threats or how hard I pressed, but she understands. If anyone understands, it's her. I don't regret any of it, though. I never regret the awful things I do to protect the family. Alamecha is what really matters, and it's more than one person.

"I'm fine," I say.

"You need to eat. With all that regeneration your body has done, you must be famished."

I can't quite stop myself from frowning. She's basically shoving my face in how many hits Chancery landed on me, but I think she means well. And the smell coming from the tray is heavenly. Angel was chef for the most powerful person on earth for centuries for a reason. The lady can cook.

"Tikka masala, naan, watermelon, and a brown butter raspberry tart," I say. "All my favorite foods. What did I do to deserve this?"

Angel sets the tray down on my desk. "You've been dear to me since you were born." Her eyes soften. "And your mother." She shakes her head. "I wanted to show you that I harbor no ill feelings toward you for suspecting me, but I would never have harmed a hair on your mother's head. I've lived to serve Alamecha my entire life, and your mother was the embodiment of the family. You're her miniature, you know."

I do. "Thank you."

"She would be very proud of your actions today, and those of Chancery. She loved you both, and you made a hard decision, but I believe it was the right one."

My nostrils flare, but I manage to hold my heart rate steady and show no other expression on my face. "I appreciate your support." Now get out of my room.

When she leaves, I don't slam the door. I'm actually relieved to have successfully navigated the first of the gloating well wishers. She won't be the last. Chancery really might be more diabolical than I give her credit for. She's punished me far more effectively with this 'spare my life' nonsense than killing me ever would have.

I sink into my desk chair and breathe in the aromas I love most. I remember the first time Mother served tikka masala, warm and savory, with a tangy aftertaste of yogurt. I absolutely will not cry twice in one day. I shovel in a large bite of food to stave off the crying jag threatening to rip through me. The flavors burst over my tongue, triggering memories of dinner with Mother I didn't even realize I'd been blocking.

I'm still furious that she left me.

I inhale the food until all that's left is the brown butter tart. The crust is a combination of chewy and crunchy that I've tried several times to recreate without success. It's still warm enough that when I dump the vanilla gelato over the top, it begins to melt. The combination is so amazing that I don't taste the difference until my last bite.

There's a faintly metallic aftertaste.

I try to leap to my feet, but my body isn't working right. My arms feel heavy, so heavy. My eyes won't focus. "Roman," I try to yell. The word emerges as more of a croak than a shout. I wrap thick fingers around the edge of the table and force myself upright.

But then my traitorous knees buckle, and I collapse on the floor. My eyes won't focus on anything, and all I can see is the tufts of my rug. I wonder if the floor in front of her is the last thing Mother saw, too. A pang of fear for Chancery surprises me, but if someone has taken out both Mother and me, she's next.

As the world goes black, I think of Mother's face. Wherever we go after we die, I hope Mother's there, waiting for me. I close my dry, achy eyes, ready to find out.

✺ 2 ✺

THE PAST

"You smell something fruity when there's no fruit in the food you're eating," Mother says.

"It could be one of twelve poisons," I say. "Nitriles, isopropyl alcohol, ketoacidosis, lacquer, ethanol, isopropanol, chloroform, trichloroethane, paraldehyde, chloral hydrate, methyl bromide, or nitrites."

"A musty smell, like fish or raw liver."

"That could be zinc phosphide, aluminum phosphide, or nickel carbonyl, and those are worse because they're stronger."

"The smell of mint," she says.

"Menthol, if it's too strong, or methyl salicylate."

"Hay."

"Easy. That's phosgene."

"Pepper," she says.

"Tear gas, but that's so strong I wouldn't eat it." I laugh.

"Rotten eggs," she says.

"Hydrogen sulfide, carbon disulfide, mercaptans, or disulfiram."

"You missed N-acetylcysteine," she says.

"That's an antidote," I say.

"An antidote that smells like rotten eggs."

"Why would anyone put an antidote in my food?" I ask.

Mother smiles. "You're learning." She moves her piece on the board.

I move mine, and she cringes. "Uh oh."

"What did you do wrong?" Mother asks me.

I squint at the pieces on the black and white marble chess board in front of me. "I didn't use my bishops."

"And you sacrificed your queen for a pawn." Mother frowns. "You know the basic pawn level structures, and you've memorized the maneuvering techniques, but that's not enough. You need to think about what I'm aiming for and how I'll attack, even if you're being distracted. Maybe especially when you're distracted." Mother points at the board. "See how I pinned you here and here? Knights are the best forks. You know that already, so act on it and play some defense."

I duck my head. "Sorry."

"Don't be sorry," Mother says. "Do better. Failure is a choice, Judica, and it's not a choice I accept from you."

"Yes, Mother."

"It's also a choice that could prove fatal."

"I know, Mother. Thank you."

A door creaks behind us and I glance up. Mother's best friend Lyssa hovers in the doorway, her face uncharacteristically solemn. Mother stands up and points at the board. "Set this up for another round. I'll be right back to play again."

I start to shift the pieces into their proper places, but accidentally knock one to the floor. I lean over to pick it up and notice that Mother dropped her notebook. She might need it. I snatch it up and pelt across the floor to where she ducked out of the room to talk. The faint rumble of voices just around the corner stops me in my tracks.

Because Lyssa says my name.

"Judica was trying awfully hard to pay attention to that chess game, and you were grilling her at the same time. You're being too hard on her. She's only five years old."

Mother scoffs. "You're acting like she's human. Only five." She snorts. "She should be doing what? Playing with blocks? Please."

"Lark's a year older, but if I corrected her that sternly, she'd be in tears."

"Judica is nothing like Lark, and your daughter won't be running the entire family the second I die. I don't like to say this, but that could be any time. I'm not young anymore." Mother clucks. "Now what do you need? I'm sure you didn't interrupt our training to chide me on my parenting techniques."

"I know raising the Heir to Alamecha is trying, stressful and difficult. I know you've raised sixteen before her admirably. I'm just saying, keep her age in mind when you tailor her lesson plans. She's not a robot. You've been drilling her every second of every day. Judica can recite basic chess strategy in her sleep. She speaks five languages regularly. She's versed in a dozen instruments, and she does an hour of combat, an hour of pain, and an hour of healing training every day. You might be pushing her a little too hard. A cracked Heir isn't any use to us."

"You of all people know why I push this hard."

"Eamon is dead. You need to stop atoning."

Mother's voice sounds angry. "I can't stop. Half of her DNA came from him, and he's *flawed*. I worry every day that Judica will turn out like her father. Melina did. And if she wasn't royal, that would be fine. But she is. The damage she can inflict with one mistake, I shudder to think—"

"Judica is wonderful," Lyssa says. "She's bright, devoted, hard-working, eager to please, and she already grasps what makes hard decisions necessary."

"Sometimes I wonder," Mother says.

"Wonder what?" Lyssa's voice drops to a whisper.

"Whether I was wrong."

A sharp inhalation. "In sparing Chancery's life?"

"Of course not. I've never regretted that decision, not for a moment."

"Then what?" Lyssa asks.

"I chose Judica as Heir the day they were born. I could have picked either twin according to the terms of the Charter, and I chose her. What if I picked the wrong infant?"

"If you'd killed Chancery, you wouldn't be agonizing over this."

"If I'd killed her, I'd probably have taken my own life by now. No, I did what I had to do, and I refuse to question that. But I wonder sometimes."

"Whether Chancy should replace Judica?"

"I don't know. I wish everything didn't hang on this choice. But that's why I push Judica. I have another option, a good option. Chancery would hate ruling, with every fiber of her being, but she would be exceptional. Charitable in ways I'm not, empathetic in ways I've never been. Sometimes I think—"

"Your sister would have destroyed Alamecha, and you know it."

"Chancery reminds me so much of Alornis."

"But she didn't rule. You did, and she couldn't have done what you have. She couldn't have brought Alamecha this far, ushered in the growth, the prosperity, the peace we have enjoyed."

Mother sighs. "I guess we'll never know."

"I know. You were the right choice, and you've made

the right decision."

"But how much better would Alornis have done in my place?" Mother clears her throat. "This line of conversation is going nowhere."

"Judica isn't Eamon, you know," Lyssa says.

"She never even knew him," Mother says. "But sometimes I see flashes of him looking back at me. The severity of her ideals, the refusal to go for the kill."

"You're wrong. That's your paranoia taking hold. Judica is her mother's daughter through and through. Alamecha is in good hands, I promise you."

"Well, I'm not entirely sure, but I have time yet to rectify my mistake, if it was a mistake. Enough about all that. Tell me why you interrupted in the first place."

"It's not critical, just time sensitive. Recall the petition from Shenoah regarding the alliance in. . ."

I creep away, notebook still clutched in my hand. It doesn't sound like Mother needs it. I've barely reached my table again when Mother comes striding through the doorway.

"Why haven't you finished yet?" she asks, one eyebrow raised.

"I, uh, well." I swallow. I don't have a good reason, and eavesdropping won't make her happy, that's for sure.

"Do it now." Mother purses her lips. "And pay more attention this time so I have to work harder to defeat you."

I scramble to set up the board, and then I focus on the positions as well as I can. Mother still defeats me in less than twenty moves, but this time my lower lip doesn't wobble, and I'm quick to point out what I did wrong. I may not be a chess champion yet, but I'll get there. And I'll show Mother that I'm nothing like my lousy father. I'm strong, and I can be the perfect leader Alamecha needs, just like she is.

THE PRESENT

I'm not dead. I know this because something metal is digging into my hip. Probably a bolt. My hands and feet are bound behind me with reinforced handcuffs. I don't know if there's life after death, but if there is, I'm sure I'll be in more pain than this.

Also, I doubt hell smells like hot dogs and body odor, and I'm practically positive heaven doesn't. Death loves hot dogs. I hope he's alright. They wouldn't have killed him, right? I breathe in and out once, then twice to calm down. There's nothing I can do about Death from inside this vehicle.

I run a critical assessment, like I've been training to do my entire life. My face is covered with a thick blindfold that's tied uncomfortably tight. I'm lying on my side in some kind of vehicle, probably the back of a sound-insulated van, based on the bumpy suspension and lack of wind. I've always had a resistance to tranquilizers of all kinds, and whoever took me clearly doesn't know or I wouldn't be awake right now. That rules out Balthasar and anyone who has worked with him, as well as Inara, Edam, and most of my guards.

The air around me is drier than home, so I'm not in Hawaii anymore. I slide my head against the floor of the vehicle until my blindfold catches slightly on something that's helpfully protruding from the floor. It takes a dozen tries, but eventually I use the small metal protrusion to shift the blindfold up enough that I can see. I'm definitely in the back of a cargo van, but it's almost as dark without the blindfold blocking my face. There's no carpet, and I'm lying on a bare metal subfloor. The helpful sharp object is, as expected, an exposed bolt. The back of the van's empty, other than me.

They'll regret leaving me alone back here, whoever they are.

I think back to my last moments. Angel brought me my food. She could be angry that I held her for so long, or for the threats I made. If she's harboring a grudge, now that I've fallen, she may have decided it's time for revenge. Maybe Chancery even sanctioned her action. I think about my sister. Could she have agreed to a petition from Angel, approving my quiet exile, or even worse, death?

I consider Chancery. She wears her heart on her sleeve for all to see. She acts on emotion, never doing the rational thing. But she's always forthright. I've never known her to deceive anyone or anything. When she disagrees with Mother, she tells her, no matter who is around. When she is upset with me, she tells me.

An image of Chancery, extending the blade she's holding out to me, eyes wide, rises to my mind. She offered me her life, when she had the power to take mine. She offered me the win I wanted, and all I had to do was slay her. She wouldn't allow anyone to cart me off, secretly or otherwise.

In fact, now that I've considered that angle, I worry about her. Someone in her court had me poisoned and removed. That person is surely a threat to Chancery, too. I would suspect Edam, who might like things far better if I disappeared, but he knows tranquilizers wear off on me quickly. He'd have whoever took me dosing me more frequently.

The other strong option is a rival family. Surely they all saw me as a much more terrifying threat. Chancery's ascension would pave the way for them to erode Alamecha's power. But if I'm still there, hovering over her, I'm a constant risk. As long as I'm Heir, I can always seize the crown again. If one of them is feeling particularly ambitious, she could remove me to gain favor from Chancery, or to prevent me from taking control again.

The fastest way to discover who took me is to regain the upper hand. If I'm ready to take them out when they open the doors to the van, I can reverse the roles and I'll be the one asking questions.

I strain against my bindings, but they don't give a hair, meaning they're a titanium composite of some kind. Whoever took me knows what it takes to knock out a royal evian. They'll probably also be on the lookout for any signs of movement from the front of the van. Which means if I utilize brute force to escape these cuffs, they'll hear it.

Torque it is.

I pivot my hands behind my back so that they're facing opposite directions and pull as hard as I can, shattering my first metacarpal on my right hand. The fire of a broken bone shoots up my arm, but compared to blades slicing open my skin, it's nothing. I don't make a sound. I slide my broken hand through the cuff before it has time to heal.

When I check my navel, I can't suppress my grin. The idiots didn't conduct a thorough check for piercings, clearly. I've kept a sterling silver bar in my navel for years, just in case I need a shim. I slide it out, the piercing healing up immediately, and use the shim to unlock the cuffs and release my left hand.

I pull up to a seated position slowly, quietly, and hope that the sound of my shifting is covered by the jouncing and bouncing of the vehicle. I use the same shim to free my feet, holding the cuffs on my feet carefully so they don't clatter against the floor of the van. I shove the shim back into the skin of my navel, forcing the skin to heal unnaturally around it so it will stay in place.

Then I crouch on the floor of the van, searching wildly for anything I could use as a weapon. Unfortunately, they did a good job cleaning out the back. Aside from prying bolts off with my teeth, and I'm not sure how that would help me, I can't find a single thing. But when they open the back door, I'll be ready for them. My hands aren't as comforting as my sword, but if they're expecting me bound and gagged, they'll be in for a shock.

I search for peace and calm, serenity. I need to be prepared for whoever comes. But my mind whirs and spins like the inside of a clock. Is Angel working alone, or for someone else? Is my kidnapping connected with Mother's murder? If so, did I uncover something and fail to grasp its significance? Could this be one step in a multi-pronged attack? Maybe Chancery has been poisoned or is under attack back home right now. The thought wrenches my stomach.

Because there's nothing at all I can do from here.

I didn't realize until this very moment that I would stand for my sister, against any or all attackers. If I could do it right now, I'd rip whoever wants her dead limb from limb. When did Mother get her wish? When did I decide to help Chancery?

Lot of good I'll do her here, crouched unarmed in the back of a van, headed for who knows where.

I need to know who took me. I run through it again. Who stands to gain if I die? It could be any of the five other families, with Malessa at the top of the list. She and Mother fought, and I attended quite a few uncomfortable meetings, but Chancery has a reputation for being forgiving. If I were Malessa, I'd suss out Chancery's plan before blindly attacking.

Or would I?

Maybe I'd take out her strongest defense, and then cut her legs out from under her. As much as I dislike him, it soothes me to know Edam's on her side. And I've seen how he looks at her. He's Chancery's to the core.

It could be someone who expects to be on Chancery's council, maybe even someone I'd advise against her choosing. Perhaps my removal was simply step one in a plan. Balthasar, if he thought Chancery might consult me over him. He doesn't seem very ambitious, but he's getting older. Perhaps with Edam's rise, he feels put out.

It could be Inara for many of the same reasons. She's next in line for the throne, once I fall, if she could eliminate Melina. I know perilously little about my reclusive, banished sister. I know she hated Chancery and fell out with Mother over our birth. But she's the main reason I don't suspect Inara. She'd be next in line, and by all counts, Melina would be hard to kill.

Now Alora, if she sees me as a wild card, could eliminate me out of a sense of protectiveness. For that matter, any of our older sisters could decide they'd like to become more involved in the day-to-day operations. Anyone with eyes or ears at the palace would know that Chancery and I have made peace and possibly worry that there won't be room for them to advise the new queen.

Or of course, there's always Melina herself. She's next in line, after me. She'd become the new Heir if I die. She hasn't expressed much interest in ruling, but she's still in the line of succession. I wish I knew a single thing about her. In spite of their arguments, Mother never said a bad word about Melina. She simply placed her lieutenant Marselle in Austin to watch my sister without ever seeming particularly concerned about the situation.

Why didn't Mother eliminate her? All those years she hovered, banished, but not removed. Cutting her out of the family entirely would have cleaned things up, I believe. I should have pressed for more details. How did I not see this as a gaping blind spot in my political knowledge during the last decade?

I trusted Mother entirely, but now that she's gone, I've been hit with wave after wave of ways in which she's let down both Chancery and me.

The van slows and adrenaline pumps through my body. My muscles tense and my breathing accelerates. I slow it with practiced focus. If their hearing is sensitive, I don't want them to know I'm awake. The van grinds to a halt, crunching over a gravel road.

I stand up slowly, arms spread, hands open, legs bent. I'm ready for whoever opens the back doors of the van.

Unfortunately, I'm not prepared for them to slide open a hidden partition between the front and the back. I didn't even realize it could open. The tranq dart thwacks into the back of my neck and I spin around just in time to see Angel's smiling face. "Look at this. The demon spawn of Alamecha, brought down by a horse tranquilizer. How delightful."

I slump to my knees and fall forward, and everything goes black again.

❦   4   ❧

THE PAST

I scowl at Balthasar. "I don't want to."

"I'm sorry," he says. "Because I've really failed you if you believe it matters what you *want* to do."

I just out my chin. "I'm your boss."

"But you're not your mother's boss, and she set me to this task. Now stop throwing a fit and do it."

I stare at the room full of coals and cringe. "They're too hot. Can't we wait until the flames go out, at least?"

Balthasar's hand reaches out and shoves me right between my shoulder blades, knocking me forward a foot and a half. I sprawl onto my hands and knees, the burning coals searing my flesh immediately. The flames lick at my shorts and I scramble to my feet, patting at the fire before it can consume my clothing again.

I scream when my blistered palms burn even worse from putting out the fire.

"Move," Balthasar barks. "You're making this so much worse than it needs to be. Work smarter and you mitigate the pain. That's the whole point."

I stumble across the coals toward the other side of the

room, the flames licking my calves and the heat rolling over the ruined soles of my feet and melting the skin on the tops. When I finally reach the far side of the burn box, I slide across the cool tile platform, slipping on the fat from my own body, and fall forward on my forearms. I'm too shaky and distracted to heal anything. I finally flop onto the cool floor, my face drinking in the contrast and my hands and feet shuddering involuntarily. I breathe in ragged breaths while I heal my muscle and skin, regrowing the hairs on my arms and legs last. Only then do I realize I didn't put out the fire on my tank top quickly enough because my stomach pulses. Burned too. The smell of my own flesh roasting nearly causes me to puke. Balthasar would never let me hear the end of that.

I groan. "I hate the fire."

"Which is exactly why we're working on burns this entire month." Balthasar walks across the coals as though they aren't even there. He crouches down in front of me, the bottoms of his feet smoking. "You're making things so much harder than they really are." He lifts my chin with two fingers. "When you're nine years old, everything seems unfair. But we are doing this for your own good, truly."

"I'm only *eight*," I correct him. "I don't turn nine until five o'clock today."

Balthasar smiles at me. "I was going to take it easy on you since it's your birthday, but if it's not your birthday yet. . ."

I jump up. "No, no, it is my birthday. It's my birthday all day long."

"Fine, fine. If you run back and forth three times in quick succession, I'll assign you to finish your training in the kitchen with Angel. I hear she's making a cake for you and Chancery. If you take everything out of the oven she needs removed today, without mitts of course, I'll count that as your healing training for the day, and we'll skip poison tolerance and detection entirely."

My shoulders droop. "I have to do the entire course three more times?"

"You need to head back to complete this circuit, obviously." Balthasar shrugs. "And then three more completions. But if you don't want to run, I could shove you again. And of course, a full training session would be more than twenty—"

I hop to my feet and race to the other side, the soles of my feet livid. I ignore them. I try thinking of anything but my feet, but they heal slower that way, so I go back to focusing on them. "No," I wheeze. "This is good. Thanks. Best birthday present ever."

I hate fire. I hate burns. I hate the smell of melting flesh.

But at least it's over quickly today. I fling my arms around Balthasar's neck when I'm done. "Thank you, thank you. Really, truly." I drop my voice to a whisper. "But could you do me one more favor?"

He taps my nose with a half grin on his face. "If you don't tell your mother, I won't either."

I nod vigorously. "I won't, I promise." I practically fly down the hall to my room, where I shower away the smell of charred flesh, and change into something nicer so I won't frighten the kitchen staff. I put on the white dress Mother gave me last week, my birthday dress she called it. I hate white, and I hate dresses, but I want Mother happy today. Because today's the day I'm going to ask her.

I really want to take a trip with her, without my twin.

She takes Chancery on trips all the time. She just took her to a UN meeting so Chancery could practice the languages she has learned. I want to show Mother that I speak Italian and German and French, and a little Russian, too. I want to impress her, and I really think I can.

I practically skip down the hall toward Mother's room, but then I hear a sound I hate. Chancery's giggle. I slow down and creep silently the last twenty steps to the doorway. The door is hanging open a few inches. It's enough for me to see them. Mother's braiding Chancery's hair in a circle around her head like a crown. Chancery yelps when Mother pulls too hard and Mother rolls her eyes.

"Stop being such a baby. You're nine years old today. It's time to toughen up."

My chest tightens at the thought. She's complaining about her hair being pulled. I spent the morning being burned alive.

Life isn't fair.

Mother reminds me of that a lot. I shouldn't expect the world to be something it isn't. Even so, I can't bring myself to barge into Chancery's room and ask Mother to take me on a trip, especially not in front of her. I'll sound like a sulky child. I'll sound like Chancery, and that's one thing I will never, ever do. I race past the doorway and on toward the kitchen.

Angel's eyes widen when I push through the door, nearly knocking her over in my haste. "Uh, sorry," I mumble.

"Happy birthday, child," she says, grinning at me.

"Thanks," I say. "Balthasar told me to report here. He says I've got to take everything out of the oven, no mitts."

Angel bobs her head knowingly. "Better than racing back and forth over the coals."

I nod vigorously. "Way better."

"Your sister Melina hated fire too, you know."

I shake my head. No one ever mentions her to me. I'm afraid if I say anything, Angel will stop talking.

"She was tough, like you." Angel sniffs the air like a dog and I miss Destruction, my Great Dane. I left him in my room so he wouldn't freak out during pain training. "Do you smell that?"

I shrug.

"The cakes are ready."

I don't groan, and I don't whine. I walk over to the oven and open it. I take each of the cake pans out, one at a time, and place them on the stone counter. They burn my fingers, but I'm careful and methodical and it only burns my fingertips. It's so much better than open flame and coals that I can almost pretend I'm just here to have fun.

"What else should we make?" Angel asks. "Because it's not much of a party if all we have to celebrate is cake."

"I've always loved frosted sugar cookies," I say.

"Which ones?" Angel's eyes sparkle.

"The thick ones, with the sprinkles."

Angel beams at me. "Good girl. Why don't you help me, and I'll give you a whole plate to take to your room."

My mother's chef is one of the most patient people on Ni'ihau. She doesn't complain when I add too much baking powder, and she lets me lick my fingers. My eyebrows rise. "My own plate?"

"We can even double the batch and you can eat some of the dough."

My jaw drops.

Angel laughs. "Birthdays should be the best day of the year." She doesn't even shout a while later when I leave one pan in for too long. "They're perfect for dipping."

We're having so much fun that she spends a little too long working on cookies.

"What's that smell?" she asks Gabriela. "Why don't I smell the prosciutto? Did you forget it? Because Beef Wellington without prosciutto is disgusting."

Angel must have been taking it easy on me, because she rips into Gabriela, chewing her out a mile a minute. Her sous chef, Frances, comes over to help me with frosting the last batch. "You're doing great," he tells me. "Can you finish the last two dozen yourself?"

"Oh sure," I say. But an idea takes shape in my mind. Mother never has time for me, because she's always with Chancery. If I ever want to have a few hours to myself, a window to ask Mother for the trip I want, I'll need something to incapacitate my twin. I've heard that humans sometimes don't feel good and lay in their beds for days on end. They call it 'getting sick.'

Evians never get sick, but maybe there's another way.

"I'll take these back to my room," I say. "Angel said I can have some for me, and I can frost them there. Is that okay?"

Frances waves me off. I take a plate of unfrosted cookies in one hand, tuck a container of sprinkles in my pocket, and then squeeze a bowl of frosting under my other arm before I dash out the door.

A big, waxy-leafed oleander bush grows just outside my window. I have perfect recall, which is how I know the exact number of times Mother has warned me that it's toxic. Eleven. With all those warnings, it's interesting that she only mentioned the seed pods are flavorless once.

But of course, one time is all it takes.

I look around the yard outside to make sure no one's watching before snatching a long, skinny seed pod. I press it until the sides split and collect the tiny popcorn kernel shaped seeds that burst free. Before I think about it too long and change my mind, I ignore every single one of those eleven warnings.

I swallow one.

And then I wait.

It takes way, way longer than walking on burning coals, but eventually my stomach begins to cramp. Then my heart rate accelerates, and my vision blurs a little. A pounding like a hammer on a nail starts inside my skull, and I focus on each symptom in turn, starting with my stomach, repairing the lining and pushing the poisonous little seed along through my system.

I rush to the bathroom, and by the time I'm done, I feel better.

Which means this is going to work perfectly. I suppress a pang of guilt when I crush four dozen seeds into pulp and then mix them into the frosting. It's not as if this could kill Chancery. I already tested it. It will just make her feel what a human would call sick. I endure far worse every day as part of my training. So really, I'm helping her. And I'll finally have a little time to myself while she writhes on her bed or huddles on top of a toilet bowl. All will finally be right with the world.

I eye the cookies critically. The frosting's a little lumpy, maybe, but once I add sprinkles, Chancery will never notice. Once the frosting has set, I pile a dozen up on a plate. Then I wonder how many she might eat all at once. What if she gobbles them all? Could she actually die? I take off all but six. Six shouldn't kill her, I'm pretty sure, and they're pretty, arranged like a flower with five petals.

"What do you think?" I ask Destruction. He barks at me, as if giving me his seal of approval. "I agree. It looks perfect."

But what if it's not? After a few minutes agonizing over the presentation, I replace two cookies with regular ones. What if Chancery's greedy and starving and bolts all six at once? I don't want to be responsible for killing my own sister. Mother would never, ever forgive me, and I would miss her too. A little. She is kind of funny, with her melodramatic squawking and little compassion projects. Who knows? If I had as much time as she does, I might try to save sickly animals and doomed humans too. Probably not, but maybe.

I open the door and listen carefully for any sound that might clue me in to Chancery's whereabouts. I'm listening so intently for my twin that I don't even notice someone is leaning against the wall behind me until I notice a conspicuously close heartbeat. I whirl around.

Roman grins at me. "Careful or you might drop those." He reaches for the plate. "You made cookies? I want one. They look awesome."

I snatch the plate inward, toward my chest. "These aren't for you."

His eyebrows rise. "Uh, okay. Who are they for?"

I square my shoulders. "They're for Chancery. It's her birthday."

"You made her a treat?" The incredulity in his voice bothers me. If no one believes me capable of making her something nice, they'll immediately realize she's sick because of me.

"I always make her something," I say.

"Like what?"

"Well, last year I made her. . . cry."

Roman laughs. "She's such a baby."

I haven't ever given her anything before. People are going to figure this out. Maybe it's a terrible idea. I should ask Roman for some help instead. He could distract Chancery so I can get Mother alone, and then I can ask her—

The bark of Chancery's horribly trained mutt distracts me. I spin around to face my twin, my ill-conceived gift still in hand, Destruction sitting on his haunches behind me.

"Happy birthday, Chancery," Roman says. "Judica made you a present."

I turn sideways to glare at him.

"Like she always does," he says, nodding his head.

He's such an idiot.

"Uh, yeah," I say. "Angel helped me. I made cookies. I thought you might like some."

Mother's only two steps behind Chancery, as always. "Judica, what a thoughtful thing to do. I am so proud of you."

Chancery's eyes light up. "You did? That's so nice!"

A pang of horrible guilt clutches at my stomach. It hurts more than the stupid seed did. "Oh." I trip over my own foot when I step toward her, nearly dropping my plate. I wish I'd actually thought to do that, although then her stupid dog would probably eat them and croak. Oh man, I'm lucky she's not in the line of succession, so her dumb dog doesn't test her food. I have no idea what the seeds might do to him. But no one feeds frosting to dogs, anyway. Right?

"Actually," Chancery says, "I got you something too. While we were in New York at the general assembly meeting." She reaches into her pocket and pulls out a tiny blue box. "When I saw it, I thought about us." She blushes. "Well, our birthday, anyway. And you know, I just thought you'd like it. Maybe it's kind of stupid."

She got me a gift? From New York? Without knowing I'd give her anything? I want to sink into the ground and never come back up.

Chancery takes my plate and sets the box on my hand. Her grin is so large, I can practically see her back molars. I want to rewind the last two hours and not have this stupid idea in the first place, but now I'm not sure what to do about it. I can't admit I tried to poison her, or it'll be even worse than a stomach ache.

"Open it," she says.

"Uh, okay. Sure." I flip up the lid on the box, and there's a necklace inside in the shape of the number eight.

"Do you like it?" She's bouncing a little on the ends of her toes, just exactly like her terribly behaved dog, Fruity Pebbles.

"Um, I'm not sure I understand it. We're turning nine, but it's a number eight?"

Chancery's laugh sounds like water bubbling from the ground in a freshwater spring, or the sound of tinkling wind chimes, or a nightingale's trill. They're all different sounds, but her laugh distills the essential element in each. It's somehow fresh and innocent and delightful at once. She may be obnoxious and demanding, but I only hate her laugh because it never fails to make Mother beam. I avert my eyes so I don't have to see it.

"No silly," Chancery says. "It's not the number eight. That's the symbol for infinity."

Right. Of course it is. Now I look idiotic. "Of course."

"You still don't get it." She touches the side of my hand. "We're sisters forever, you and me. More than sisters. We're best friends forever. From Mom's belly to the grave, you and I are the same, right down to our DNA. I got one for myself, too." She pulls a chain out from under the collar of her dress. "See?"

I open my mouth, but words don't come out. I snap it shut again.

"Plus," she natters on, "the letters of our first name look like the necklace, kind of. The J hooks this way, and the C this way." She waves her hands in the air. "Like the two sides of the infinity symbol, if you hook them in the middle. See how the chain pulls at the end of the symbol, like the letters of our name have been hooked together into one design?"

I swallow. I need to get away from her right now, or I'm going to tell her not to eat the cookies, and then I'll have to tell her why. "Cool. Well, thanks. I better get ready. I've still got combat training and it starts soon."

"Of course," Chancery says. "Thank you so much for the cookies. Now I feel really bad that I didn't make you something more personal. I'm so sorry. There's always next year."

"Right," I say. "Always next year."

I practically sprint down the hall to where Balthasar's waiting to slice me into ribbons. This time, I don't avoid his blade.

After a few miserable minutes, he yanks back and straightens from his crouch. "What's going on with you?"

"What do you mean?" I ask.

"You're not even trying. I'm carving you like a roast chicken. This isn't pain or healing training, so what's going on?"

I shrug. "I don't know what you mean."

Balthasar frowns. "Get your head in the game."

This time, when his broadsword swings for me, I meet it with a double handed grip and gritted teeth. The impact travels up my arm, but I deflect his attack. I stop thinking and focus on the fight. Nothing matters here, in this ring. Not trips, or necklaces, or Mother or the throne or my duty.

A loud boom startles me out of my combat fury and I stumble. Balthasar turns toward the sound and I follow his gaze. Mother must have burst through the double doors so quickly that they flew into the walls behind them. Her eyes are blazing when they meet mine.

Oh no, did I miscalculate? Did I kill her? I can't hide

the fear in my eyes, so I drop them to my feet. "Is everything okay, Mother?"

"I recently searched your room." Her voice is melancholic.

"Okay." My hands tremble more than they did when I was healing the burns this morning. What if I killed her? What will Mom do?

"I found eight more cookies on your countertop. The frosting on two of them was laced with the same oleander seeds in the *gift* you made Chancery. Were you planning to poison anyone else? Or *just* your sister?"

I clear my throat. "Is she—"

"No. You didn't kill her, thankfully. Only her dog."

I open my mouth to tell Mother that I didn't mean to kill Chancery or her dog. I open my mouth to apologize. But if I apologize, that means I made a mistake. That means my plan didn't work as I intended. It means I'm not perfect. And that would be worse than being vicious, or angry, or jealous. It would mean I'm weak. Like my father. Admitting his fault and apologizing is something Eamon would have done.

I force the tension from my shoulders. I can't apologize. I can't make this right, and I have to live with that knowledge forever. I think about Destruction dying and close my eyes, but Mother can't know I'm hurting. Mother can't know my plans went awry. What would I say if I wanted to kill Chancery, but failed? What would I say if I tried to do what Mother thinks I did?

For a split second, I consider what Chancery would do in my place. She'd run past Mother, ignoring her vexation, and chase me down. She'd fall at my feet and apologize. She'd probably confess that she was jealous and wanted time with Mother on her own. Then she'd beg for my forgiveness with a few tears to season the entire thing. If I did that, we could be friends. But Mother would remove me as Heir.

And Mother loves Chancery, not me. Mother spends her time voluntarily with Chancery, not me. So I wouldn't be Heir anymore, and I wouldn't be beloved, either. I'd be caught with nothing. A cheap facsimile of my twin, not inherently sweet, not strong enough to deal with the realities of the throne.

Mother would have no use for me at all.

So I say what I must. I killed my sister's dog, which is sickening, unforgivable, but my sister is still alive. "Well, there's always next time." I choke down the disgust I feel. I bury the regret. Instead I focus on my frustration, my resentment, my jealousy. I fan it until my eyes spark and my fingers tingle. "I guess there's some sport in that, right?"

Mother crouches down in front of me. "No, Judica, this isn't a game. There can't be a next time. You must promise me that. You must never try to kill your sister again."

I try not to, but the frown shoves its way through, pulling the corners of my lips downward. "What if she betrays me? What if she's a threat to me? To you? To Alamecha? What then?"

Mother shakes her head. "You mustn't ever kill your sister. She would never betray you, or me, or Alamecha. Never. Do you hear me?"

I nod, tightly, not having to try quite so hard to expand my resentment. "I hear you." I sound practically sullen.

"You don't need to fret over this. I'm drawing up paperwork today that will name you as Heir, formally. Chancery isn't a threat to you. You know that, right?"

I should be reassured. Mother clearly wants me to feel better about things. She's worried and wants to protect darling, perfect, contrite Chancery. But I'm smart enough to know that if Mother can draw up paperwork naming me, she can also change that paperwork. Which means it's completely worthless. Pointing that out is probably equally useless. "Yes, Mother. I believe you."

She pats my head. "Good girl. I don't expect you to do anything about this, because I don't think anything you do or say would be well received, but your sister is very upset right now."

She loved that stupid dog. I liked Pebbles too. He always licked my hand and bumped my leg so I would scratch him behind his ears. I didn't mean for him to die, but she thinks I meant to kill her, my own sister. "I know." My lower lip wobbles.

Mother's mouth tenses. "The thing is." She clears her throat.

"You want me to apologize to her."

Mother nods. "That might help, but we might need to wait and do that tomorrow."

"What am I supposed to do at our party tonight?" I ask. "Ignore her?"

"That's the thing," Mother says. "She doesn't want you there."

I open my mouth, but I have no idea what to say. She's right. I tried to force Mother to spend time with me, cutting Chancery out. It's fitting that I should miss this celebration, lose out on even more time with Mother for my selfishness. Not that it fixes anything, but I get it.

"I told her you should be allowed at your own party," Mother says. "Of course. But I think I have a solution that will work out better for everyone. We'll host your party first. You can greet everyone, and spend some time with your friends."

Is she really so clueless she thinks I have friends? "Okay."

"And then after an hour and a half, you can return here,

to your room, and Chancery will come out. You can both enjoy the party, but we don't agitate her further," Mother says.

I hate the idea. Chancery gave me a necklace an hour ago to tell me she'll always be my best friend. I grab my shirt, feeling the metal underneath. But my options are to apologize and explain it was all a huge mistake, that I was simply greedy for time alone, or to let this stand.

In a bizarre way, I'm getting what I want. I won't be sharing my party. But for the first time ever, I'm realizing that if I don't share, I get half the time I had before. I thought I knew what I wanted. I thought I was being smart.

I was an idiot.

And yet, when Mother stands up to leave, she looks at me with respect in her eyes. I'm terribly afraid that she's proud of me for trying to kill my sister. Which is both undeserved and unwanted. I've never wanted to blurt out the truth more than I do right now. I want to beg Mother to forgive me, beg her to plead with Chancery to understand.

Chancery won't look at me with respect. She won't blush and give me corny jewelry. She'll look at me with loathing, with contempt, and maybe even with fear. I swallow and force myself to meet Mother's gaze calmly.

Because any kind of apology Chancery would accept would require me to admit that I made a mistake. A fierce queen is respected. A ruthless queen is feared. A terrifying queen is obeyed. But a flawed one? She's replaced. I've learned my lesson for this year.

Be perfect at all costs. Even when it hurts more than burning coals.

❧ *5* ❧

THE PRESENT

What wakes me is the cold. Not like a dog's nose or watermelon on a hot day. No, nothing friendly, nothing welcoming. This cold hits me like a flexed palm, striking my body with a painful ache. I've clearly been cold for a long time, because my fingers and toes are stiff. But I don't know where I am, or how long I've been here, so I can't let on that I'm waking up. I don't open my eyes, but I reach out in other ways.

I'm lying on my side with my arms in front of me, clasped as if in prayer. The stone underneath me is hard, unyielding, and inconsistent. I'm guessing it's limestone based on the texture, which I can feel easily because I'm wearing only my underwear and sports bra. One particularly rough stone rubs against my ribs with every breath. I quickly suppress my shiver before anyone who may be watching might notice. It's humid, but not as humid as Hawaii. There's a chill in the air outside, I suspect, but I both hear and feel the regulated air entering the room from a vent in the ceiling. I'm inside a building somewhere in the developed world. I hear a heartbeat behind me. It's evian.

I don't open my eyes. I don't breathe any faster than I would while sleeping.

"She shouldn't wake up for almost another hour," the heartbeat says in a gruff voice.

"Unless she's stimulated," a woman says, the sound piped in from a speaker in the ceiling. She's not inside the cell with me and the gruff-voiced man. Her voice is high, shrill-adjacent even. Maybe she's nervous, or maybe she always sounds upset and unhappy.

"What did you want me to do to her exactly?" The man sounds disgustingly eager.

"Don't be crass, Egan. Shake her."

He shakes me, but I don't respond.

"Nothing, boss."

"Do it again."

He kicks me in the ribs.

"I said to shake her."

"She'll heal."

The woman's voice tsks but doesn't reprimand him again.

He clearly takes her failure to censure him as encouragement and kicks me again, harder this time.

I grunt.

"See?" he asks. "Told you a kick would do the trick."

I blink and blink and blink and my eyes finally process the veritable flood of data. Egan's heavy, black boots are retreating and fury floods my abused, prone body. My hand shoots out and grabs the heel closest to me, then I wrench it hard. Egan is a very solid man, but that doesn't keep him from toppling to the flagstones next to me.

I'm practically giddy to discover that I'm not restrained in any way.

I can't prevent the small smile from creeping across my face. I roll to my knees and spring to my bare feet, taking in the details of my confines out of my periphery while I focus on the threat in front of me. Egan's dark brown eyes widen, his nearly black eyebrows slanting downward angrily.

I kick him in the throat, collapsing his windpipe. Then I use my foot and hand to flip him on his stomach, and I pull his arms behind him and upward. He's choking in front of me, oxygen deprived and dazed, but he'll heal the injury to his throat quickly enough and recover use of his lungs. If I don't kill him first.

I apply pressure until I've dislocated both shoulders. He wriggles underneath me. I'm grateful he can't scream yet, but I don't pay much attention to him, not anymore. After all, it's not Egan who truly interests me. He's not my captor. He's a pawn. I look around at the three solid stone walls, and the one mirrored one. Then I glance upward, casting my eyes around for the speaker from which the villainous voice emanated. There are two things in the ceiling, nine feet from the ground. A speaker and an air vent.

"I assume you can see me."

"I can."

"Then you can watch while I kill your man in front of you."

"I can."

"If you think I'm bluffing—"

"Oh, I know you're not. I've heard all the rumors, and I don't doubt them for a second." The mirror shimmers and suddenly becomes a window. No more than eighteen inches from me stands a woman whose face surprises me. It's not abnormally beautiful, not for an evian, anyway. It's not full of rage. It's not scarred, or plain, or distinctive, at least, not in particular.

But I've seen it before, a very, very long time ago.

Flawless, deep golden skin. Tawny bronze eyes. Full-bodied, rich mahogany curls that shine and bounce with a toss of her head. High, pronounced cheekbones, and an aquiline nose. Full lips that are slightly open as if she can't help looking like an airbrushed model, but she wishes she could.

The recognition is immediate, but the placement takes a beat. I scan my memories, reaching further and further back until I finally reach my oldest and fuzziest memory.

"You were there in the room on the day I was born."

Her full lips close and then curve into a knowing smile. She bobs her head, her eyes glinting with pride. "I was, but it's impressive that you recall my presence."

"Who are you?"

"I'm your sister."

A shiver claws its way up my spine, like a cat scaling a tree trunk without regard for the damage done.

The woman holding me in this cell is Melina, the sister who tried to kill Mother almost eighteen years ago. The sister Mother exiled instead of killing. The sister who wanted Chancery dead. "Oh."

"It's about time we met, don't you think?" She touches her throat with one delicate hand. "But we could talk more easily if you'd free poor Egan."

"He kicked me," I say. "Twice." I don't mention that he insinuated that he'd be willing to behave much worse. She was there. She heard it.

She sighs heavily. "He did, and he shouldn't have. But I'd say the collapsed throat and dislocated shoulders qualify as punishment enough for his inexcusable rudeness. If it helps, we don't see many guests."

"Is that what I am?" I ask. "In that case, I'd really like some clothing."

The respectful glint sparks again in her eyes. "I'll have appropriate clothing brought in. We had to ensure you weren't concealing any more shims like the one you cleverly poked through your navel." Melina's tone reproves me for nearly escaping from the van earlier, but the look in her eyes belies her inflection.

I tighten my hold on his arms and shove them higher. He has healed enough to grunt in response. Good, I want her to realize I mean it. Egan's in jeopardy. "While we're on the topic, clothing will be nice, but I'll only free your ill-mannered lackey if you agree to release me."

Melina laughs just like Chancery. It's uncanny, really. I wonder whether our father laughed like that, like wind in the trees, a bird warbling with joy, the nicker of a horse when he hasn't seen me in a while, the squeal of a child with a lollipop. Was our father's laugh distilled from a fount of pure joy as well?

"I can't release you, little one. I'm sorry." She bites her lip. "Truly."

I swallow and try to think of everything Mother ever said about her. I draw a blank. Why didn't I press for more information on my own sister? She was flawed, that much I recall, but how? Why? I was too afraid I'd hear Mother describe my own flaws to ask. And inasmuch as Chancery made me crazy sometimes, she was a known quantity. Mother's reticence to discuss Melina made me uncomfortable enough that I preferred to pretend she didn't exist.

"Fine, then answer my questions and I'll release him."

She leans closer to the glass and responds in a low voice that barely carries through the speaker. "I don't actually care what you do with poor Egan. I'm too smart to send anyone I truly value into the cell with you. I've heard the stories. You adapted well to the Heir training, taking to it like a monkey to the trees, or a shark to water. You excelled far more than I ever did, from the accounts I've heard."

I squeeze tighter and tighter as she talks, taking out my frustration on the target at hand. Egan moans, and I knee him in the back. *Shut up, you useless waste.* If Melina truly doesn't care whether he lives or dies, I have no leverage. I stand up, releasing him. I ignore the noises he makes as he relocates his own shoulder by slamming into the wall. He doesn't get either arm on the first try, which makes me grin a little in spite of myself.

He crosses the room toward the floor to ceiling metal door on slides, and I follow him. Go ahead, sister. Press the button to free your useless goon. I'll be right behind him.

"Oh, I don't think so, Egan. Get comfortable in there. We won't let you out until I'm ready to put darling, treacherous Judica back to sleep."

I swear under my breath, but file the information away. She's not killing me, at least, not right away.

"You worked hard to create your reputation of ruthlessness, efficiency, and pragmatism." Melina flattens her hands against the glass and leans closer. "I know precisely what that kind of reputation costs. Thousands of hours spent suffering unspeakable pain, healing over and over, only to be injured again, and fighting nearly fatal matches so you'll be ready when it's time. Stretching and developing your mind through countless lessons, languages, historical facts, game theory. But it's never enough, is it? No matter how much you learn, there's always more, like trying to drink straight from a fire hose. I know this, because you see, I earned my reputation the hard way too."

I wish I knew what exactly she was known for, other than trying to kill Chancy after our mother refused.

"I told Mother this would happen, you know." Melina shakes her head. "I predicted this from the very beginning."

I don't know, in fact, what in the world she's talking about. "You predicted you'd kill Mother, and then Chancery and I would fight, and Chancery would win?"

She laughs again, but this time I sense the difference

between her laugh and Chancery's. Her laugh starts off at the same place, Delightsville, but it goes off track somewhere around Happytown and there are notes of delirium, of insanity behind it. The end of her laugh is unhinged somehow, unbound by any solid emotion or empathy.

"You grew very still for a moment," she says. "Do you mind if I ask why?"

"You sound like her, like Chancery." I wonder how she'll react to her name, since she swore to kill her from what I heard.

"Ah, sweet, gentle Chancery. I sound like her, do I?" She shakes her head. "You're so entertaining, and I would be lying if I said I wasn't relieved to hear that Mother finally died. But I feel sorrow, too, more than I expected. But no, I certainly didn't expect her to live quite this long when I challenged her to a fight to the death eighteen years ago."

"You lost," I say. But after proclaiming it's true, I wonder. Did she lose? Who was unable to kill whom?

"I challenged Mother the day you were born. I knew you and Chancery would eventually come to blows. Mother promised me that it would never happen. She vowed that you two would become fast friends, but you can't force people to get along. Having one child destined to rule doesn't really make for the best dynamic. There's a reason all three sets of female twins born in the last century of an empress's life have resulted in full blown civil wars."

I lift my chin. "Chancery and I worked things out."

"Oh, sure you have. When was it you were hacking at one another with swords? Oh, right." Her grin this time doesn't touch her eyes. "Yesterday."

So I've only been out for one day. Good to know.

"I need some information from you." She leans closer to the glass.

I lift my eyebrows.

"Why did Mother change her mind? Why did she cut you out?"

My heart contracts.

"Angel tells me you saw her face, so it's no secret that she worked for me. She told me that Mother changed the paperwork naming you as Heir just before she died. She said she named Chancery as her heir, but hadn't finished the paperwork. Unfortunately, she had no idea why Mother did any of that." She pins me with a glare. "But you know. Of course you know why you were displaced."

I look away from her.

"I need to understand," she hisses. "Tell me what motivated the change." Her eyes bore into mine.

I shrug with practiced indifference. "That's too bad."

Her lips compress until they're practically white, and then she spits her next words. "You will tell me eventually."

"Or what?" I ask.

"You may have endured the pain training, the healing training, the torture preparation, the poison tolerance and identification, the one-on-one combat, the weapons training, the multi-opponent drills, and everything else. You may be savvy with political intrigue and family power lines. You may know the names and alliances of every known evian." She presses her face up against the glass, pressing both palms hard on either side of her face. "But I completed the same rigorous program as you did, and I did it for longer. The only reason you supplanted me was that you were *born*. It had nothing to do with skill or ferocity. So if you think I don't know how to crack you, you're wrong. And I will have that information. It's just a matter of how hard I have to pry before I jostle it loose, and how much damage I do in the process."

"Okay." No sense arguing with a crazy person.

"Wouldn't you rather save us both some time and agony and tell me what I want to know?"

Tell her that Mother thought Chancery was the subject of some super-secret prophecy that Inara hadn't even heard of? Inara was Heir far longer than Melina, and she had no idea.

"Why do you need to know?" I ask. "Maybe you should have waited a little longer before murdering our mother. She might have told you herself, though I doubt it. She tended not to over-share. Not like some family I've met." I lift one eyebrow pointedly.

Melina slams the inside of her left forearm against the glass, and I realize there's writing on it. I squint a little to make out the words.

With the might and power of God, the Eldest shall destroy all in her path and unite my children as one. Only through her blood can the stone be restored to the mountain.

I look up at her and realize my mouth is hanging open dumbly. I close it with a tiny click.

She drops her arm and slams her right forearm against the glass. More words.

Together, with the strength of her strongest supporter, she shall open the Garden of Eden, that the miracle of God shall go unto all the Earth to save my children from utter destruction.

I don't know what to say. Mother said no one but the Empress could access the prophecies from Eve. I shake my head. "I don't know what that is."

Melina frowns. "You never knew our dad. He was very persistent. Mother would never have shared this with me. There was some kind of vow made by the governing queens. But she told Dad and he passed it along to me. He thought it would be me, you know. He was convinced I'd be the key to this kind of sweeping change, redeeming and purifying the corrupted Earth from itself. He convinced me, you know. I was absolutely positive that this referred to me."

"Because you're the Eldest?"

"It was a reasonable assumption," Melina says. "After all, I was the Eldest of Mother's children with her new Consort. I was the eldest of this new bloodline, and I was Mother's Heir. It made sense."

I lift my eyebrows but don't comment.

"It took me a little time to process how wrong Dad was. How wrong I've been for years." She leans close again, her eyes shining like garbage fires. "It's Chancery, isn't it? Mother realized Chancery is the Eldest."

I've never stammered in my entire life. Until now. "Sh-sh-she isn't the eldest. She's seventeen, just like me."

"But she's the eldest of two twins, twins who shouldn't have both survived. I thought Mother made a dire mistake many years ago, but now I've realized that I had everything backward. I had the right idea, of course, but I missed the mark. That happens more often than you'd think, with these prophecies. They describe something so far in the future that they seem unclear until all of a sudden, they're crystalline."

"You aren't making any sense."

"Mother discovered something," Melina says. "Something about your sweet, kind, generous sister. Angel tells me Chancery espouses radical ideas. She says your twin was always making suggestions that Mother change things that no one would ever countenance changing. She advocated for sweeping reform that Mother discounted as nonsense. Angel says Chancery isn't like other evians. She says she's special."

She's jealous, I realize. She doesn't want Chancery to be this prophesied queen. Because that means she's not important at all. I shake my head. "Chancery loved Mother, and she followed everything Mother ever told us."

Melina smiles again. "You haven't been able to explain why Mother changed her mind so quickly. Why flip on the selection of Heir without provocation? No, there's more to this story."

"What are you going to do to me?" I ask.

"Oh, darling Judica. I've been on your side for so many years. I argued for you, and I left our people for you. I challenged Mother when she wouldn't kill Chancery, you know. So you should believe me when I say that I don't want to do this."

Do this? What's this?

"My mistake was understandable." Melina begins pacing. "As Eldest, I needed a staunch supporter. One supporter, not two, and every single history book decries the problems created by twins." She spins around and fixes her gaze on mine. "What do you know about the Hundred Years' War?"

Now she's giving me a history lesson? "The humans think Plantagenet and Valois were fighting over the crown in France."

"And?"

"And it was really Senah and Denah fighting over control of Malessa."

She nods. "And?"

And what? "The third time is the charm. After that enormous disaster, all the empresses vowed to kill one of their daughters if they ever have twins."

Melina smiles. "Mother didn't hide that from you, at least, she didn't try to disguise her infraction. Her rebellion from what was required of her."

"No. She didn't." My voice is flat, which is just as bad as

scowling. I need to cover my feelings better. I'm projecting nearly as badly as Chancery.

"Did she tell you that Denah and Senah were best friends for nearly fifty years?"

I don't drop my jaw. I don't widen my eyes, but my heart rate accelerates. Luckily, I doubt she can hear it through the communication devices. I know I can't hear hers.

She grins as if she can. "You didn't know that. You had no idea that their arguments came after a period of great peace and prosperity."

I reach for my inner calm. I need to take back control of this conversation, but it's hard to feel calm when you're half-naked and stuck in a rock-encased cell. "Clearly Mother left a few things out."

"It would appear so. The two of them were inseparable, but as time wore on, they weren't as eager to share. Evians are very, very good at sniffing out opportunities, and driving a wedge between those two, well, it was too good to pass up. Over time, the two sisters both picked up special allies who whispered in their ears. Their respective allies worked on them, playing them against one another. They were a powder keg from the start. And powder kegs can be relied upon to do the one thing they always do best. It's inevitable, unless they're preempted."

"Boom," I say.

Melina nods. "So you see, it's nothing personal."

"What's nothing personal?" The skin on my arms crawls.

"I actually thought it was Alamecha's fatal flaw: our inability to kill family members, even when it was clearly necessary. First Enora couldn't kill Chancery. Then I couldn't kill Mother for sparing her. Which would have then been followed by my murder of Chancery, right? Otherwise, what was the point?"

"You thought that was our flaw? Refusal to kill?" I think of Mother, beheading Lyssa without a single pause. I contemplate the justice she's dealt out impartially for nearly twenty years in front of me. Mother never had trouble killing people she loved. She always followed the law, to the letter.

Melina stops pacing and meets my eye. "I thought it for a while, yes. And then from what I heard, even when Chancery spared you and you had the chance, you didn't step up to take her out. The dragon among heirs, the insane berserker, brought as low by empathy as the rest of us poor saps. You didn't kill Chancery when you had the chance either."

Berserker? I don't roll my eyes, but it takes an effort. "Chancery and I have a lot of things to work out, but I don't begrudge her the throne. In fact, if you tell anyone this, I'll deny it, but I'm relieved she beat me. For the first time in my life, I've shed the anvil wrapped around my neck that was dragging me down to the bottom of the sea."

"You're missing the point," Melina says. "It's not about whether you will fight her, not anymore. That's why I left, that's why Mother and I fought, but I was so lost I didn't see up from down. I thought her failure to kill your gentle twin would result in a protracted war that would damage Alamecha specifically and evians at large. I thought it was my duty to stop that. But I missed it. I missed something so obvious that I could kick myself."

"Don't let me stop you," I say. "In fact, let me out, and I'll help with the kicking."

Melina rolls her eyes. "I missed the thread that ties this all together. The answer was staring me in the face, but I was too blind, too obtuse to see it. It's not that we can't kill people who matter to us. Mother beheaded her best friend last week, for heaven's sake."

I gulp as that image replays in my mind. She's right. We don't shy away from hard things. "What's your point?"

Melina drops her voice so low I strain to make out her next words. "Mother beheaded Lyssa to spare your sister, I'd bet my life on it. I'm not sure how or why, but every crazy, insane, bizarre thing Enora has done has been for *Chancery Divinity Alamecha*. I couldn't kill Mother. . . to kill Chancery either. You could have defeated her, but you couldn't do it either. At every step, Chancery should have died, but God spared her again and again and again."

God? I want to scream. *I* spared her. *Mother* spared her. *Melina* spared them both. God doesn't factor into it.

"He needs her," she says. "And He protects his tools."

Fantastic. She's bonkers.

"And now the biggest threat facing Chancery is standing in front of me. I messed up last time, thank goodness, but this time I'm positive. You may not be willing to admit it, but I've got other methods to confirm my suspicion."

"What suspicion?" Crazy people don't behave in predictable ways.

"You're Chancery's Heir."

The non-sequitur throws me for a moment, but her leaping on that can't be good. "Only for a short time," I say. "It won't be long before Chancery manages to birth a girl, and I've seen how Edam looks at her. She'll name him as Consort before the end of the year, I'm sure of it."

"Edam, Senah's boy?"

I gulp.

"I heard that the two of you. . ." Melina lifts both eyebrows. "And he switched, just like Mother? Never mind. It doesn't matter."

Like Mother? "Why exactly did you bring me here?" I

ask. "Because you went to a lot of trouble when you could have just called me to ask me these questions."

"Ah, I couldn't have done this over the phone. I did wonder whether you'd have come if I issued a polite invite."

"Probably not," I admit.

"And I needed to see you."

"You needed to see me?" A sense of unease creeps between my shoulder blades. "What are you going to do?" Before she responds, I already know what she's planning.

"I've been impressed by reports of you, little sister, at every turn. I have, regrettably, been forced to look on at your success from afar. Notwithstanding my distance, the reports from spies and allies have all been extremely promising. And now that I'm finally seeing you in person, all grown up." She shakes her head and beams at me. "You're every bit as magnificent as they all told me. Dad would be so very proud."

I flinch like she slapped me.

"Do you miss him?" she asks.

I lift one eyebrow.

"Well, you never met him. But what I mean is, do you wish you had known your father?"

I square my shoulders. Just say it. Own up to your plan.

"It doesn't matter. The point is that Chancery's the Eldest, the empress of prophecy, and you may be the one person who could take her down. That makes you the biggest threat to her, to Alamecha, and consequently to the whole world."

"You're going to kill me."

Melina sighs heavily. "I don't have a choice. You've seen the prophecy. Utter destruction."

Egan pulls a gun from an inside pocket and I want to kick myself for not patting him down. I tense, preparing for a shot, when I realize it's a dart gun. She is planning to kill me, but if she's darting me, she isn't doing it yet.

"Since you won't admit anything, I'll need to independently verify. Or maybe I'll get the information out of you yet. But for now, it's lights out," Melina says.

I could avoid the dart, but what's the point? They could release gas into the room through the air vent, or they could fire way, way more projectiles. The more I struggle, the more they'll double down on protocols. And I need them to be as lax as possible if I want to have any hope of killing my insane, treasonous sister. And I want to kill her, badly. She didn't deny killing our mother, and she even admitted that she couldn't kill *Chancery*.

But I don't suffer from this Alamecha epidemic of sparing family members, and I have no qualms whatsoever about killing Melina. She will pay for killing our mother, and I'll collect on that debt myself.

❧ 6 ❧

THE PAST

Stephanie pins my hair up in a complicated knot on top of my head. After the last pin slides into place, she steps back. "What do you think?"

She's a miracle worker. My hair is thick, shiny, and curly. It's hard to work with, and I don't have the patience to reconfigure it all the time like my sister does. Mom's stylist has braided the top part in a line running straight back from my forehead, and then artfully brought the various pieces together to form a beautiful configuration in the center of the top of my head. I look older, sophisticated even. But my neck is uncovered, and as beautiful as I look, I hate it.

It leaves me . . . exposed. Like my skirt has flown up around my shoulders, like everyone can see my flaws. "It's too much."

"Nonsense," Mother says. "It's a New Year's Eve ball. Chancery's hair is up, my hair is up. Yours should be, too."

I swallow. She wants me to look like them. "If you say so."

Mother nods. "I like it, but you should like it too."

"How about if we leave the top part up." Stephanie's hands move across the crown of my head at lightning speed, pins falling to the ground around us. My hair falls around my shoulders in a waterfall. "But we let the rest down. You'll look formal, but fierce."

She finally stops and spins me around to see. My hair is braided in a line across the top of my head in a Mohawk, but the rest falls down around my shoulders, tumbling in a riot of curls. I look more like me. Not quite my utilitarian braid, or severe ponytail, but less alien than the debutante updo.

"I like it," I say.

Mother sighs. "It's acceptable, but—" She shakes her head. "It looks fine. It's more *you*, that way."

"Thanks," I say.

"Thank you, Stephanie," Mother says. After her stylist leaves, she turns to inspect my dress. "You look elegant, Judica, even with your hair down. As much as it hurts me to admit it, you look older. You don't look seventeen. You look closer to twenty-five. I wish I could still dress you in pinafores and pigtails."

I roll my eyes.

The corner of Mother's mouth turns up. "But I can't. Not anymore, and I think quite a few young men have begun to take notice."

My heart races, just a bit, but I quickly regulate it. Can't have Mother thinking she's struck a chord.

But of course she notices. "Is there someone you're hoping to see tonight?"

I shrug. "Not really."

"You have dozens of options Balthasar trained right here in Ni'ihau to choose from. None of them have caught your eye?"

Caught my eye? Am I shopping for a handbag? "Umm, no."

"Would you tell me if one of them did?" Mother's eyebrow goes up.

I clear my throat. "When did, uh, when did you decide that you loved Althuselah?"

"Loved?" Mother asks.

"Or you know, when did you decide you liked him?" I shrug. "Either way."

"Althuselah?" She pauses. "Wouldn't you rather talk about your father?"

I flinch. "You didn't love him."

Mother's finger taps her lip. "I don't suppose I really did, no. I wanted to love someone, but we didn't quite get there. I missed being in love and I longed for a partner, but you're right that your father didn't turn out to be quite who I hoped he would be."

"What about Althuselah?"

Mother's eyes focus beyond the wall she's staring at, as if she's watching something beyond comprehension. "I was only sixteen the first time I saw him, his bare chest gleaming with sweat."

"His *chest*?"

Mother nods. "It was covered with blood, of course. Everything was a complete mess in the years leading up to Mother's death, you know. It wasn't entirely her fault, what with all the insane Viking attacks she dealt with for so many centuries. So many half-evians were unhappy around that time. Mother wasn't exiling them, but they didn't have a place. They didn't belong among their own people, so they banded together and called themselves Vikings. They claimed our God had forsaken them, had forsaken us all, and then they made up their own pantheon. They were just strong enough to irritate us, and we felt too guilty to completely eradicate them. In fact, many of their parents commanded the armies sent to deal with their attacks. Droves of humans in our armies died fighting them. It was utter madness." Mother shakes her head. "But Mother was tired of it all by then and she wasn't at her best."

"When was that?"

"Eleven-Thirty-Six." Mother sighs. "My mother had killed so many humans, put down so many tiny squabbles, but most of it was for the good of the rest of her subjects."

"Why hadn't you seen him before?" I ask. "Wasn't he trained in your household?"

Mother shakes her head, a sly smile on her face. "He wasn't."

My eyebrows rise. "Wait, they didn't sell their sons?"

"Oh, they did," she says. "Mother had several dozen sons of monarchs trained within our family ranging from fifteen all the way up to nearly a hundred years of age. I didn't like any of them."

"Wait, why was he covered with blood?"

Mother licks her lips. "Balthasar and Althuselah were brothers, and they were actually fighting against Alamecha."

"Whoa, what?"

"They were sons of Reshaka. She kept them and raised them to be her own warlords. They hadn't taken over yet, obviously. They were only twenty-eight and twenty-six, but the sight of the two of them, mowing down Alamecha warriors..." Mother closes her eyes as if savoring a favorite memory. She's more sadistic than I realized. "I should have hated them on sight, but they worked together so artfully, perfectly attuned. The two of them were a living work of art."

My mouth drops open. "You married someone who wasn't raised in the family? What did your mother say?"

Mother beams. "She'd never have allowed it. But she died when I was only twenty-two. I had entirely fallen for Althuselah by then, and Balthasar was the greatest supporter of our star-crossed love."

He left his family for her. I breathe in deeply, and sigh wistfully. "How did you know he was the one for you?"

"I didn't. I hoped he was and got lucky."

"That's so romantic."

"It was stupid." Mother's lips are pressed together.

"Your love story spanned eight centuries. I think that's evidence you're wrong."

"Althuselah loved me back, and that alone was a miracle. I was a headstrong, mercurial mess back then. He could have been pursuing any sort of agenda, including one for his mother, or later his sister. There are long games, under-lying political plays that are hatched in ways I couldn't even contemplate at that early age. In fact, if he'd followed his orders, Alamecha would have been subsumed by Shamecha years ago."

"But it wasn't."

Mother brushes white dog hair from Duchess off her skirt. "It wasn't." She strides toward the door. "And now it's time for us to attend our own party."

I stand up to follow her, but a tentative tap at my door halts me mid-step. None of my guards would knock like that.

"Come in Chancery," Mother says. I should have known.

My sister pokes her head around the door. Her eyes are yet a different color today, burnt umber. Why can't she pick one hue and keep it? She has darkened her skin too, to the color of rich, moist, lava-infused earth, offset by bright, shimmering, golden hair. Just like Mother said it would be, it's up off her neck. Instead of a tight, smooth knot like mine, hers is a big, messy bun, with dozens of braids entwined in it. It looks breathtaking.

She looks like she's trying too hard, and I wonder whose eyes she's trying to catch.

It'll probably work, because ridiculous or not, she's utterly, flawlessly gorgeous. I hate her and her stupid copycat face. And somewhere, deep down, I wonder whether she wears our face better, and with more ease. I'd like to try darkening my eyes or skin, but with as often as she changes her appearance, I can't ever change mine or no one could tell us apart. At least, not until one of us spoke or tapped pathetically on a door.

I resume my movement toward the door, because I will not let her appearance change my course. Roman's face comes into view behind Chancery, where he's guarding my room. His eyes meet mine, and he glances pointedly at her hair and mimes his horror.

I suppress a snort. Mother would be furious if she knew we were secretly laughing at Chancy, but Roman always gets me. Chancery's hair couldn't scream 'look at me' any louder. Why is Mother encouraging it?

Oh, right. Because Mother never judges Chancery. Ever.

"I'm ready," I say.

It's not wasted on me that Chancery's dressed in gold brocade with a full, pin-tucked skirt, while I'm wearing silver so dark, it's practically black. Her dress bells around her like a princess, while mine hugs my every curve from shoulder to mid-calf before flaring slightly, just enough that I can walk. She looks like light and airy goodness, and I look like the grim freaking reaper. We all have our roles to play.

No use fighting mine.

As usual, Mother's dress reflects both of ours, silver at the bottom on one side and gold on the other, the two blending together in a swirl up and around her hips, and then separating again in the bodice, with a gold strap on the opposite side of the gold at the hemline, and silver on the other. Mother's dresses are always jaw-dropping, and this one's no different. One day she's going to invite me to help her choose the design instead of Chancy. One day I'll attend the party she and Chancery have before each of our events. But not this time and probably not the next.

I certainly won't ever *ask* to be included. I'm not that pathetic.

Mother walks through the door and I follow her closely, letting Chancery trail after us both, as she should. Third in line, and don't forget it. We pause before entering the celebration in the anteroom behind Mother's throne. She enters first, as always, and I follow after, flanked by the head of my guards, Edam, and his first lieutenant, Roman.

I don't have a date, but neither does Chancery. That's something. As usual, Frederick steps up to take Mother's arm and leads her to stand in front of her throne.

"I'm delighted to be here with all of you," she says. "On the eve of a new year, we always gather as a family, to welcome those who matter most. And I'm the luckiest of mothers, to have not one, not two or three or even five daughters here." She waves her arm down a line of women in front of us, all of them smiling in a way that looks just like her. "I have eleven daughters who were able to make it tonight. My oldest, Magdelina, hasn't come to visit in nearly a decade. I'm especially pleased to welcome in the New Year with her. But I'm delighted to see Margerite, Avina, Falin, Annekah, Danika, Rivena, Alora, Inara, and of course, Judica and Chancery."

Mother sits down on her throne. "As delighted as I am to celebrate tonight with my family near, I'd also like to acknowledge how many friends have made an effort to be present. We have allies from all five families in attendance, including Alamecha's ambassadors from each. With the wide variety of guests, and in celebration of the peace we're currently enjoying in the world, I'd like to suggest we embrace a rather human tradition among us."

Mother gestures for Chancery and me to take our seats on either side of her.

"As your Empress, I'm not ordering you to kiss someone at midnight." She glances sideways at me. "But I'm going to strongly encourage it."

Murmurs erupt all around us.

"Too many of you are putting off marriage and family. If we want Alamecha to remain strong, we need to be focused on what matters. To that end, I've opened the rooftop balcony and set up an oceanside dance floor as well. This party will expand to cover three separate locales. Each will feature its own ambiance and music, from live bands to orchestras, to popular music of our day. This main ballroom will focus on classic Victorian ballroom dances like waltzes, quadrilles, and reels. The balcony will include Latin music, featuring salsa, mambo, merengue, and bachata. And finally, a popular human DJ, Christopher Comstock, will be mixing music for dancing out by the beach. I'm sure between those options, all of you will find a location where you'll be comfortable mixing and mingling with the evians assembled to celebrate."

No one can top Mother for doing the unexpected. She didn't even prepare me for this one. Which is how I watch, dumbstruck, as Chancery stands up and squeezes Mother's hand before bouncing down the steps and out the door toward the beach. Lark joins her near the door, their eyes sparkling with excitement.

"I told you it was an amazing surprise," Chancery says a little too loudly.

"Let's go," Lark practically squeals.

Out of the corner of my eye, I notice that Edam's eyes follow Chancery the entire time, resting on the door once she's gone. Is he interested in her? Or does he just want to dance to modern music for once? The idea of him wanting to flee me to be with her rubs me the wrong way, but it's not like I can control his feelings.

"You don't need to stay with me all night," I say. "You can certainly assign someone else to work in your place."

Edam's eyes dart to mine guiltily. "I would never—"

I roll my eyes. "Oh please. Just go." I raise my voice. "Fesian, do you mind guarding me tonight?"

Another of Edam's lieutenants, tall, bulky, with hawk-like features, Fesian gambols over to my side. "It would be my pleasure." His eyes run across my face like he's eyeing a prize. Oh, no. He thinks I called him over to kiss me at midnight. Do not blush, Judica. Don't do it.

Roman clears his throat. "He worked last night, Your Highness. Might Nightingale be a better call?"

"Yes," I say desperately. "She would. Is she—"

"She was on the schedule for tonight," Roman says. "But as it's a special occasion. . ."

Edam took her place in the lineup as head of my guard, a position always held by Balthasar's second-in-command.

"It's not like anyone is on high alert tonight," I say. "Please, go."

I glance around and realize there's been a mass exodus of almost everyone under the age of one hundred. But it's too late for me to high-tail it out of here now. Plus, Margerite is approaching. I haven't talked to her in a very long time. Unfortunately, by the time she's done catching up with me, I'm stuck. I'm certainly not about to follow Chancery out to the beach like a human-wannabe.

It's not like this is a big surprise. I mean, I've been planning on dancing waltzes all day. Beyond that, I've danced waltzes on New Year's Eve for years and years. It's expected.

I hate it.

"Would you do me the honor of this dance, Your Highness?" Roman asks. Something about his tone is different somehow, richer or deeper, maybe.

I look up into his eyes, and my heart skips a beat. It was only one single beat. Surely no one noticed.

But Roman smiles like he did.

"Uh, sure."

When he takes my hand in his, my heart sprints like I'm running a race. What's going on? Is something wrong with me?

"I absolutely, positively adore. . ." Roman leads me over to the middle of the dance floor. "This song. Don't you?"

Work, ears, work. What in the world is the band playing? Who the heck cares, anyway? "It's Skater's Waltz?"

"Exactly," he says. "I don't miss the typical third-beat lilt that most Viennese waltzes use."

I lift one eyebrow. "Don't tell me you're secretly learning melodics."

Roman laughs, a rich, full sound that puts a twinkle in his eyes, and a warm undertone in his cheeks. "Nothing so dire, I assure you. I appreciate music and atmosphere, that's all."

And somehow, the night doesn't seem so terrible anymore. His arm around my waist settles something in my chest I didn't realize was fraught. Yet, simultaneously, my fingers and toes buzz in a way I've never experienced before. I'm aware of his every shift, his breath on my face, his hand in mine. When the Skater's Waltz ends, I realize I don't like it after all.

It's far too short.

"Would you care to dance another?" Roman asks.

My heart swells inside of my chest, but another voice answers him before I have the chance. "I'm sure she can dance again in a moment, but I need a word with my daughter. I'm sure you understand."

Roman drops my hand and steps away, bowing deeply. "Of course, Your Majesty."

I follow Mother quickly back to her seat and drop into mine beside her.

Her voice is barely audible. "Not him."

My mouth rivals the Sahara for lack of moisture. I can barely force myself to swallow. "What do you mean?"

"Was I unclear?" Mother lifts her nose and sniffs.

I open my mouth and then close it again. "No, I suppose not. You don't want me to kiss Roman, but I'm not sure why you'd even think I want to."

She lifts her eyebrows. "You don't?"

I shake my head. "No, of course not."

"I must have been mistaken, then."

Mother is never mistaken. I close my eyes. "Why?"

"Why what?" she asks softly, so softly.

"You bought him from Adika to be part of my honor guard." Which makes him one of my options.

"I buy lots of racehorses, but I only put my money behind the ones who turn out. It's all a gamble until then. You know already that he's tenth generation," Mother says. "I bought him because *not* to buy any sixth family's children would be an insult. None of the other options are tenth generation. He's beneath you, Judica, and beyond that, he's underwhelming in every single way."

A kick to the stomach wouldn't have shocked me more. "He's underwhelming?"

"This isn't the time or place." Mother inclines her head at the ambassador from Shenoah, who is now eyeing us askance. "But there are certainly men who are more deserving of your attention."

"Like who?" I want to take the question back, but it's too late.

"Fiorem, for one, or Charles. Or Edam. My top choice would certainly be Edam."

Chancery's top choice too, by the looks of things. "Because Balthasar likes him?" I can't help my frown.

"He's a warrior," Mother says. "He's a shining star, burning a path across Alamecha, carving a place for himself. You deserve a partner who brings something to the table, someone you can rely on to protect you from all the threats that will come after you."

I fear Mother's warrior prince already fancies her other daughter, but if Mother wants me to choose him, then I'll make it happen. I close my eyes and search for things about Roman that bother me to make it easier to shun him. I'll need to immediately put some distance between us. But I can't think of anything. I do think about his hand at my waist, his eyes on mine, and his voice in my ear.

I shake my head. "Well, I'd better head out to the beachside dance floor, then." My voice sounds tinny to my ears. "I think all three of the men you mentioned are out there."

Mother's grin is sly, like a cat with a mouse in its paws. "Don't let me stop you."

I do not stomp down the stairs. I don't race past Roman or Nightingale toward the exit, either.

"Is everything alright?" Roman catches up to ask.

I plaster a smile on my face when I realize he can tell how I'm feeling. I've allowed Roman to draw too close to me. He can read me too clearly. Even Mother never knows when I'm upset, but thanks to that miscalculation, it's going to hurt to pry him loose. It must be done, however painful, because I'm nothing like my father. Mother said he was overly emotional, too passionate about people and things. She said he went down when he should have gone up, he grew hot when he should have been cold.

But I always do precisely what she asks of me, no matter how difficult. No matter how painful. Always.

Which is why I casually slide across the veranda toward the dance floor set up a few dozen paces from the exit of the palace. I brace myself to see Edam mooning over insipid Chancery and her stupid ever-changing skin, hair, and eyes. I don't answer Roman's thoughtful inquiry. I don't react to Nightingale's shared glance with him. None of that is any of my concern.

Edam's leaning against one of the tables around the edge of the dance floor. Music pulses through the wooden squares, shaking the chairs, the tables, and guiding the mass of bodies throbbing in unison. I pause for a second, transfixed. Even Edam taps his foot, his hip shifting in time with the bass of the song.

This is a definitely a song I've never heard in my life. Roman stands one pace behind me, and I'm acutely aware of his presence. Too aware. "Nightingale, Roman, go and dance. That's an order. I'm not in danger here, surrounded by family and other guards. Enjoy your evening for once."

Tiny wrinkles form between Roman's eyebrows, and his eyes cloud for a moment, but then they're gone, and I wonder whether I imagined it. He's my oldest friend. He probably didn't feel anything other than sorry for me earlier. I'm such an idiot.

I tear my eyes away from his high cheekbones, his startlingly white teeth and full lips and force myself to look at Edam. He's already staring at something. I follow his gaze . . . to my twin. Of course. I clench my fists, but I force myself to take a calming breath and analyze what I'm seeing. She and Lark are dancing with their hands in the air, their hips swaying, their mouths moving with the lyrics.

How can they possibly know this song? When would they have time to hear anything like this?

"Would you care to dance with me?" Roman's voice comes from only a few inches behind me.

Nightingale may have disappeared amidst the chaotic mess, but Roman's going to be harder to lose.

"I've never heard it before," I say, "but it's oddly compelling."

"It is."

When I turn to face him, he's looking right at me, and I can't help but wonder whether he wasn't talking about the music. I may need to be more direct, on all fronts. I brace myself and spit the words out, hoping against hope they won't hurt his feelings. But a part of me hopes they do. "Roman, it's almost midnight, and I've got Mother's edict to think about."

His grin is pure pleasure. It almost kills me.

I clear my throat. There's no going back, not from this. "So can you buzz off? I think you're scaring him away."

Roman's face blanks immediately and he swallows hard. "Totally. Of course. Sorry, I just wanted to make sure you were safe, but I can do that from a distance."

He melts into the crowd so quickly that my head practically spins. Gone. He's gone. He'll probably never look at me the way he did tonight ever again, but I can't think about that right now. I can't. I have work to do if I want to make Mother happy.

Edam's moving from the edge of the group. Oh, no. Am I too late? He's sliding between dancers like a panther tracking his prey, moving toward Chancery like a spear driving toward the heart of a warthog. Purposeful, calm, intense.

I want to melt away and find Fiorem or Charles, or anyone else, but they were second best. Mother's top pick is right in front of me, and clearly he finds my face attractive. He's heading for the one person on the island who looks just like me. Besides, it has been his sole purpose since birth to become my Consort. It's the reason Mother bought all of them, trained all of them. It's their highest goal.

Which is probably the only reason Roman was dancing with me at all.

I've shown zero interest in Edam up until this point, which is probably why he's aiming for second best. It makes sense. All he needs is a redirect, a bump toward the greater prize.

Chancery has been drawing his attention slowly for weeks, like a lodestone pulls iron ore. Watching it has been irritating in the extreme. But that tactic won't work, not for me. I'm not magnetic, I'm not alluring, and I'm not fun-loving. I'm too direct for any of that, so I'll need a simpler plan. I walk toward the punch bowl, which happens to put me on a collision course with Mr. Panther himself.

He nearly bowls me over and pulls up short, a dismayed look on his face. "Excuse me, Your Highness. I didn't see you."

"No, you really didn't," I say. "You nearly ran me over."

He bows stiffly. "My sincere apologies."

"Actually, there's something you could do to make things right."

Edam's mouth parts slightly. I analyze him for possibly the very first time. He's exceptionally tall with broad shoulders, and he has deep blue eyes with dark blond fringed lashes. His features are severe, but perfect, like an ice sculpture of the famed Greek Adonis. "What can I do to serve, Your Highness?"

Right. I told him he could help me. "Well." I look down at my feet, encased in strappy silver sandals. "You may not have been paying attention, but it's nearly midnight. And my mother gave me very specific instructions." He has no idea quite how specific. I inwardly groan.

"Oh." Edam's mouth opens and closes like a fish flopping around on the sand. I want to throw him back, but I can't. He's too perfect for that, and I always do exactly what I should. Always.

I lift one eyebrow in a way I hope is coquettish. "Surely you would do me a favor."

He bobs his head stiffly. "Of course. Yes."

Great, I've effectively told him he has to kiss me. I want to sink down beneath the sand and never come back out. What's my plan? Will I order him to marry me next, and then smile simperingly while he stiffly stands beside me, wishing for my sister?

But then the DJ is counting down from thirty and it's too late to take it back. Edam wraps an arm around my shoulders, a heavily muscled arm, and my heart races again, for the second time in the same night.

Maybe this can work. I certainly find him attractive. When the DJ says ten, somehow everyone around us knows to count with him, chanting the numbers. Ten, nine, eight, seven. I look up at Edam, his eyes meeting mine. He looks away quickly, his teeth biting his full bottom lip. Four, three, two, one. His head dips toward mine, his teeth releasing his lips so they can descend over mine.

His mouth is warm, and I don't want this kiss to end, but it does, too soon. Edam lifts his head and bows slightly before slipping away from me. I want to cry, because it's not supposed to be like this, is it?

But then I catch Chancery's eyes. I've been the Heir for nearly seventeen years. She's known that Mother chose me, that she will never rule, because I was chosen. She's trailed behind me for almost two decades, acknowledged to everyone that I'm the better choice. And yet, I've never seen this expression on her face before. Never.

She's terribly, consumingly, furiously jealous.

It almost makes up for the uneasy feeling that I did something *wrong* tonight. After all, if Mother thinks it's the right thing, and if Chancery wants to be me for once, I'm on the right path. That must be true. So the next time Edam glances this way, I beam at him and wonder whether my twin notices.

✻   7   ✻

THE PRESENT

Egan and Melina are gone when I wake up. Or at least, I assume Melina is gone. The glass has shifted back into a mirror, and I don't hear any heartbeat other than my own.

I also really, really need to pee, which reminds me. I can't recall the last time I had anything to drink. My throat is dry, my lips are peeling, and my throat is scratchier than parchment paper.

It absolutely kills me to remain prone on the ground, my face pressed against the stone floor, my shoulder bent at an awkward angle, and my neck torqued. But if I move, they'll realize I'm waking from their tranqs sooner than I should. They'll up the dose or the frequency or both, and my odds of escape will drop to zero.

While I was out this time, they restrained me. My hands are shackled in front of me, titanium cuffs connected by almost delicate chain links. If I had to guess, I'd say Egan pressed for the additional precaution. I might do the same if someone collapsed my windpipe. I shouldn't have let anger supersede strategy. Idiots do that, and I am not an idiot.

I lie entirely still and assess my surroundings. Stone walls, floor, and ceiling. Roughly an eight-by-eight foot cell. Large enough I can move around, but not big enough that they can't see nearly the entire space with a single camera. Luckily, the camera in the upper corner faces the mirrored wall and I'm far enough forward toward the back wall that it shouldn't catch my face. I'm not facing the mirror, so I can open my eyes and they still won't have any idea I'm awake as long as my breathing doesn't change and my heart rate doesn't accelerate.

I've had plenty of practice regulating those.

Escape is my top priority, preferably before Melina kills me. She could have done it earlier, but she didn't. That means she wants something from me. At a base line, she wants to know what prompted Mother to change the heir-ship paperwork. She may want more, but as long as I don't provide that information, she will be forced to wait for evidence of it through another channel. That buys me time.

An alternative is that she's waiting for someone to arrive who needs to witness the execution. I really ought to find out which so I know how much time I've got. If I have more time, I can formulate a better plan. Less time, I'll have to wing it.

From what I can see, my options aren't plentiful. One. Overpower a guard in order to break out while I'm being fed, moved, or interrogated. High interest times. Two. Tunnel out. Unlikely, given the cameras and complete stone surroundings. On top of that, I'm not sure what's on either side of me, so I could be tunneling into another cell. That would really suck. Three. Smash the glass of the mirror wall and escape through the interrogation room. Bonus points if I can strangle or impale my zealot sister in the process. The restraints might help with that, but if it's leaded glass, it's unlikely to work no matter what tools I bring to bear. Obviously this cell was created with evians in mind. It ought to use the highest resiliency materials available.

No matter which way I choose to go about this, I need more information.

What do I know about this entire set up? Melina lives near Austin, Texas, unless she relocated without Mother knowing. Mother kept a rigorous presence around her to prevent that sort of thing, so for now I'll assume I'm in Texas. That means it's relatively temperate weather, but no one has basements because of the water level. Which means I'm unlikely to be underground. That makes things easier. Without windows in here, it's likely I'm in an interior room of some kind of home or compound. If I'm surrounded by cells, or if there's an iron shell around the stone, my entire escape attempt may be DOA. In any case, I'll have to overcome the camera situation. Blacking it out would immediately be noticed, and I have no electronics on my person, so there's no chance of creating a loop in the feed. I have to assume it's monitored, whether on site or remotely, and any disruption or strange behavior will immediately be noticed and addressed.

My hands are bound, but I've got these helpful, almost beautiful shackles. In spite of Melina's previous assurances, I'm still in my underwear. A glint of something draws my attention downward. I can't see much without shifting, but I can see my own clavicle, which is where the glint originates. The figure eight necklace Chancery gave me so many years ago rests against my chest. It passed Melina's rigorous search, apparently deemed unimportant.

Mother's gone, and now Chancery thinks I've fled. She probably assumes I'm plotting against her. A tear leaks from one eye and drops to the dusty yellowish stone underneath me. I hold my heart rate steady somehow, but barely. It feels like it's breaking right here, in this empty, depressing cell. My sister trusted me, loved me, in spite of all that I've done. She forgave me, even though I never apologized. She brought me a gift pledging we'd be together forever, friends and allies, and I poisoned her for it. Over and over again I spurned her attempts to make peace with me. There's no search party coming, and I have only myself to blame.

Maybe I deserve to die here. If Melina's right that my death would bring Chancery and Alamecha the best chance at peace, I should lay down and let her kill me. I could even confirm her suspicions and set her mind at ease. But I'm too selfish to roll over and give up. I like living too much.

An image springs to my mind of the air vent and the speaker. The ceiling was stone as well, but those two things require incursions in the stone. Maybe there's something I can do with that. . .

My stomach growls and I think about how long it's been since I last ate. Evian bodies can heal most anything, but they need nourishment to do it. I need to replenish, or before long I'll be healing as slowly as a human. Well, not that pathetic, but closer than I care to admit.

A sliding sound behind me startles me and I flinch. A scraping sound follows. I sit up slowly, pretending the noise woke me. Another sliding sound before I can even spin all the way around. A silver tray rests on the floor with four bowls and a liter of water in a plastic container on top of it. The smell of some kind of beef stew, bread, chunks of cheese, and grilled vegetables fills my scent receptors and I practically moan.

Get it together Judica. I scrabble toward it pathetically, my shackled hands reaching for the bowl instinctively. No utensils on the tray, but I can drink stew. I bring the bowl to my mouth, but something hits me oddly. I look at the stew and sniff deeply. Beef chunks, gravy, potatoes, carrots, rice, celery, onions, and something else I can't pinpoint. What is it? A slight tang of solvent. Think, Judica, think. What smells like solvent? It's faint, so faint, but it's there.

Gamma-Hydroxybutyrate.

I swear under my breath. I'm starving. I need food. But if I eat this, I'll pass out again. They're counting on me needing the food badly enough to accept it, or they're hoping I'm not well-trained enough to spot their crap. But Mother prepared me too well to be fooled by this.

And if I delay my escape much longer, I'll grow weak enough that I can't succeed. I need to act now.

The weight in my hand tells me something I wouldn't have otherwise believed. The idiots sent me metal bowls. I dump the cheese out of the smallest bowl and into the stew bowl where it will melt. Then I carry the empty bowl to the very front of the room, mostly out of sight of the camera. I glance at the ceiling from my periphery. I'll only have one shot at this. I smash the bowl against the stone floor under my cuffs repeatedly until it's flattened and then I use the now flat metal to pry out a stone. Then another. I continue to pry frantically for a few minutes. I have a nice pile of rocks and a small hole dug when I hear a scuffle outside my door. I fly across the room and grab my stew, hurling the melted cheese blob at the camera. It hooks over the top, covering it entirely. So far, so good.

Now or never. I leap at the ceiling, hands extended, fingers scrabbling at the air vent and the speaker circle. I don't get a good enough grip to support myself, but I shift the metal cover on the air vent and dent the speaker box before I slam back to the ground, twisting my ankle badly when I land. I focus all my energy on my ankle, healing it as much as I can, but I don't repair all the damage. No time, not with me half-starved. The door latch grinds and I fling myself back into the air, my fingers slamming with every ounce of force I can muster into the vent and the speaker cover.

My nails shatter, my skin tears, and two fingers break, but I dig my broken hands around the edges of the speaker hole, twisting into the tangle of wires inside. My hands and arms shake with the strain of holding the rest of my body against the ceiling with so little tension. My core muscles shake, my legs wobble, and my thighs cramp, but it works. I'm suspended from the ceiling, outside of their range of view.

The door slides open and two men walk inside, both holding guns. They aren't tranq guns, not this time. They walk straight toward my pathetic twelve-inch hole, just like I hoped they would. It's directly beneath me.

This part I can do, this I was made for.

I drop down on them, landing directly on top of one and startling the other. I fracture my arm in the process, but luckily it's just my left. The guard who breaks my fall has a knife in his leg sheath. Idiot. I wrap the chain connecting my wrists around his throat and use my toes to relieve him of his conveniently accessible knife. I toss it in the air and snag it with my unbroken right hand. Then I whip it around and slice his throat. He flops around on the ground melodramatically, hands flailing. He'd do better focusing his energy on healing the damage instead of trying to attract attention. If he thrashes too much, he might actually lose too much blood and die.

Unfortunately, this idiot wasn't the only one who entered my cell. The other guard lifts his gun and fires, punching me in the shoulder with a hollow tip round at point blank range. I grit my teeth and breathe through the pain, not diverting resources to try and heal it, not yet.

Shoulder wounds aren't deadly. I throw the knife at his throat, punching through into his spine. He stumbles back, and I rush him, yanking it out and slashing both eyes.

I probably should have severed his spine or removed his head, but that's messy and time consuming with a six-inch knife. Besides, healing eyeballs, from what I hear, is one of the most painful and time consuming processes our body can complete. He'll be occupied with that for at least an hour. I try not to relish the sound of the guard's screams. I shouldn't revel in defeating my enemies, but we all have our flaws. I take the gun from his weak fingers and tuck it into the waistband of my underwear. I really need some clothing, but I don't dare slow down to try and take any blood-stained shirts or pants from the guards.

Besides, I couldn't get anything over my handcuffs even if I did.

I snag the keycard from the blind guard and tuck it under the shoulder strap of my bra. Then I set the knife on the ground so I can pat down the other guard until I find his card too. Can't have them healing quick and following me out the door. I hold the knife in my teeth and I limp toward the door, ignoring the jabs from my sprained ankle. I don't even bother using my left arm, knowing the hole that hollow point punched through my shoulder will take forever to heal in my current state. My fractured arm shoots bolts of pain up into my shoulder, and my broken fingers complain, but it's minor compared to the pulsing pain of an open gunshot wound.

Healing slowly blows.

I scan the plate on the wall with one of the keycards. The door slides open with a chime just as the cheese falls off the camera and schlops to the floor. I blow Melina a kiss and step outside of my cell, tucking the keycard back into my bra strap and tossing the knife back into my right hand.

I expect a beehive of activity. I expect guns pointed at my head, or poison gas grenades.

I do not expect to be standing in a relatively dilapidated shed. Good grief. The light is so low that I blink repeatedly to help my eyes adjust, and then marvel at the lack of security outside of my stone room. A small door leads to the sterile gray room where I assume Melina stood earlier. A variety of gardening tools clutter up the space around me. I look around frantically for something to get me out of these cuffs, and notice rat droppings in the corner.

I'm embarrassed for my sister, and I like my chances at escape if this is her holding facility.

I don't see anything likely to remove these cuffs, but at least there's a black shirt hanging on a hook. The name on the label on the front reads Diana, and it smells like turpentine and mold, but it's better than naked. I think. I tug it on over my head with thick, slow fingers, and then tear the sides of the shirt so they can drape down over my arms around the stupid cuffs. I try half-heartedly to knot the sides, but it's too hard. Tattered rags to cover my underwear? Better than nothing.

I focus on healing the bloody mess of my shoulder next, working on the musculature one section at a time. The harder I push, the dizzier I become, but the skin finally closes over the hole, and I rotate my shoulder up and down in small circles. Gah, that was the slowest I've ever healed in my life. I grit my teeth and flex my hand. Yep, forearm's still fractured. I close my eyes and shove at my cells, flogging them into doing their job, one tiny cellular regeneration at a time.

When I put weight on my right ankle, wonder of wonders, it has actually already healed on its own. My fingers are swollen, but clearly improving as well. Next up on my list of short term wants: pants. With the luck I've had today, when I find some, they'll probably be covered in maggots.

When I duck outside of the shed, I look around slowly, cool air pebbling the skin on my legs. It's dark outside, and stars wink at me from the sky above. The shed is set in the back corner of a large yard, probably at least two full acres. A white limestone wall six feet tall circles the outer perimeter, but the main house is a sprawling stucco mansion that rises three floors high. Light spills over the manicured back lawn from a row of seven or eight foot tall picture windows across the back on the first floor. I duck behind a plumbago bush and listen for anyone near me. I can't hear anyone else.

Would there really only be two guards tasked to watch me in my cell? What kind of operation does Melina run here? Why would Angel betray Mother for *this*? I can't believe I could have punished Angel and instead I released her.

I let Mother down, but not again. Not today.

Five cameras are mounted across the back half of the house, rotating back and forth to provide eyes on the entire yard. I watch the pattern for several minutes, aware of time ticking down the drain. The camera on the far left finally clears my position and I vault up on the side of the stone wall. I can barely make out the land spreading out before me, rolling hills gently sloping downward for nearly a mile. But the lights nestled at the bottom of that expanse tell me we're a little far flung, with more civilization that direction. I could slink over the wall and be free within minutes.

The possibility tugs at me. Melina has countless people here in her compound, and I have a gun with five hollow point rounds, a purloined knife, and two useless keycards. Technically, this isn't even my fight anymore. I'm not responsible for revenge, justice, or the pride of the

Alamecha name. I'm barely even Chancery's Heir, soon to be replaced by her first daughter. The thought of her marrying and starting a family with Edam sends my jealousy into flare, but I tamp down on that reaction. I'm not what Melina fears. I won't tear our family apart. I wrap my left hand around my necklace. I need to be alive to have any chance at making things right.

As much as I'd like to escape posthaste, that's not who I am. I don't run, even when I'm afraid. Actually, fear usually amplifies my desire to attack.

I drop back down into Melina's yard and refocus on the cameras. Once I've worked out the pattern I'll need to follow, I wait for the first camera to track left. Then I sprint for the live oak. I stand as straight as I can behind its large trunk while the middle camera sweeps my area.

On the proper count, I spin around the trunk and crawl behind the day lilies until I've reached the first picture window. I peer through it from behind a hibiscus.

Miraculously the entire bottom floor looks empty. Where are the armed guards? Where are the snipers, the perimeter guards? What's going on here?

I reach for the handle on the sliding door, the chains connecting my cuffs rattling irritatingly, but before I've shifted it even a hair, a loud alarm sounds from the corners of the house. 'Alert, alert,' it blares obnoxiously.

I huddle down further, but this time the place springs into the beehive I expected before. I glance back at the shed and notice one of the guards is hobbling out. I swear under my breath. I should have killed them after all, and shattered that dumb camera, too. I scuttle back toward the perimeter wall, knife in one hand, firearm in the other. A tall woman with half a dozen earrings running up the side of her ear turns the corner and her striking golden eyes widen when she sees me.

"Judica," she says, her voice breathy. "It's really you. I've wanted to meet you for a long time."

I shoot her in the face and she crumples to the ground. Heal that, Miss Chatty.

I spring over her body, hoping against hope that my sadistic, insane sister will follow her around the corner. But she doesn't. Six armed guards do instead.

The first one fires an exploding round that hits six inches away from my leg. Shrapnel from it shreds the skin and muscle covering my outer calf and ankle. One piece lodges painfully in the bottom part of my fibula. I bite my lip and start to fire. I hit the first shooter in his throat, the second, a short woman, in her chest, and the third in both his shoulder, which doesn't slow him, and his thigh.

Now I'm out of ammunition.

I fling my knife at the fourth guard before she can hit me, the knife point reaching the barrel of her gun as she fires. The round explodes in front of her and I turn away from the gore, leaping to the top of the wall. Another shot explodes beneath my feet, missing me only because I surprised them.

I glance up toward the house and meet Melina's eyes. She's staring down at me from the central window on the third floor. Her lip is curved into a half smile, almost like she's proud. I clench my empty hands and strain uselessly against the cuffs. This isn't a fight I can win, not shackled, starving, and unarmed.

I've failed Mother again. I grab a hunk of rubble from the top of the wall and hurl it at the last guard, knocking his weapon from his hand. Then I leap from the wall. A bullet clips my forearm and blood sprays downward, all over my bare legs. I don't pause, my feet barely finding purchase in the rubble and mesquite scrub brush. The bottoms of my feet paint the rocks with blood I can't see clearly in the dark. Hopefully my pursuers will struggle, too.

I stumble and fall, but the sound of Melina's people giving chase keeps me moving. I can't run as quickly as an automobile, but I'm not taking roads, either. My foot comes down hard on a cactus and I bite down on a scream. No reason to alert Melina's goons to my exact location.

After what feels like eons, I stumble into the outskirts of the town I saw from the wall. I run past a dozen houses, then two. Finally I see one that looks perfect, because it's almost exactly like the other thirty I've passed, right down to the brick mailbox, rustic brown shutters, and brick and stone façade out front.

I check the back door and, as if karma has finally decided to reverse course, it's unlocked. I won't even need to smash the glass. I creep into the back door and crouch down, listening. Blood pools around my feet and drips down from my forearm onto the white tile floor.

Splat. Splat. Splattery splat.

A clock ticks in the next room. Otherwise, all is still.

I need food, pants, shoes, and to bust out of these dumb restraints. Then I'll split. I won't harm these humans, because I don't want to do anything to alert Melina to my location.

A light switches on and a deep voice exclaims, "No way."

I hold my hands up, blood-streaked palms facing out. "I mean you no harm."

"Are you Wonder Woman?" a human around my age asks in a subdued voice behind me.

I spin around and notice that her pajama pants feature flying squirrels. Am I wonder who? I shake my head.

"Don't be an idiot," the young guy standing by the light switch asks. He's holding a baseball bat in his right hand, but it's not raised. "Those aren't vambraces, they're cuffs. She's got to be a nutjob who escaped from that Decatur Inpatient Institute for the Mentally Ill." His chest puffs up and he flexes his arms. "Don't try anything, and we won't report you. Just head back out the way you came."

"Your back door was unlocked," I explain. "I wasn't breaking in."

"The door being unlocked doesn't mean you're welcome," the girl says. "We left it open for Dad, so he won't wake us up. Again."

"Shut up," the guy hisses.

"What?" she asks.

"Don't tell her we're alone," he whispers.

I'm pretty sure that even a human could have heard him. These two aren't very coordinated.

"She's not going to hurt us," the girl says. "She's injured. And if she's not Wonder Woman, she's trying to hide from someone herself. We shouldn't kick her out. We should help her."

The boy's eyebrow cocks on the left side. "Are you? Hiding, I mean?"

I nod dumbly. "I need food and a change of clothing and I'll leave right away, I swear. I won't hurt you."

The boy frowns and lifts the bat menacingly. "Anyone who has to say 'I won't hurt you' is bad news."

The girl exhales loudly. "Cut it out, Billy, and put that dumb bat down. Obviously we're helping her. She's saying she won't hurt you because you're threatening her, the poor thing. Nothing interesting ever happens around here. Hazel is *not* going to believe this."

❧ 8 ❧

THE PAST

I've never worked so hard not to show emotion in my entire life.

My mother is dead.

I am alone. And with her last breaths, she replaced me. My entire life has been a complete waste of time.

I watch impassively as Chancery flies away in Alora's jet. I do not allow tears to well in my eyes. I do not allow my heart rate to increase or my breathing to hitch. I do not frown, or cry, or gnash my teeth. I turn and walk back to my room as though nothing life-altering, heart-shattering, or practically incapacitating has occurred. While Chancery trains, and agonizes, and mourns, I will hold the other families at bay. I'll manage Alamecha, and reassure our human leaders, and handle internal family disputes.

But that's not all that I'll do.

Chancery thinks I killed our Mother. Nothing I can say or do will change her mind, but I know that I didn't. Today, while the evidence is still fresh, I have the best chance of finding the clues that will lead me to whoever did. They must pay for throwing our family into turmoil and stealing the last years of guidance and support she would have provided. I won't simply kill them. Whoever did this will suffer, but first I have to find him or her or them.

I close my eyes and evaluate the facts.

Mother was poisoned.

It wasn't Chancery.

It happened during her birthday celebration so it could have been a human, although that's unlikely. Mother's policies have been the most pro-human of any empress ever. But they're so short lived, they might not even realize that. Humans do things for idiotic reasons all the time.

More likely, she was taken out by a rival family.

I wish I had been present earlier and had the peace of mind to watch each family representative present in turn. Not that it would have been conclusive, by any means, but one of them might have given something away. Poison, while not as aggressive as a challenge, is personal. It's sneaky. It's cowardly, too.

What baffles me is that we take precautions against poison. Consistent precautions. Which means someone knew about all of them and found a way around them. First, Mother had a tasting dog. She had servants and guards who tasted her food as well. Her chef Angel had protocols in place too, many of which extended beyond her.

But of course, Angel would know the ins and outs of every single one. She's one of Mother's oldest friends, and Mother trusted her implicitly. But Mother trusted Lyssa too, a woman who lied to her for the better part of twenty years. Clearly Mother's not immune to deception. Friendship is a liability. It blinds you to the truth. I already knew this, but Mother's demise is a good reminder. It's the reason I have no friends.

Angel surely knows she's a top suspect, even if she's

almost too obvious. Even so, I'm positive Balthasar locked her up and secured the kitchen. That would have been my second order of business, after shoving all the guests on planes and off the island.

I was too distraught to think about it, but my tray last night held leftover party food, and this morning's breakfast consisted of yogurt and granola. All things no one needed to prepare, things that could have been tossed on a tray and dropped off in my room.

I need to talk to Angel right away, before she's been interrogated by anyone else. I make a beeline for the kitchen. Balthasar's already there, reviewing files with Job.

"What does this mean?" Balthasar asks, pointing at something on a piece of paper.

"It indicates that all of the food served at the celebration was clear of any toxin, sir," Job says. "As was every other object both in her rooms and at the celebration."

"Were all standard protocols observed?" I interject. I can't have evidence disappearing at the hands of the one who created it.

Balthasar and Job both salute me and offer a short bow.

"Yes, Your Highness," Balthasar says. "We had four guards on the—" He coughs. "Four guards watching over your mother until Job retrieved her. She's been attended by four men at all times since, even in Job's lab. Hestus has stepped in to check everything Job did. The two of them did not study together, nor did Job have any say in the person chosen to parallel him."

I nod. "Fine. Good. And Job, you've tested my mother's garbage from yesterday?"

Job nods. "Yes, Your Highness. It was disposed of in a separate area, per standard operating procedure. Everything was clear, but there wasn't a lot of waste. Angel knows how much they eat, and frequently they consume all that she makes."

"They?" I know who he means, but I'm going to make him say it. I can't have people tiptoeing around me.

"Chancery." Job clears his throat. "Her Royal Highness."

I do not frown. I do not scowl. I do not growl at him referring to my sister as the Empress. "Of course."

"Your mother regularly eats deviled eggs." Job closes his eyes as if he's in pain. "Ate. She regularly ate deviled eggs." He clears his throat. "She regularly ate deviled eggs, and that's a fairly simple dish to. . ." He trails off.

"It's an easy thing to poison," I say. "You can say it. I won't collapse or sob or create an embarrassing display causing everyone around me to feel uncomfortable."

Job nods. "Of course not. Unfortunately, your mother liked them enough that she ate everything that was provided."

"But you pumped her stomach," I say. "Obviously."

"I did, but we found very, very little inside of it. She had been quite busy and evian stomachs process food efficiently." Job shifts from foot to foot. "We ran as many tests as we possibly could on the teaspoon of contents, but they yielded nothing."

"Her intestines?" Balthasar asks.

"The same," Job says.

"What about Cookie?" I ask. "My sister accused me of killing her, but I didn't. Since she was poisoned, isn't it likely the culprit was something both Cookie and Mother consumed? Perhaps something that Duchess wouldn't eat?" Chancery already said it. She and Duchess didn't eat eggs, but Cookie and Mother did.

"I had the same thought," Job says. "We pumped Cookie's stomach as well. While it's not conclusive, we found trace elements of a toxin we haven't yet identified."

"How can you know you've found poison, but not know what it is?" I ask.

"Are you asking for the science behind it?" Job's eyebrows rise. "If so, it's that we located portions of the bowel that had become necrotic—"

I throw up my hands. "Nope. It's fine. I was merely wondering, if you identified that something is a toxin, how can you not determine the nature of that toxin."

"Ah," Job says. "You can see how the body reacted to it, and you can swab for trace amounts. Until we've spent enough time analyzing the sample, we won't know its exact origin. And beyond that, as we run tests, the sample available to us diminishes."

Aggravating. Also, out of my wheelhouse. "Well, I don't want to keep you from that," I say, "but I'd like to confirm that Mother's body is in cryo."

"Absolutely it is," Job says.

"Thank you. I promised my sister we'd delay the funeral until her return. Please feel free to resume your analysis or study in any area you might need. We really need to know as much as we can about the cause of death."

"Agreed." Job bows and strides from the room with purposeful steps.

Balthasar falls in next to me as I walk toward the portion of the ballroom where Mother lay yesterday. The tape outline is too macabre for words. "You've pulled all security tapes of Mother for the past two weeks?"

He nods.

"And you have a team reviewing them for anything, with a focus on any consumption of food, I assume."

"I do." Balthasar's voice is low and tense. "We're going to catch whoever did this. They will pay."

I widen my eyes. "You don't think it's me?"

He shakes his head. "I'm not blinded by sibling rivalry

like Chancery. You loved your mother. You'd never have harmed her."

A tightness in my chest eases and I fight back the emotion that tries to drown me. "Thank you."

Balthasar's eyes are the softest I've ever seen them. "I'm very sorry for your loss. I know words can't help, not really, but you're not alone in your grief."

In that moment, I can only think of three people I know beyond a doubt didn't harm my mother, and he's one of them. Balthasar's sorrow is genuine, and it clearly runs deep. I'm positive Chancery never would have harmed a hair on Mother's head, and I'm sure Roman wouldn't have done it. He's too loyal to me. Everyone else is a suspect as far as I'm concerned.

"I'm ready to interrogate Angel now," I say.

Balthasar's foot stumbles, but he recovers immediately. "Of course. Let me take you to her."

"You haven't spoken to her yet?"

He shakes his head. "I assumed you'd want to be the first. She's had no visitors, and the speaker in her cell is not turned on. There has been no outside communication, no way to prepare a cover or work out details."

If she really did this, that all would have been done in advance, but it's still helpful to know Balth hasn't slipped. "Perfect."

He walks next to me, matching my steps perfectly the entire way down to the holding cells that recently contained Lark. I wonder how Chancery's holding up right now. Lyssa, Lark, her dog, and now our Mother in the span of a day and a half. I don't often feel sorry for my twin, but I do right now. I can't imagine feeling even more pain than I already do.

Angel is sitting cross legged on the stone floor of her cell, her hands resting on her knees. She's meditating.

Could she be dead enough inside that she might feel complete peace after mother's death yesterday? Her calm demeanor certainly doesn't convince me that she's grieving a close friend. But then again, we all process our feelings in our own ways. I dismiss my guards to wait outside the door, but Balthasar leans against the back wall, arms crossed over his chest.

Even now I'm being trained, supervised, and measured.

Memories of time in the kitchen with Angel flood my mind, but I brush them away savagely. She's not a friend, a mentor, or a teacher, not right now. She's a suspect. "Angel." My voice is smaller than I wanted it to be. I repeat the name, louder the second time.

Her chin lifts, and her eyes open. The corners of her mouth turn down, and her eyes well with tears. "Oh, Judica."

I wipe away a tear that pops out unbidden in response to her simple exclamation. "Angel, I am here to ask you some questions. I'd ask you not to employ any emotional devices or manipulation. I've been through the requisite courses of study, taught by you in fact, and I'll spot any attempts you make."

I'm interrogating the leader of my mother's spy network. She has probably interrogated more people than any other person in Alamecha. The irony isn't lost on me.

"Mother trusted you implicitly, and you're the one person who had complete unlimited knowledge and access to everything she consumed. As you know, she died by poison."

Angel nods.

"Start with the beginning of the day and walk me through the protocol for the preparation of Mother's meals."

"I wake each day at four a.m. I oversee the operations

of the entire kitchen, and I personally create the food consumed by every member of the royal family in residence here at the palace. You, Chancery, your mother, and Inara. Your mother ate breakfast every morning at six-thirty a.m. She liked a spread of food, but she especially enjoyed egg products. Omelets, deviled eggs, fried eggs, Eggs Benedict, soufflés, etcetera."

I know all of that, but she needs to lay it all out, so I don't interrupt.

"I would begin with inspection of the eggs, all of which came from our own chickens. Sometimes I even collected the eggs myself. It allowed me to check for signs of illness or unrest among the chickens, and I like to keep the staff on their toes. I would whip the eggs, prepare the breakfast items, including pastry, and then taste it all myself. I had the person carrying the food taste it as well. In such a way, anyone who might come in contact with the food is also eating it. These things will be reflected by the video feeds. I plated the food, and then walked it to the edge of the kitchen. Once it leaves my custodianship, there are always two guards who accompany the server to your mother's breakfast room. Some days, if I had something to discuss with your mother, I'd carry it myself."

"Did anything strange happen over the past few days? Anything at all, no matter how small?"

Angel looks at the ground and shakes her head slowly. "I've been going over the past week in my mind, over and over. I can't think of a single thing that was out of the ordinary." She looks up at me. "From a food perspective, that is. There was the bizarre EMP that someone set off. I assume you're looking into that. In my experience, very few things are as unconnected as we would like them to be."

I grit my teeth.

"But from a culinary perspective, we throw parties quite

often. Your mother's nine-hundredth birthday is a large event, and I made a very large, very fancy cake, but she hadn't even taken a bite of that. The rest of her diet remained the same as it always is. The same people working for me. I haven't had a new member join my staff in eighteen months. We have prepared the same foods for several months, on rotation of course, and I've had the same suppliers for the last eight months or more. The same ovens and stoves and storage containers have been used. Most of the produce is grown either here by my people, or by my agents on Kauai." Her shoulders tense. "I lost the best queen we've ever had, and I have no idea how or why." She meets my eye. "Are you positive it's poison? Could it have been something else?"

I arch one eyebrow. "Acute onset old age? A stomach grenade planted by a flea that went in through her nose? What else, exactly, could it have been?"

Angel's voice is flat. "I notice Job's not down here with me, but he had access to her as much as I did."

"He checked her weekly as the court physician. I doubt anyone would say that's quite the same as three meals a day and intermittent snacks."

"There's one thing that struck me as odd last week," Angel whispers.

I step nearer to the cell, almost touching the titanium bars. "What was that?

"The day before your mother died, I brought dinner to her. Chancery was showering, and as you know, the power was still wonky. It was a strange night."

I nod. It was a bizarre day all around.

"Your mother asked me to vow to always do whatever it took to protect the family."

"That's part of your oath when you're placed on the Council."

Angel nods. "It is, but that oath ends upon death of the monarch you serve. She wanted me to promise her specifically, regardless of timing, or anything else. I'm nearly as old as her, so it seemed odd."

"What did you say?"

Angel shrugs. "I agreed, of course. I loved your mother, and I love Alamecha. I'll always serve."

The night before my mother died, she asked Angel to make an oath that would outlast her life. Like she knew she was going to be poisoned.

"Could she have done it herself?" I ask, regretting the words as soon as they leave my mouth.

"You think your mother poisoned *herself*? After destroying the heirship documents, but before completing new ones?" Angel's head cocks sideways. "Doubtful."

Of course she didn't. The whole idea is absurd. "Never mind. But I wonder whether she knew."

"The Empress is always in danger," Angel murmurs. "And Enora lived a very long life."

I shake my head. "She would have done something to stop it if she knew."

"Maybe."

"What do you mean, maybe?" I ask.

"Did you see your mother after she killed Lyssa?"

"I was there," I say. "I watched the entire thing."

"I'm asking if you *saw* her. Did you notice her quiet desperation? Have you ever killed a friend?"

I square my shoulders. "I've never killed anyone at all."

Angel's eyes soften. "Of course you haven't, not at seventeen years old. But trust me when I tell you that the first time you end someone's life, it takes a toll. I pray you never have to kill a dear friend, but if you do, it saps your resolve and deadens your soul. Enora felt her own mortality that day, I'm sure of it."

"So you think she begged the promise from you because of what happened with Lyssa?"

Angel shrugs. "I don't know why she did what she did, but that was my assumption at the time, yes. I didn't think much of it, other than Lyssa's death caused your mother to examine how much longer she'd be with you and your sister. But then when she died. . . The timing seemed strange."

"Fine." I take one final step, my face almost pressed against the bars. "What are you afraid of, Angel? What makes you squirm the most when you consider you may be locked up in here for the rest of your days?"

"Motive." Angel's mouth turns up in a smile. "You're wondering about my motive."

She taught me to interrogate people, and I'm sure botching this one. But she would see through any attempts at subtlety, so what's the point?

"Look through all my belongings, child. Talk to everyone in my family, every one of my children. I had access, and I had opportunity. I could have killed your mother every single day of her life. But I have absolutely no motive to do it. I've spent my entire life serving her. I respected her immensely and I loved her deeply. I would have died for your mother for the past eight hundred years, and I'll die to honor her memory or protect her family now. There's not a scintilla of evidence that will contradict that, and I don't fear waiting here in this cell until you come to the same conclusion, because it means you are looking for her killer." She opens her mouth, then closes it again, without saying anything else.

"But?"

"While I'm in here, you have who knows who making your food. You have a poisoner on the loose, and it makes me nervous. And I don't want you to waste too much time on me while the evidence is still fresh."

"I should release you so you can keep me safe, like you didn't keep my mother safe? And you're worried about me being in here talking to you, only because I'm not tracking down other leads?" I slow clap. "Brilliant performance, masterful really."

"You think I murdered her." Angel's shoulders slump. "I'd probably think the same. Opportunity, knowledge, and expertise. That's fine. Do what you need to do, and I'll cooperate any way that I can, any time you need me. I swear that I won't struggle or try to escape. Ever. Eventually you'll see."

"What if I don't want to wait? What if you've convinced me that you had the chance, and no one could have done it without your knowledge?"

She shrugs. "Then you execute me, and the whole debate ends."

"But you know I won't do that, spymaster."

She smiles. "You're many things, Judica. Savage, brilliant, coy, direct, and audacious. What you aren't is premature. You think things through, and you come to the logical conclusion. You'll eventually see that I had nothing to gain from your mother's death. Nothing at all, in any way or conceivable form. Unlike Lyssa, there are no skeletons in my closet, no dire secrets, no treasonous lies. I'm exactly who I've always appeared to be, which is why I make such a perfect Intelligence Director. No one can blackmail you when you have no secrets to expose."

Everyone has secrets. I intend to find hers. But I won't find out anything else here in this cell.

"I'll be in touch." I spin on my heel and climb the stairs, guards taking position in front of me, and several steps behind, sandwiching Balthasar between them along with me.

He follows me, one step behind. I had forgotten he was

even there during the interrogation, he was so silent and motionless.

When we reach the main hallway, he puts a hand on my shoulder. "That was hard, to interrogate a master. And what's more, a master you respect. You did very well. You handled it very much as your mother would have. She would be quite proud."

My heart swells, but I can't hug him here, and I can't break down in the main hallway either. "Do you think Angel had anything to do with it?"

Balthasar considers for a moment before answering, his eyes distant, clearly filtering through his memories of our recent interaction. "Enora the merciless." He chuckles and shakes his head, walking down the hallway until we reach the door to my room. He inclines his head toward my door.

I push it open and Balthasar follows me inside, closing it behind us.

"Everyone called her merciless, and they were right in many ways. Your mother never wasted time on tears and general theatrics when something had to be done. She chopped her best friend's head off without batting an eye."

"She had her reasons," I say, defending her reflexively.

Balthasar laughs. "Of course she did, young pup."

"Treason is a good one."

"Treason," Balthasar says. "Pah. She was protecting sweet Chancery."

I can't quite contain my shock.

"Your mother told me most everything, and what she didn't tell me, well, I've known her for a very, very long time." Balthasar frowns. "I *knew* her for a very long time." He breathes in and out once, then twice. "But she trusted Angel, and I do too."

"She miscalculated something," I say. "Someone she trusted killed her."

Balthasar's entire face crumples and tears well in his eyes. I've never seen this man upset, much less crying. It's not pretty. He makes an odd sound, almost like a bark. "I failed her, and obviously I should have stepped down years ago."

Without even thinking, I hug him tight. "You didn't fail her. All of us did everything we could."

"It wasn't enough, and now you need someone better than me to run this investigation."

I pat his back awkwardly.

He stiffens. "You shouldn't be comforting me, not you. This is backward."

"Grief doesn't play by the rules." And strangely, hugging my mother's brother-in-law, her warlord, somehow it's soothing, like we're all broken, and we're all doing the best we can together.

Probably because it's the first time since Mother died that I haven't felt utterly and completely alone.

A moment later, Balthasar straightens up. "I'm not the man Enora deserves to pursue justice for her death, but I'm what we've got."

"I'm glad you're with me on this," I say. "We got very little from Angel, but I have some ideas, direction, if nothing else. How about you dig into her room and her motives, and I'll look into Mother's office and check the video feed of her for the last few weeks."

Balthasar grunts. "Is Roman the new captain of your guard?"

I gulp. I forgot about that. With Edam gone, I need a new one. "Sure, yes."

"Not a bad call. He's motivated, that's for sure."

I narrow my eyes at him, but I don't ask. "Let's eat dinner together and review what we've discovered."

He nods. "You need to train today, too. Make time, and use Rivera, Sloan, Crewel, and Dmitri."

Four guards, four different attack specialties. He's not taking things easy on me. For some reason that makes me feel better, not worse. He knows Chancery will be preparing, and he wants me ready for it, but I'm not worried about her. She can't catch me, not anytime this year in any case. No use fighting him over it, though. "Sure," I say. "Sure I will."

"Dante." I call the senior guard once Balthasar has rounded the corner. "Where's Roman?"

"Reviewing the footage of your mother, Your Highness. He insisted on handling it himself."

I'm not even surprised that he's already thought of it. "Let him know I'll join him shortly, and send for the four Balthasar named to meet me at the training arena."

After a long and challenging session, I stride down the hall toward the security bay.

Roman greets me with a tentative smile. Poor guy has no idea how to act around me. I'm sure he wants to be sympathetic, but I'm not exactly the gushy, needy type of boss. "I'm fine, everyone. Assume that at all times."

Roman's shoulders relax, and Lorn shifts in his chair, his foot resuming its typical tapping.

"Have we found anything?" I notice the time stamp on the video footage. Twelve days ago, which means it was Mom's meeting with Larena and the Secretary of the Treasury for the United States. She sips her tea and I have to regulate my breathing and heart rate. Why is every single thing hard right now? I shove my feelings down so deep I doubt I could find them again if I tried.

"No," Lorn says. "Nothing interesting, anyway."

"Even the slightest detail might matter," I say.

"Thank you," Roman says. "We hadn't realized that. In fact, what else can you tell us about how to do our job?"

I scowl. "I know you're being thorough. But make sure you watch all of the feed, both of you. Something might click that otherwise might not if you split it out."

Roman pauses the video feed and crosses the room in a few long strides. He whispers. "I know you need to know. I won't miss anything, I swear."

More than knowing, I need to do something about her death. I can't stomp around helplessly any longer. I turn to leave. "Make charts and lists of every person with whom she comes into contact. Names, and the circumstances in which they interacted. Then compile a 'best of' track for the feed so I can watch relevant sections myself. I'll be reviewing her correspondence from the last month in her office when you need me."

I tear my eyes away from my mother's face on camera. Gazing longingly at her won't bring her back, and it won't avenge her murder. I'm not Chancery to wallow in grief and self-pity at the expense of action.

Mother's office is well organized, as I knew it would be. First, I review the correspondence from the other five empresses. The missives contain the usual amount of griping and sniping, but nothing too surprising, except for a letter from Venagra. I was born just two years before her, which makes her barely sixteen. In spite of her tender age, she's furious with her own mother, Melamecha, and offers an alliance with Alamecha if we will pledge our aid in overthrowing the throne so she can ascend. There's no way to know exactly what Mother said, but I can guess. It would be an attractive offer, and Mother could have turned Shamecha into a fiefdom with that kind of access, but she'd never work with someone who showed that kind of disloyalty and ingratitude. I imagine Venagra's eyes are still stinging from Mother's reprimand.

I sort through letters from various Alamecha evians next. I had no idea Mother's subjects were so whiny. Graig copied my idea. Nimerick lied about me. Dax went back on our agreement. Mother should have invested in a whipping post to deal with most of this. But I find a partially drafted response to Graig, and she's so even and reasonable. Her response makes his letter complaining look hot-headed and petty.

The pain that tears through me feels like lemon juice on an open wound. I curl inward and clench my fists until my nails slice into my palms. Even that isn't enough. Great heaving sobs wrack my body and I cry on Graig's dumb, whiny missive. How can she be gone? How? She was the one person who truly loved me in the entire world. No matter how badly I let her down, she would hug me and tell me it was okay. No matter how epically I failed, she always forgave me with grace. She led our family with strength and purpose. I still had so much to learn. The gaps in my knowledge terrify me.

I hate the idea of doing everything without her.

But she taught me to be better than this. Finally, my tears dry up and I straighten. I wipe at my face and sit upright. Eventually, these idiotic fits of weakness will stop, but until they do, I need to make sure I'm never in public when they hit. Thankfully, no one witnessed that breakdown.

I plow through all of it, making notes about each letter. I could go back and recall everything I see, so notes aren't strictly necessary, but it helps me integrate my thoughts. I shred my notes as soon as I've finished making them. I don't like to leave evidence of my suspicions. It feels good to be doing something, even if it's only digging into leads.

It's cathartic enough that I don't stop to eat. No lunch tray ever comes, which means the kitchen is chaos incarnate with Angel's incarceration. I wonder who Balthasar would trust to fill in for her until she's been cleared. The last time I saw Roman make his own lunch, he slathered more mayonnaise on his sandwich than cold cuts. I can only imagine the mess Balthasar makes of cooking. No thank you.

I'm nearly done with the piles and piles of correspondence when there's a knock at the door.

"Come in," I say.

Larena enters, a box in her hand. "I've got next month's rotation schedules for approval."

And she's bringing them to me. I suppose there's no one else. I suppress a groan. "That's fine. Put them there."

I don't want to wade through the eye-crossing lists of which guard will be on duty for each of the various tasks. I have no idea how Edam had the patience to create them every month, but the concept of approving every single one overwhelms me. Even an island as small as Ni'ihau boasts a wide variety of tasks that need rotations: kitchen work, grounds, security, training, reconnaissance, placements for ambassadors, negotiators, and on and on and on.

But someone has to do it, and I can't very well appoint a Council without officially being Empress. Even if I was Empress, I'm not sure who I can trust, which means I'll need to go through these lists and make sure people who distrust one another are doubled up to lower the likelihood of conspiracy.

Alamecha is a mess.

This would break Mother's heart nearly as much as me being at odds with Chancery. I dig into the lists, seeing patterns in the match-ups. There's clearly a method to each chief's selections. Harold always falls asleep on watch, but he's the best shot we have. Octavia almost never sleeps, but she's a lousy marksman. Louis offends almost everyone he interacts with, while men and women both adore Edeline from word one. I understand that things need to run smoothly, and I laud Mother's leadership for their thoughtfulness, but I have different goals right now.

Octavia is my great niece, daughter of my much older sister Vera's third son. I can't have her paired with Harold, who is Vera's nephew. Vera is ninth in line for the throne, after me, Chancery, Melina, Inara, Alora, Rivena, Danika, Annekah, and Emmeline. It's small, but it's still a motive, and crazier things have happened.

But when everyone is a threat, how can you narrow the field?

Mother's phone rings and I jump. I calm my shaking fingers and then pick up the receiver. "Hello?"

"I thought I might reach you here." Job doesn't sound pleased.

"What's wrong?"

"I've found trace elements of poison."

"You already told me that." I frown.

"We had found it in Cookie Crisp's stomach. We had identified necrotic bowel in your mother's stomach. We had not found poison in her body until now."

"Wait, does that mean—"

"I found traces of the poison in her hair."

I gulp. "This didn't happen yesterday."

"It has been going on for quite some time," Job says. "You should be looking for someone who had consistent access to her."

"Was the poison consumed? Or could it have been delivered in another way?"

"It's too early to tell. It could have been administered

through topical application, or through the air, though then it would likely have affected others around her."

And Chancery is fine. And Mom's dog Duchess seems perfectly healthy as well. "Understood. Please don't share this information with anyone."

"I won't, but recall I have a partner."

Right, a partner we assigned. "Ask him to keep this to himself as well. Tell him if he doesn't, there will be consequences."

I hang up the phone and process the new information. If the poison is in her hair follicles, it wasn't a one-time thing. Someone who saw Mother often wanted her dead. Off the top of my head, I can only think of Inara, Larena, Angel, me, Chancery, Balthasar, Frederick, and a few others who had consistent access to her. As easy as it feels to focus on Angel, I need to broaden the net. Everyone who might have been around her frequently or consistently in any capacity is a suspect.

I'll get a list from Roman before too long detailing everyone she interacted with for the two weeks before her death. But that makes me think about the schedules I just reviewed. Some of the patterns in the rotation schedule had major variances. I wonder why, and whether the same was true of the last two weeks. With my hand still on the phone receiver, I pick it up and call Amelia.

She answers on the first ring. "Yes, Your Highness?"

"I've been reviewing the rotations for next month and I had a few questions."

"I live to serve."

"Yes, yes. I noticed that you have a handful of people who show up on the calendar at erratic intervals. Can you tell me the reason for that?"

"I'm not sure I know what you mean."

I rifle through some papers. "Okay, you have Greta

handling the front flowerbeds for five days. Frankfurt for the next five, and so on. In fact, almost all of your rotations run in days of five for each task, and then each worker has two days off in between before they're brought in to handle another section of the grounds. But on the fourth rotation on the front flowerbeds, you have Quentin for eight days in a row, and then Greta for only two."

"Ah, I see what you're asking. You're wondering why don't we stick with the five in a row. Why is Quentin stuck working eight? That's your question."

"Even so."

"Well, your mother utilized humans for this type of work for a long time, but when you and erm, well, when you were born, she opted to forgo the use of humans for any tasks around the island."

Mother told me it was to keep us from growing unduly attached. Humans are like pets that might turn on us, but we would want to save them, help them. She worried that we could become distracted by them. "Fine."

"Well, using evians to do this type of work, it's. . . Other than the prestige of serving here, there isn't a lot to draw people to this job."

If she hems or haws any more than she already is, I might use her as a punching bag in tomorrow's training. "Go on."

"We have found that we need to be flexible with our workers so that they will keep the job here. Instead of merely offering two days off, our staff has flex days. They can take any five additional days per month, and the rest of us work around the days they choose. That way the benefits of being stationed at the capital can be enjoyed."

"Networking, you mean."

"Even so."

"Basically, you set the schedules, but then you post

them or something, and your staff can request to change them around however they like." Which makes them almost entirely useless.

"Within reason."

"Once the rotations have been posted, are they permanent?"

"Emergencies arise."

"We don't get sick, Amelia. What kind of emergency are you talking about?"

"Well, when the staff wants to work elsewhere, or on a different day, sometimes they trade."

I may as well throw these rotations in the trash bin. "Is there a record somewhere of who actually worked each shift? Do they have to document why they're trading and with whom?"

"This isn't Woodstock," Amelia says in a huff, like that should mean something to me. "Of course we have records."

"I need to see them for the past month."

I call each of the chiefs of the various sections and ask for the same information, because I need to know who was scheduled to be with Mother, and who made arrangements to be there instead.

A few hours later, Roman brings me his list of the people he saw interact with her. The number of people Mother interacts with daily is staggering. How is it so high?

From all the various information sources, I compile a list of my own. People who were scheduled to be with Mother, and other people who traded places with someone in order to come in contact with her.

It takes me seven hours to tease anything that makes sense out of the tangle of names and schedules, but when I do, I don't even need Roman's list. One person traded five times in the past month in order to clean Mother's bathroom. He was assigned to work on her bathroom crew eleven other days as well. Which means he had access to mother's soap, face cream, and sink sixteen days out of the last thirty. I've been so focused on food that I ignored other mechanisms of transference.

And it's someone I know. Roman's first cousin, Nihils. I stop and tidy up Mother's room. I should get something to eat. Tomorrow's going to be a busy day.

�֍ *9* ֍

THE PRESENT

"First things first," the girl says. "We need to get you out of those cuffs. They look miserable."

"Hold up," the guy says. "We should find out why she's wearing them in the first place before we take them off."

I sigh. "I'm Judica Alamecha. A full explanation would take quite some time, but to cut to the chase, my older sister Melina wants to supplant me and is trying to kill me. As soon as she can verify that she would step into my place in the family hierarchy. I managed to escape from the cell where she was holding me, but I haven't been able to free myself entirely yet." I lift my hands.

The blood drains from both of their faces.

"This is where you tell me your names," I say.

"I'm Ambrosia," the girl says. "And this is my brother Billy. His real name is William, but I've never heard anyone call him that."

The boy scowls and something about the way he looks at his sister, with a mix of irritation and affection, makes my heart contract painfully. Chancery will never look at me like that. "I go by Will now."

Ambrosia rolls her eyes. "He's a freshman at UT and bent on reinventing himself into someone fancier, but he'll always be Billy to me."

"Your sister's really trying to kill you?" Billy drops the bat and opens a drawer, his brows drawn together in concern. "That's messed up."

He emerges with a screwdriver. I have no idea what he's planning to do with that, but it's not going to work. What I need is a shim. "Do you happen to have any paperclips? Or a small metal wire of any kind?"

Ambrosia ducks out of the kitchen and reappears a moment later to dump a handful of paperclips on the table.

Two paperclips later, I'm sliding my hands out of the cuffs and rubbing the abraded skin underneath. Blood oozes slowly from the skin around my wrists, and I feel genuine empathy for these humans. A little food and I'll be good as new, but they're like this all the time. So fragile, so weak. I couldn't live like they do, afraid of every small injury.

"That was amazing," Billy says. He's watching me now the same way Ambrosia did when she said I was the Wonder lady.

"Who's the wonder person you mistook me for?" I ask.

Ambrosia's nose scrunches. "You've never heard of Wonder Woman? Where has your sister been keeping you?"

"I haven't spent enough time studying human historical icons," I admit. "But I can't blame my sister for my deficit there. She only held me captive for a few days."

"She's not real," Billy says. "Wonder Woman, I mean. She's a cartoon character from comic books, but they made her story into a movie. A pretty epic movie, actually."

"Well, I'm flattered," I say. "But right now, I'm also starving. Is there any chance I could get something to eat?"

"Maybe we ought to get you bandaged up first," Billy says, eyeing the puddle of blood on the floor, and the scabs forming around my wrist. "Did you run through a cactus?" His eyebrows rise precipitously.

Two dozen or so needles stick out at odd angles from the skin around my ankles. I cringe. At least they haven't noticed the gunshot wound on my forearm.

"Trust me. Food first, bandages later."

"Maybe we should call Dad," Ambrosia says quietly. "He could help her."

"He wouldn't even answer," Billy says. "And if he did, he wouldn't come home to help."

"What does your father do?" I ask, hoping that's the right way to ask a human about her parent's job.

"He's a surgeon. A trauma surgeon."

"Quite impressive," I say. At least, I think it is to them. Doctors go to school for a long chunk of a human lifetime. Several years, at least. "But really, if you've got some food for me to eat, I'll be grateful and I won't impose on you beyond that."

Their chronic and never-ending kindness is starting to skeeve me out. Surely one of them is waiting for me to turn around so they can knife me. Humans are greedy creatures, always grasping for things they don't understand. Quick to shoot or injure without care for those around them. Human history may not be my best subject, but I've studied enough to know that at least.

Ambrosia lifts one eyebrow dubiously, but she crosses the room and opens the refrigerator. "We've got kale, kombucha, Greek yogurt, peaches, plums, strawberries, spinach. Does any of that sound good?"

Great, they're health nuts.

"Do you have any lean protein sources?" I ask.

"Eggs," Billy says. "We've got loads of eggs."

I flinch, but luckily they don't notice. I can't avoid them forever. "Sure, that's great."

"How do you like them?" Ambrosia asks.

"Here." I shuffle across the floor, grimacing at the bright red trail of blood I'm leaving behind me. "I'll do that."

Billy's voice sounds abnormally high. "You sit, okay? We'll make you some food."

"A lot of food," I say. "I'll take every single egg you've got. Scrambled, fried, whatever's fastest."

Ambrosia shoots me several strange looks, but she pulls out a frying pan and starts cracking them into the pan, a full dozen, stirring as she does.

Billy holds out a plate, and she dumps the entire mess on top of it. He carries it over and offers it to me like you might feed a feral cat, holding it out as far away from his body as he possibly can. "Is this okay?"

"Sure," I say. "It looks perfect." Saliva floods into my mouth, and I lick my lips. "Is there any chance I could have some water, too?"

"Oh sure," Ambrosia says, rushing across the room to grab me a glass. She fills it at the faucet and then freezes. "Is tap water okay?"

They're worried they'll offend someone who illegally entered their home by offering water from a pipe? "It's perfect. Thank you." I begin shoveling mouthfuls of eggs as quickly as I can. As they hit my stomach, my gut processes the energy and begins sending it out to my cells. After the last bite, I drink the entire glass of water without pausing for a breath. Then I close my eyes and suppress the sigh of relief that wants to rip out of me as my body finally heals as it should have all along.

I really could use three times as many eggs, a few dozen waffles and another few glasses of water. I've lost a lot of volume. But I doubt they have any more eggs, and other things are more pressing. My bladder is about to burst, for one.

"Could I possibly use a bathroom?" I ask.

Ambrosia doesn't answer, and I focus on her to try and figure out why. Her eyes are riveted on my feet. Cactus needles litter the bloody ground around them, because as my body healed, it forced the needles out. And of course, they're unaccustomed to bloody injuries miraculously healing in seconds. Right in front of them.

"I can explain."

She lifts her face to mine and her mouth turns up in a smile. "I told you she was Wonder Woman."

I shake my head. "I wasn't kidding when I said I don't know who that is, but it's certainly not me."

"She didn't know who she was either," she says. "But she was the daughter of a god, and she couldn't be harmed, not really. Just like you."

"No, no, no. You have this all wrong. I'm flesh and blood, just like you are. I can heal quickly, yes, but it's not what you're implying."

Billy's face is much less rapturous than his sister's. "Why exactly did your sister want you dead?"

I stop myself from asking, 'Which one?' but barely. "It's a really, really long story."

Billy crosses his arms. "My dad won't be home for hours. I've got plenty of time."

Ambrosia rolls her eyes. "Chill out, okay? We can interrogate her more after she's cleaned up." She takes two steps down the hall and waves her hand at me. "Bathroom's down here. I'll give you some clothes."

I follow her gratefully down the hall and duck into the

bathroom. The shower water feels as close to heaven as I've ever been. When I step out, wearing clean clothing and boasting an empty bladder, Ambrosia is waiting for me.

"You still looked hungry, so I made you a smoothie." She holds a large glass out to me. "It's the only way I can choke down Dad's healthy junk. I do think it's good for you, though, and you look like you could use some vitamins right about now."

She's kind of hilarious. I choke down the first two-thirds of her 'healthy' smoothie as fast as I downed the water. I still need calories and fluids badly. I'll take anything, and this doesn't taste half as bad as Roman's attempt at making ice cream last year.

"Now that you're clean, care to answer a few questions?" Billy's holding the bat again.

"You want to know why my sister wants me dead, and how I healed so quickly." Humans are so predictable.

"Actually," Billy says, "I'm most interested in what your plan is, because I think it's about to matter."

I hear voices at the house next door.

It could be nothing. Maybe they're just visitors. "What time is it, exactly?"

"Ten minutes after midnight," Ambrosia says.

"Any reason your neighbors might have company this late?"

Billy glances out the window. "Those people have cover-alls on with a patch for the local power company. It's not a social call. If I had to guess, I'd say they're pretending to work for the power company in order to search for someone."

I swear under my breath. Melina's still looking, and I'm out of time. I need to get out of here, pronto. I slurp down the last of the smoothie. "I took note of your address outside. I'll have some money sent to you as a thank you for the clothing and food, but right now, I've got to go."

Ambrosia glances at Billy. "What's your plan here? Those people are going door-to-door, searching houses for you. But it's not like they can check every crevice. Why don't you hide?"

I can't exactly explain they would hear my heartbeat, no matter where I hid, or at least, that would take more time than I have. "Let's just say my sister can track me."

Billy lifts his eyebrows. "Did you do something bad?"

Too many to list. "Yes."

"Would you harm us?" Ambrosia asks.

I wouldn't unless I had no other choice. They are, after all, only humans. I figure that counts as a no. I shake my head.

"We need to help her," she whispers to Billy. "Get her out of here."

"How are we supposed to do that?" he asks.

"Your sister's people have no idea how many people live here, let alone are currently at home," Ambrosia says. "So she and I will pretend to be sleeping and you can tell them you've got two sisters."

They'll hear my heartbeat and know it's different.

Unless I speed it up for a few moments to fool them. Could I do that? My eyes notice the pool of blood drying on the kitchen floor that trails through the house to the bathroom. Not to mention the handcuffs in the corner. If I'm going to take them up on their offer instead of trying to flee like a rabbit, we have work to do, quickly. Melina's people are coming.

I either trust these humans or flee and hope they can't catch me in a place I don't know and have no contacts. I may have surprised Melina's people when I ran earlier, but they're organized now, and surely prepared to take me out with tranqs. Or maybe something more lethal. The odds of success for this plan really come down to how well Billy can lie, and what Melina's people will do if they realize he is.

I shake my head. "I can't risk it. They'll press you for details, and if they realize you're lying, they'll take measures. Bad measures."

Billy scowls. "That decides it. You're staying here. Go. I'll clean this up."

I snatch the handcuffs and take them with me, Ambrosia only a step behind. Billy's already scrubbing the floor with a towel.

"This is my room." She points. "And I've got bunk beds already so when my friends come over, they have somewhere to sleep."

I bob my head, allowing my heart to spike from the stress. It's still half the speed of hers. Gah.

"Does your dad have any weapons?" I ask quietly.

Ambrosia gulps. "Uh, you mean like guns?"

I shake my head. "Guns wouldn't even slow them down."

She opens her mouth and then closes it.

"Does he have a sword, maybe? Sometimes humans keep decorative ones, I've heard."

"Humans?" Her voice is high and wobbly.

I frown. "I'll explain later. I'm not an alien, okay. I'm just different."

"I figured that out when you healed up in three seconds after eating some eggs."

I bob my head. "Look, I could really use a sword, but if you don't have one of those, even butcher knives are better than nothing."

I flinch when I hear a knock at the front door.

"Oh, Dad went to Japan once. There's some kind of samurai something hanging in his office over the door."

"Where's the office?"

"By his bedroom, right back there." She points around the corner, and I race out.

Billy's answering the door fifty feet away.

"Sorry to bother you this late," the man at the door lies. "But there's a dangerous fugitive on the loose in this area. We need to find her before she can kill again."

Who knows how Billy will react to that one. It's not even, strictly speaking, a lie.

I tear down the hall and into the master bedroom, then through it into a side room that's stacked high with books. So many books. Are offices full of books or am I in the wrong place? I look up at the door—nothing. I almost groan in defeat, until I notice another door in the back that probably opens to a closet. Hanging above it is a Musashi Platinum Katana. I could do far worse. I snag it and sprint back to Ambrosia's room. There's a ladder up to the bed, but I hear footsteps in the hall.

No time.

I vault up and over the guard rail on the bed and slide under the covers with my new sword.

Ambrosia swears softly below me. "That was awesome."

She's impressed easily, but then she is human.

The door cracks open. "See?" Billy says. "Just my sisters."

My heart is racing, possibly too fast. Human hearts slow down at rest, don't they? I wish I knew exactly what it should sound like. Ambrosia isn't helping me down below, her heart racing like she's sprinting a race.

"They aren't asleep," the man says.

"Of course they are," Billy says. "It's past midnight."

"Their hearts are racing, their breathing elevated," a woman's voice says. A voice I've heard before.

I close my eyes. It's the lady I shot in the face. I suppress a groan.

"We're going to need to take a closer look at them," she says. "Trust me when I tell you that you do not want to shelter the woman we're pursuing. She killed a kid not much older than you last week. She's not . . . normal."

Also true. Footsteps approach the bed and I tense to spring out.

"Wait," Billy says. "I've got 9-1-1 entered in my phone and I will call them, right now. I *don't* trust you, and I don't want you terrorizing my sister. I think I'd know if I was harboring a fugitive, and I'd hand her over. Please leave before you make things worse."

Melina's people stop.

"You said your sister." The woman's voice is practically gleeful. "As in one sister."

This time it's me who swears under my breath.

I throw the covers over the woman's head and leap from the bed, unsheathing the sword. I drop the sheath and stand on the balls of my feet. "Get out Billy. Run, Ambrosia. Now."

"Oh, that's touching," the man says. "She's pretending to care about the humans."

"Precious, actually," the woman says, her gold eyes sparkling. I'm a little annoyed to discover her face looks fine. She healed that point blank shot quickly, which is why guns are so useless.

I tilt my head back and forth, analyzing the scene in front of me. The woman's unarmed as far as I can tell, and the guy has pulled two guns. Exploding rounds, I'm assuming. Fine. I can handle that, but not with Billy and Ambrosia here.

"Get. Out."

Billy shakes his head. "We may be weak, but this isn't

right. Judica didn't threaten us, or scare us, or try and kill us. You two are the only ones doing that."

He drags the stupid bat out from behind the doorframe and bonks the guy on the head with it. I'm furious he isn't listening, but for a human, Billy's got an arm on him.

The man drops both guns when he crumples to the floor. The woman is so surprised her mouth lolls open. I'm only a hair less shocked, but I'm not about to let them kill the kid over it.

I spring forward and kick both guns toward the wall. Then with two smooth strokes I slice off both of the man's hands. The blood spray disgusts even me, and I'm pretty inured to this type of thing.

Of course, I know that removing his hands won't kill him. Ambrosia and Billy don't.

Ambrosia vomits in the corner of her bed. Poor kid.

Billy drops his bat and stares at me, aghast.

"He'll survive," I say, "and his hands will regrow. Don't worry about him too much—"

A knife thwacks into my throat mid-word, air rasping out of the hole when I try to talk. Melina's golden-eyed friend is really pissing me off. She's hiding behind the edge of Ambrosia's desk now, like a coward.

I yank the knife out and drop into a crouch, soaking poor Ambrosia's carpet with my blood. I cough, making an even bigger mess. But when the woman throws a second blade, I'm ready. I deflect it with the sword, and it lodges in the wall instead.

Time to give her a little of her own back. I throw the wicked, serrated-edged knife I pulled from my throat at the woman, expecting her to dodge and reclaim it, which she does. But she wasn't expecting me to roll and come up with a sweep to her left thigh. My borrowed sword swings underneath the desk and bites into the meaty part of her leg. And yet, I'm greedy for more. My throat is nearly healed, but I don't appreciate being taken by surprise.

I thrust at her solar plexus with my free left hand, knocking her backward, and then I spring on top of her, borrowing one of her own blades to press against her throat.

"You have one second to give me a reason not to end you. Permanently this time."

She grins. "I don't have one. Your sister's planning to kill you."

"You're lucky I'm not like her, then."

I slit her throat and stand up. Mine is already healed, but I'm guessing it'll take her much longer.

Ambrosia is in shock, staring blankly at me, mouth open, face pale.

Billy's holding a towel against the guy's stubs. I have no idea what color it began, but it's the dark purply-maroon of blood now. I could walk out and they wouldn't stop me, but I have no idea what Melina's people will do to them. And if I'm being totally honest, I kind of like them. I don't want them to die, not now, not after they've tried so hard to help me.

"They'll both survive." I wipe my throat and chest off with the sheet on Ambrosia's top bunk. This shirt can't be saved. "But they'll also alert Melina as soon as they can move and talk and dial, which means backup will be here soon. You two can stay here and wait for them, or you can leave with me."

"With you?" Billy asks, his eyes wide.

I bob my head. "Melina will interrogate you at a baseline. I'm not sure quite what else she'll do to you for harboring me."

Ambrosia tears her eyes away from my now-healed

throat and says, "Cutting her like that." She coughs. "That won't kill her? She's like you?"

I shrug. "No one is quite like me, but she'll recover, yes."

The woman at my feet has begun coughing, so I jab my sword into her leg, straight down through the bone.

She cries out, blood bubbling through the hole in her throat.

"I'm giving her things to heal so we have time to escape. Killing her would be cleaner, but. . ."

"You're not the monster they say you are," Ambrosia says.

I can't meet her eye. "I did kill someone, and I'd do it again. I probably will kill again, and soon. I don't like that fact, but I won't go gently into the night."

Her eyes are sad. They remind me too much of Chancery's. Kind, brave, generous.

"I'm leaving," I say. "Come or don't." I change my shirt and use the cleanest parts of the discarded one to dab at my new pants. Then I crouch down to grab the sword's sheath and walk out the door, stepping over the man's grotesquely unattached hands and tracking his blood down the hall.

By the time I reach the back door, both of them have joined me. Billy even has a backpack slung over his shoulder. "We're sticking with you. Maybe we can help out more."

Doubtful, but who knows? "Stranger things have happened."

"Maybe we head out the back door?" Billy says. "Less light that direction."

I nod. "Good idea."

"We could take my car," Billy says.

I shake my head. "There's no chance that kind of noise

wouldn't be detected. Melina's people would be on us immediately. No, we've got to put some space between us and her people before they heal enough to call her."

We duck out the back door and I set off at a jog, wincing at the noise Ambrosia and Billy make, even on pavement. Their footfalls are louder than the slaps of bare hands across rosy cheeks.

Also, there's no good way to carry my purloined sword. I guess you take a baldric for granted until you don't have one. I end up tucking it through the neck of my shirt and a loop on my pants, which angles the whole thing sideways, stretching the collar on my borrowed t-shirt. The three of us, looking about as covert as a buffalo on the flat, open plains, blunder down the street.

We miraculously reach the edge of the neighborhood before Ambrosia exclaims. "Oh no!"

I spin around, looking for assailants, assessing risk. I see nothing but houses with dark windows and flowery landscaping. "What's wrong?" How did a human notice something I missed?

"I just realized, Dad is going to freak out."

I think about the blood and severed hands. Oh boy.

10

THE PAST

Iapproach the staff quarters as quietly as possible. It's early enough in the morning that the hall is empty. I tap on the door softly.

I hear rustling inside, and I wonder how annoying it is not to have completely soundproofed walls. I didn't realize the staff walls weren't reinforced.

The door opens a crack, and Nihils' eyes widen with alarm.

"Hello," I say.

"Uh, Your Highness. Can I help you? Is there a problem?"

"May I come in? I'd like to talk to you." And poke a knife into your eye until you scream.

"Oh." He glances up and down the hall as if looking for my guards, who were quite hard to ditch, or anyone who might save him. "Uh, sure." He opens the door a few inches.

I shove it open further and press myself through. He's standing in his room in basketball shorts and nothing else, but I couldn't care less what his chest looks like. I've got bigger problems than insufficiently defined pectoral muscles, even on an evian who should be working harder. I mean, geez, a hundred sit-ups and push-ups a day and he'd be ripped.

His eyes dart from the door I slam shut behind me to the sword strapped to my back. Good. He's appropriately nervous.

"I have a few questions," I say.

"Because I traded shifts."

He may be lazy, but at least he isn't painfully stupid. "Yes."

"I wondered when someone would notice."

I cross my arms. "I noticed."

"I didn't hurt your mother, I swear to you I didn't." His heart rate remains steady, his smell is neutral, and no perspiration has spiked since he answered the door. That actually magnifies my existing suspicion. Why isn't my presence and interrogation more terrifying? He's acting like I'll find his secret candy stash, not as though I've discovered he positioned himself to poison his Empress.

"For your sake, I certainly hope that's true." The more time I spend here, the more convinced I become that he can't be the mastermind behind my mother's death. If he was involved, it was as an intermediary, a delivery boy, and nothing more. Which means, if my suspicions pan out, I should be pumping him for information on his boss.

"I have a reason for changing those shifts," he says. "A reason that has nothing to do with your mother."

This better be good. I stare at him and tap my foot.

He swallows. "It was because of a girl."

"I'm going to need more than that," I say.

"If you check the chart, you'll see that I had kitchen duty on all of those days. I'd have come in contact with your mother anyway by delivering her tray. But I didn't want to see Cina, and if I'd kept kitchen duty, I would have."

"Why exactly didn't you want to see her?" I raise one eyebrow. I know Cina. She's feisty and outspoken and I like her, and like most evians, she's attractive.

"We made out, and it was hot." He looks at the ground. "But then she wanted more than I did, and it was easier not to bump into her."

She'd have known he switched, and hopefully gotten the message. Good grief. Someone who takes the coward's route to avoid seeing a girl is no one she'd want anyway. "You're an idiot."

He tosses his hands up in the air. "I won't argue with that, but it worked."

So he's not nefarious, just rude, cowardly, lazy, and imbecilic. Fabulous. Of course I'll need to check out his story, but it looks like this may be a dead end. Before I wanted to cut him, and now I'd like to punch him out of frustration. Because now I'm back to the starting line. Empty handed again.

I spin on my heel and head for the door. "Enjoy your morning."

"I'll try," he says.

Roman's waiting in the hallway outside, glowering terribly. "You can't dismiss your guards, *Your Majesty*."

I huff. "I can do whatever I want to do."

He grabs my upper arm. "Don't be stupid. Not now." He lowers his voice. "Please."

"Worried about your job?"

His heart accelerates, but he drops my arm and steps back. "Yes. My job disappears if you die, and we have a killer at large right now. And worse than that, you're searching for him or her. Alone."

"I can protect myself, you know. Calm down."

"There's a reason people use the phrase, 'watch your back.' It's because even perfect princesses can't watch their own back. That's my job. And if you don't let me do it, I get crabby."

I want to huff or dismiss his complaint, but I can't. Because he's right. Running off alone to chase a killer is just as dangerous as trusting the wrong person to guard me. Mother taught me better than this. I need to separate myself from emotional baggage and trauma and start being smart about all of this, which means doing the things I was taught to do, and not taking reckless, unnecessary risks. I could have at least asked Balthasar or Roman to come along.

"I'm sorry."

Roman tilts his head. "Words I didn't expect to hear."

I roll my eyes. "Let's go."

He doesn't chastise me further on the way back to my room, but when we reach the door, he takes up a position outside with Dante.

"What happened to Riose and Lorn?" I ask.

Roman's shoulders straighten infinitesimally. "They're mine to deal with as I see fit."

"I tried to elude them and failed. I had to give them a direct order," I say. "Don't discipline them for obeying me when I yelled them into doing it."

He stares straight ahead, not meeting my eye.

"Roman."

His eyes gleam when he turns to face me. "They must obey you, but they obey me, too. Don't cut my legs out from under me, Your Majesty."

In obeying my orders, they violated his. I sigh. "Fine. Do as you see fit." I trust him to figure this out. Something they'll respect him for, but that won't be so bad they resent it. I lower my voice to the barest of whispers. "And I promise not to do this to you again."

He nods almost imperceptibly, but I know he's forgiven me. It's enough.

I collapse into my desk chair and pull out the schedule I recently approved. I need to talk to this Cina to verify Nihils' story. She's on kitchen duty today, which could mean she'll bring me a food tray, or it could mean she's chopping carrots. I wish I could simply tell Angel to send her to me, but Angel's in a cell, and requesting that anyone else do something like that is too big a risk.

I miss the days where everything made sense and I trusted the people Mother trusted.

But an integral component of success in finding something like my mother's killer involves not broadcasting to everyone where I'm looking. My overbearing accusations with Nihils were clumsy. Mother taught me better. I can be patient. I can be stealthy. I need to, if I want justice, and I do. I burn for it. My eyes blur over the schedules, all the names, and I notice a pattern on the edges of my vision before it slips away.

I'm over-simplifying this. Usually you'd keep things as simple as you could, because the more angles, the more likely something goes sideways. But if you were poisoning a monarch, a brilliant, well-loved monarch, you might need a little added complication. What if it wasn't one person in charge with just one other, like Nihils? What if it was a group of people?

I close my eyes and tap at my head. I need to start looking for patterns of people who might have, together, had consistent access to her. And if they had to trade to gain access to her too, then they'll be easier to spot. This is going to take some time, especially since I need to check on them one at a time, without anyone suspecting me. And

I'll need to plan some more obvious interrogations to do more publicly so the real culprits will believe they're being overlooked.

Angel's a good cover for that, because I'm growing increasingly sure that she's not at the heart of this. It's too obvious.

The names swim in front of my eyes, almost a distraction. I've seen all the lists. They're in my brain. I close my eyes and try to focus on assimilating the data I've already stored inside. I think about the lists of people scheduled, and then the lists of people who actually worked each shift. It's complicated further when I cross reference it with the various areas where each of the assigned people worked, based on Roman's list of who came in contact with Mother. For instance, lots of people traded shifts, but didn't end up crossing Mother's path. Others traded then, and noted their reasons, but haven't traded since. Now that Mother's dead, their fake reasons would evaporate. Unless they were real and ongoing issues.

I compile a chart in my brain of people who changed their assignments and how many times, and then I start writing that list down so that I can compare it to the others. Dozens and dozens of sets of people could have, working together in pairs, poisoned my mother. Thirty-two sets of people who came in contact with her each day between the two of them, in fact. If I include sets of three people working together, the number rises dramatically. And I'm not even sure whether she needed to be poisoned every day, or whether every other day was enough. If I include pairings where they saw her every other day, the number goes far higher.

Clearly I need more information from Job.

I groan.

If I'm looking to narrow the field, there are only three

sets of individuals where one of them traded shifts to have access to my mother on a daily basis. One of those sets includes Cina, which seems like a pretty big coincidence. Another includes Nihils.

"Breakfast tray." Roman's voice is muffled.

My stomach rumbles right on cue. "Come in," I say.

The woman carrying the tray is Cina. Steady breathing, steady heart rate, steady expression. Do not act bizarre, Judica, do not give anything away. Handle this better than you did with Nihils.

"You can set that there," I say.

Cina sets the tray of food on the end table and bobs her head. What do I ask? How do I keep her here? I need her to talk to me. My mind is entirely blank. Chancery would put her at ease. Everyone loves her. They probably already spent time braiding each other's hair. What would Chancery say if she were here? Something stupid, about how she looks, or what she's wearing.

"That's a cute—er—pair of pants." Her pants are plain and black. I can't channel my inner Chancery. I don't have a speck of that inside of me.

Cina looks at the door and then back to me. "They're standard issue for kitchen work."

I've never noticed that all the kitchen staff wear black pants. "Oh. Is that new?"

Cina shakes her head and eyes the door.

Think, Judica, think. "I really like black," I say. "So I'm always looking for new things in that color." She's going to think I've lost my bloody mind.

"Well, Angel ordered nice ones this time. They're actually really comfortable and they breathe well. They're made by a company called Rag & Bone."

"Uh, I'll have to look that up." Well, good job Judica.

Now she thinks I've taken an interest in clothing chains. And I've learned absolutely nothing helpful.

"As you know, Angel is in custody," I say. "I thought you might be able to help me figure out how some things in the kitchen went, and whether her story was accurate."

"Of course," she says.

I ask her a half a dozen questions about food preparation and plating, and then about the protocols and how well they're followed.

She answers every question. "But if you want my opinion, and maybe you don't," she says, "I don't think it was Angel. That woman has always been completely obsessed with following every rule, which involves everything she does being in plain sight, on camera, and witnessed by more than one person. And on top of that, she adored your mother. Truly."

Angel's obsession with following the rules could be covering her own duplicity. It sounds almost like overkill. "Did my mother ever talk to you when you brought her food? Maybe she asked you things, or mentioned anything? Small details, even." I close my eyes and inhale through my nose. Why am I so bad at this? I torture secrets out of spies without blinking. I never give away a hint of information at public events. Why is it so hard to get information without letting on the reason I want to know? Why is it so impossible to be casual and friendly?

Cina's chin tilts. "You're hurting and I'm sorry."

I scowl. "I'm not hurting. I was just wondering whether she ever said anything to you."

"My mother died a year ago. I recognize pain when I see it."

She's nicer than I expected her to be, especially to me.

"I'm sorry though. The Empress never really spoke to me. I'm not sure she noticed I was even there, other than waving her hand to show me where she wanted it when I brought her a tray."

Alright, I've tried being sneaky and so far all it's gotten me is condescension. Maybe stealth isn't my style. "If she never spoke to you, why did you trade five different shifts in order to carry that tray into her room?"

Cina's heart doesn't speed up. Her breathing doesn't, either. I can't smell her perspiring and she doesn't clench her fists or shift from foot-to-foot. But her eyes dart sideways and she licks her lips before she says, "I needed more time to study. I was on yard duty and it's non-stop work from clock-in until clock-out. When I'm on kitchen duty, there's a lull between jobs and I can actually catch up on my reading."

I lift an eyebrow. "What are you studying for, Cina?"

"I'd like to be a diplomat, Your Highness. I need to learn three more languages."

"You didn't place there."

She shakes her head. "I didn't even apply, because my mother hated the idea. She wanted me to stay here, close to her."

"But now your mother's gone, and you can re-apply."

She nods.

"You only have to work ten-hour days. That gives you plenty of time to study."

Cina opens her mouth, then closes it.

"You're lying about something and I want you to tell me what and why." I stand up.

She swallows again.

"What will Beverly tell me when I call her in?" My palm itches for the hilt of my blade. She's lying, and if she had anything to do with Mother's death. . .

The blood drains from her face. "Why would you call her?"

"You traded shifts with her. Repeatedly. I'm assuming she'll tell me the reason you gave for all those shift swaps."

Cina bites her lip.

"Roman is right outside that door."

"Don't call him," she says. "I'll tell you."

I fold my arms over my chest. "I'm listening."

"I wanted to see someone," she says.

My forehead furrows. She must mean Nihils. But he traded to avoid her. And her swaps didn't put her in contact with him. I close my eyes and review my lists of work assignments to see whether there could be any truth to what she's saying. Only one person was working in the same location as her for each of her five requested changes. She traded with Beverly, but she moved onto a shift where she was working with Gwendolyn.

It makes no sense.

Cina breathes in and out deeply. "There's only one good thing about your mother being dead."

"Excuse me?"

"When your secrets come out, you don't need to worry about her disappointment anymore."

Her mother would be disappointed in her, if she were still alive, and she figured out what I just did. "You didn't harm my mother," I say. "You traded for another reason entirely. You traded shifts to see Gwendolyn. You *like* her, don't you?"

She nods slowly.

"You're what the humans call 'gay'."

She closes her eyes.

"It's not a crime anymore," I say. "You don't have to hide."

"I don't even know whether Gwendolyn likes me," she says.

"You could ask her."

Her half smile unnerves me. "I won't be executed for liking women anymore, that's true. Your mother eliminated that law when *in vitro fertilization* was discovered. But it's not accepted, and it's certainly not celebrated."

"There's still a stigma," I admit.

"Everyone assumes I am the way I am because of a deletion," she says. "And I'll be obligated to have a child every ten years that I'm alive whether I want one or not. Women who choose not to marry are obligated to do that. There are consequences, injustices."

"You can stop once you've had fifty children," I say. "It's to make sure that your kind doesn't lead to under population of the evian species."

"My kind?" She purses her lips. "Okay."

"It's a reasonable request. Fifty children is on the low side for most evians, after all." And for all we know, it is a deletion. "Did you even try kissing guys? I mean, maybe you don't like all of them, but neither do I. You're a cute girl. You can be picky."

Her utter calm reaches me far more effectively than theatrics would have. "I am not deficient, and I didn't *choose* this, any more than you chose your eye color. I can pretend it's not true, like some evians can change the color of their eyes, but it doesn't alter the truth of who I am."

"So you did try to like guys?" I don't much care whether she likes men or women, but I do need to know whether she kissed Nihils.

"Of course I tried," she practically wails. "Several times." Her nostrils flare. "Is that all you need?"

Maybe she kissed Nihils after all, but it seems quite unlikely, even if she did, that she'd want more than he wanted out of that kind of fling. "Who, exactly, did you kiss?"

Her eyes flash. "I know you're in pain, but this is none

of your business." She stomps her foot, and then as if she realizes who she's talking to, she gulps. "Your Majesty."

"Answer one last question and I'll leave you alone. I've heard that on occasion gays will feign a relationship to keep people from suspecting. Or they'll try and make things work with someone of the opposite gender even though they aren't attracted to them."

"Uh, okay."

"Did you do that with Nihils? Did you ever kiss him?"

Her lip curls. "What is your deal with him? You can't possibly like him yourself. But, no. Gross. If you're wondering why I traded with him, it's because everyone knew he was always willing to trade. The guy wanted people to owe him. It's strange, but it's who he is. He always trades things for other things."

"So he doesn't know you're gay."

She shakes her head vehemently. "No one knows, not even Gwendolyn."

If she's telling the truth, and I believe she is, then Nihils lied to me. He didn't make out with Cina, and she never wanted more out of their interaction than he did. He should have done better homework before making up his cover.

I need to talk to him, but he can't know that it's an interrogation, not this time. If he's distracted enough, he won't be able to fabricate clever lies on the spot. I'd never have uncovered this one if Cina hadn't been closeted. I got lucky, and I can't rely on luck.

"You can go," I say. "But you may not discuss the details of this conversation with anyone. Do you understand?"

She bobs her head.

"Not your best friend, your brother, your sister, your father, your lover, and certainly not Nihils. I don't care who they are, you can't talk to them about this. It would be treason. Are we clear on that?"

"Crystal clear, Your Majesty." She walks to the door. Just before she opens it, she turns around. "Your mother was doing her best. I really believe that." Cina blurts out the rest quickly. "But you could do better. You can fix some of the things she got wrong." She pivots on the ball of her foot and practically runs from the room. "Your sister cares about her people. It would be nice if you did, too."

Part of me wants to slap her, but part of me thinks about what she said. Mother was known for her sweeping changes, her radical reforms in the way we manage the world. She freed the humans, essentially, from servitude and gave them latitude and opportunities no other empress had ever risked. She eliminated a whole host of laws, such as those proscribing homosexuality, as long as the evians who chose that lifestyle still did their duty by perpetuating our species.

But what if Mother's whole world view was still too narrow? What if she cared less than she should have for the individual people? I can guess what Chancery thinks. She doesn't fault Lark for being half-human, because it's *who she is*. She probably thinks Cina didn't choose to like women instead of men. Actually, Chancery, in her heart-of-hearts, may not even consider evians to be superior to humans. She spouts the same sort of nonsense Mother claims destroyed our father and their marriage.

Equality.

It would destroy our entire way of life if that kind of morality spreads. I shake my head. Mother was radical to a point. She believed in freedoms as long as they didn't upend the world order, throwing us into unregulated chaos. Mother was right, and I'll follow her example. Which is exactly why Alamecha needs me ruling instead of Chancery.

But for now, I need to focus. I've got to question Nihils again, but subtly, which is not my forté. He's not one of my guards, but he occasionally rotates through the multi-opponent training days, which means no one would question my fighting him in the ring. But to get any time for questions at all, I'd need to defeat every opponent *but* him, and then take a little time to defeat him.

And he has to believe it's a coincidence, and not a plan I have crafted. I flip through the schedule until I reach this week. Cina waltzed into my room right as I needed her, and now, as I look down at the schedule, I realize Nihils is listed tomorrow for my multi-opponent combat training team.

I don't believe in a God who interacts with his or her children. If he or she existed, surely there wouldn't be so much death, so much destruction, so much misery. And the God described in the human Bible is at once too distant, and too caring to be believable. But for the first time, I feel like perhaps God checks in periodically to tip the scales toward the pursuit of justice.

Either way, when I see Nihils again, I plan to walk away with some answers, or he won't be walking away at all.

11

THE PRESENT

"It's okay," Billy says. "I'll text him."

Laughter pours out of me. I can't seem to stop it. "You'll text him?" My eyes water.

Ambrosia stops walking. "This isn't very funny."

"You're going to text your dad about severed hands?" I burst into laughter again. "Will you say they're fake? Some kind of prank?"

"He's a surgeon," Ambrosia says. "He'll know they're real."

"You two should stay here, close to the house," I say. "You can return in a few hours. I'm sure Melina's people will be gone by then. I doubt they'll be upset with you, but it won't be like you can tell them where I've gone anyway. I won't tell you."

"Actually, I've got a buddy who's a paramedic," Billy says. "My best friend. If I called him, he'd come pick us up. He could even take us to the hospital where Dad's operating. Your sister can't stop an ambulance, at least, not without attracting a lot of attention."

Melina's people are clearly circling, probably drawing

nearer to me every second. Hopefully I can fight my way through, but ultimately I'll need to get out of Austin somehow. They'll know that as well, and probably be watching the easiest ways to leave. Main highways and so on. Airports are problematic, since I have no identification. Something humans insist upon to fly, as I understand it.

"So should I call him?" Billy holds up his phone.

"Wait, you have your phone," I say dumbly. I'm clearly suffering from the incarceration. He was talking about texting, so obviously he has his phone.

Billy nods.

Because he wasn't kidnapped, duh. I'm too stupid to live. Of course he has his phone. Why didn't I think of this before? I could call Roman and ask him to come. Melina won't be watching planes coming *in* to Austin. Just the ones departing. I bet Roman would come right away, and he'd keep it all a secret from Chancery until I know what to do. My fingers practically itch to call him and ask for help. Then I wouldn't have to continue to rely on the charity of humans, and I wouldn't need to risk their lives again, either. Of course, it'll take some time for him to get here, so Billy's plan may still be my best bet in the short run.

"Fine, call your friend."

Billy does, and he tells him to pick us up about three blocks from here, hopefully in a less populated area.

"Can I borrow your phone?" I ask after he hangs up. "I need to make a long-distance call."

"Like, outside of the United States?"

Ambrosia giggles. "You're worried about a few bucks in phone charges? There are two disembodied hands lying in sticky pools of blood on my floor. You don't tell Wonder Woman no to save twenty bucks."

Billy shrugs. "I guess not." Billy tosses his phone to me.

"It's not out of the country. Just Hawaii." I dial Roman's

number slowly, but before my thumb taps the talk dot, I pause. Could this endanger Roman? What does Chancery think about my absence? How upset is she about the bombs I sent before she defeated me? She might be furious and wishing she'd killed me, in which case, she could be relieved I'm gone. Or maybe she's realized what a favor I did for her. It's not like I hit a populated area, and the only casualties were a few thousand humans.

Only a few thousand humans.

Yesterday I wouldn't have thought twice about those words. Humans are, I've always believed, lower than dogs. They're worthless, except as commodities, pawns from which we only seek to optimize production. They aren't like us, not at all. The human leaders I've met are notable exceptions, the best of the best, the trained performance dogs we can work with. They don't bite our hands or poop on the carpet because they've been conditioned to act as we expect them to act. But even so, they aren't as good as an evian. Not even close.

The idea of half-evians always horrified me. Who would sully themselves to the point of copulating with a human?

And yet, I've only spent a few minutes with Ambrosia and Billy. They're both full-blooded humans: normal, untrained, unremarkable. They aren't as strong as me, or quite as intelligent, but they're kind, generous, interested in justice and morality.

I like them quite a bit more than the human leaders I've worked with in government, men who allegedly represent the very best humans have to offer. The President, for instance, seems only to think about himself and his friends. He would never have called in a favor to help someone who turned up on his doorstep. I've never even seen him pretend to care about right and wrong.

Maybe the humans I've met aren't the best of the best,

or maybe I've been misled. Billy and Ambrosia are helping me for absolutely nothing in return. Billy took down an evian, for heaven's sake. They're good people, better than quite a few evians I know, and not nearly as dense as I expected. I shake that thought away.

Focus, Judica. Will Chancery be watching Roman? Will it harm him if I ask for help? Would she detain him, or even kill him in pursuit of my location? Roman's smarter than that, and I don't think Chancery will shoot first and ask questions later. It's not in her personality.

I hit talk.

Roman picks up on the second ring. "Hello?"

His voice is richer than I recall, deeper too. I've missed it, like I miss strawberry shakes. Like I miss Death. Actually, more than I've missed both of those combined, and I really like strawberry shakes.

"Hello?" His tone has shifted to annoyed. "Is someone there?"

"It's me," I squeak out.

"Where are you?" he asks. "Is it really you? Say something else. Anything. Are you safe?"

I savor the sound of his voice. I consider not speaking quite yet, so he'll talk more. But he's worried, and delaying feels cruel. "It's really me," I say. "Melina took me with help from Angel."

"So she did kill your mother. When she went missing too, we all suspected. We all thought." He coughs. "Chancery still thinks you're dead."

"It's all my fault," I say. "Angel made a promise to Mother, and I think she felt she was honoring it by delivering me to Melina. Melina plans to kill me as a favor to Chancery."

"I don't understand," he says. "Chancery doesn't want

you dead. She spared you and then refused to contain you in any way."

"I'll explain later. Can you come get me?"

"Yes. Tell me where." He drops his voice. "In fact, if you'll let me tell your sister, I bet I can bring a small army."

"No," I nearly shout. "Don't tell her."

"Have you changed your mind?" he asks. "Is she our enemy?"

Our enemy, just like that. My heart does a tiny somersault. "It's complicated. I'll explain when you get here. Bring a pilot and no one else."

"Where am I headed?" he asks. "I assume you're in Texas, if Melina took you."

"Austin, yeah. Meet me at—" I glance at Billy and shrug.

"How about Maxine's Gumbo House?" he says. "It's near that small airport, the Austin executive one or whatever."

"Dad's a pilot," Ambrosia says. "Or he used to be before Mom died. He used to fly us to lots of places in his tiny plane. Our favorite place to eat was Maxine's, coming or going."

"You get that?" I ask.

"Tell me you're okay," Roman says.

"I'm fine."

"Who are you with?" he asks.

"Two humans who have gone above and beyond."

"I'll be there as quickly as I possibly can," he says. "And I'm saving this number."

"Thanks." I hang up and pass the phone to Billy.

"Your boyfriend?" Billy asks.

I shake my head. "The head of my guard."

"Of course," Ambrosia says. "Why wouldn't you have enough guards that they need to have a boss?" Her eyes look a little wild.

"Let's go, okay?" I ask. "We can call your dad later, and I promise once I get home, I can make all this go away. You won't be in danger or in trouble."

Billy lifts one eyebrow, but after a second or two, he nods and takes off at a jog again. I follow him with Ambrosia on my heels. Every snapping twig and wild squirrel causes my heart to race. I don't even bother modulating it, since they can't hear it anyway. Luckily, the jog to the corner is uneventful. Billy's friend is waiting in an ambulance as promised.

"Frank," Billy waves. "Thanks for helping. I'm telling you, this is an absolute emergency."

"It better be," Frank says. "Because we've got to take you three straight to the emergency room for evaluation." Frank jerks his head toward the woman sitting on the passenger side with a sour expression on her face.

"I'm Barbara, Frank's trainer. We don't usually take calls in this unconventional method. You should have called 911 and taken whichever ambulance was dispatched."

I step toward her and extend my hand in the way humans like. "I'm Judica Alamecha. I promise you that your willingness to help will be richly rewarded."

"Richly rewarded? What are you, a secret Nigerian prince? Because I told you no when you emailed me, too."

I glance at Billy, but he shakes his head.

The sour woman rolls her eyes melodramatically. "I'll settle for a valid insurance card, okay?" Barbara doesn't shake my hand, but she does mutter to Frank. "Altered mental status. Did you notice that stupid toy sword on her back?"

"We'll work the paperwork out with the hospital," Ambrosia says, "because our friend Judica here is having *severe* chest pain. Right, good friend?"

"Oh, right. Yes. It's severe." I clutch at my heart. "Shooting pains that feel really, really bad."

Barbara frowns again, but she opens the back of the ambulance and shoos us inside. "Fine, get in." I climb in and start to sit on a jump seat. Ambrosia widens her eyes at me and I reluctantly climb onto the stretcher. Billy climbs in after her.

"We insist you take her to Scott & White in Pflugerville."

"We'll pass about four other emergency rooms to get there."

Ambrosia puts her hands on her hips. "Did I ask your opinion? We're requesting a particular ER, and you have to take us there. HIPAA says so."

Barbara's scowl intensifies, the lines between her eyebrows like quotation marks. "Frank says your dad's a doc. You brats are always a pain."

"Our dad works at that hospital," Ambrosia says. "And I don't trust anyone else. He's a cardio-thoracic surgeon there."

"Surgeons are the worst of the bunch." Barbara closes the first ambulance door. "Fine, let's go." She slams the other door shut.

"We're like rats in a cage back here," I say. "No way to get out."

Melina's people could be surrounding us at this moment. She could be bringing a bomb, or rabid dogs, or an army with exploding rounds. Crazy people don't give up easily, and this has been far too easy so far.

"What's wrong with you?" Billy asks. "You're acting like you really do have chest pain."

"I don't like being trapped inside a metal box on wheels with no visibility."

"You're worried your sister will find us," Ambrosia says.

"You don't understand," I say. "She's strong like me, and she has a small army at her disposal." How did Mother ignore Melina? She's clearly a threat. First she needs to kill me. Who knows what she'll need to do next to fulfill her bizarre prophecy. Maybe steal Chancery's baby and offer it as a sacrifice.

"It's a forty-minute ride to the hospital," Billy says. "I think now might be a good time for you to share a little about what the hell is going on."

I bite my lip. "I'm evian, which is to say, I'm a direct lineal descendant of the woman you know as Eve, the mother of all living."

Ambrosia and Billy share a glance that says, *Okay, whatever you say, crazy person.*

"Look," I say. "You've seen me heal quickly." I pick up an oval metal basin. "What is this?"

Billy clears his throat. "It's a bed pan."

Why would a bed need a pan? Who cares? I grab either end and bend it in half, then I bend it in half again. "I'm stronger than a human. I can't demonstrate in here, but I also run faster, have a photographic memory, and so on. I'm not this wonder woman you mentioned, but I am what you might call super-human."

"Why haven't we heard of evians?" Ambrosia asks. "Wait, evian. Like the water?"

Mother and her oddball sense of humor. "Yes, like the water."

"Do you, like, only drink that kind of water?" Billy asks. "Is that the source of your power? Will regular water harm you? Because earlier, that was sink water. It wasn't Evian."

Oh good grief. "Look, you've never heard of us, but we secretly rule the world, okay? The last thing we want to deal with is disgruntled humans hatching ridiculous plots against us, and frankly, you don't live long enough or pack a large enough punch to really do us much damage. It's easier for us if you don't know we're here."

"So presumably your sister's evian too?" Billy asks. "Why would she be after you?"

"In this particular instance, she happens to think I'm a threat to my twin sister, Chancery. My older sister Melina believes the only way to keep Chancery safe is to eliminate me. See, the youngest female always becomes the new queen of each evian family. I was the ruler, but our Mother changed her mind. She named my twin in my place."

"That made you mad, I assume. And now you want to kill this Chancery?" Billy asks.

I shake my head. "We fought, but we've worked things out. Our mother made her the ruler at the last minute, and I have accepted her decision. I won't get in Chancery's way, and in fact, I plan to help her with whatever she needs. Forever. Our family matters, and I'll do whatever it takes to keep us strong, including killing my older sister before she can do anything else to harm Chancery."

"But she didn't want to kill your twin, right?" Billy asks. "She only wants to kill you."

"She's unhinged. She's fixated on me right now, but I'm telling you. Mother banished Melina for a reason, and that reason is becoming very apparent."

"So you don't intend to go back until you've done exactly what she accused you of doing," Ambrosia says softly. "Killing someone, namely her."

I shrug. "Sometimes bad people need to die before they do more damage to the world around them."

"Spoken like every dictator ever," Billy says.

I don't bother telling him that all those dictators were only figure heads for various evian empresses. The crazier the dictators seemed, the less efforts the empresses had to make to explain away their actions. "As soon as I eliminate her, I'll go back to Chancery. Trust me when I say that you'd love my twin. She's as benevolent and kind as they come. Which is exactly why she needs someone like me around to keep her alive."

"The twin you wanted to kill needs your help to survive?" Ambrosia asks. "Really? Or do you think she's relieved you're gone?"

Chancery's not prepared for the job she's taken upon herself. She's in too deep and likely drowning, but the question is still a good one. Does Chancery even want my help? Or was she happy to hear that I left? And if she's relieved by my absence, should I even return? I blink repeatedly. "I've been so caught up figuring out how to get back that I never considered what might happen if I *didn't* go home."

"I would want you back, Rosy," Billy says. "No matter what fights we had, or how mad you made me."

Ambrosia beams at Billy and my heart contracts. I wish I knew whether Chancery felt the same way. Maybe Roman can tell me more when he arrives.

"What happened to your mother?" Ambrosia asks. "You haven't said anything about your parents."

"My father died before I was born," I say, "and my mother died recently. Very recently."

"Oh," Billy says. "I'm very sorry."

The sympathy in both their eyes clues me in.

"What about your mother?"

Ambrosia frowns. "She died almost a year ago."

"Why?" I ask.

"Cancer," Billy says. "My dad's friend is an oncologist, and I think Dr. Hermes did as much as he could, but it wasn't enough."

"Your father faults him for it?" I ask.

Ambrosia nods. "He does, just not as much as he faults himself."

"Explain," I say. "How is her death your father's fault?"

"Dad's a surgeon," Ambrosia says. "He considered doing the surgery to remove the tumor himself, but it's not his specialty. Dr. Hermes convinced him to step back. But they couldn't get all the cancerous cells and Mom. . . Well. She didn't make it. Dad thinks he should have done it himself or found another doctor, a better doctor. Dad says he screwed up her care by trusting too much to his friend."

Humans don't live very long, so I'm not surprised she died. But I'm not too familiar with what cancer is, exactly. "What does that word mean, cancer?"

"It's where your cells replicate too fast and in the wrong places," Billy says. "And they often form tumors. Those tumors are aggressive and damage various parts of the body."

"It's an illness where your body goes haywire, causing functions to shut down?" I ask.

Ambrosia nods. "Basically, yeah."

"Does your mother's death indicate that any of you will also become ill?"

Billy shrugs. "I guess that's my dad's fear. He's been researching cancer with every second of free time, like if he works hard enough, he can find the cure even though people have been studying for decades without much luck."

"The thing is," Ambrosia says, "Mom had breast cancer, and that's hereditary. He thinks I'll die in my thirties."

In her thirties. She might die after living less than twice as long as I have. I can't even imagine what that would feel like, knowing your life is so fragile and having no control over your future. "But your father can't stop something like that, right? If you have cancer?"

Ambrosia shrugs. "Someone has to cure cancer eventually, so he figures, why not him?"

"He's doing so much research and so many cases," Billy

says, "that he never sees us anymore. So whether we live a long time or not, he won't remember a thing."

"Dad's always been a perfectionist," Ambrosia says, "and he's gotten so much worse since Mom died. I try not to let it bother me so I can enjoy the little bit of time that he's around."

The ambulance stops, and I don't know why. I unsheathe my sword and stand on the balls of my feet, ready to take down anyone facing us on the other side.

But when the doors open, no one is waiting to hit me with a tranquilizer.

Frank's mouth drops open and his eyes glance nervously from my sword to my face and back again. "Uh, we're here," he says. "Are you alright?"

"We're fine." Billy hisses at me. "Put the sword down, crazy." Then he slides around me and hops out of the ambulance. "Thanks, Frank. I owe you one. Seriously."

Frank shakes his head. "Don't worry about it. It's what friends do."

"Your boss seemed pissed," Ambrosia says.

"Nah, she just doesn't want to get in trouble, but it's fine, really. Chest pain or not, you needed a ride somewhere safe, and you got it."

"Thank you." I climb out of the back, and Ambrosia follows me.

A tall man with black hair that's greying at the temples strides out the ambulance bay doors. "William? Ambrosia? What are you doing here?"

Billy kicks at a spot on the concrete. "Hey Dad."

"Are you both okay?"

Ambrosia nods. "We're fine, but our friend might need some help."

"Who is your friend?" the tall man asks. "And what does she need?"

"Uh," Billy says loudly, "her name is Jud—Judy er, Meecham, and she's not safe."

"Not safe? What does that mean?" His eyes shift to me, taking in the spots on my pants that I didn't take time to change.

"She's uh, she's in bad shape," Billy says. "I didn't know what to do, because I found out she's . . . she was assaulted. On the street."

The man's mouth drops open. "I'm very sorry to hear that. Well, let's get her inside right away."

"What was that?" Ambrosia whispers as we follow him inside.

"You're covered in blood. What was I supposed to say?" Billy asks. "We both know there won't be a scratch on you."

"Dad is going to ask a lot of questions," Ambrosia says.

"Technically, I was assaulted," I say.

"If you tell them you're too nervous to talk about it, they'll let you sit in here for a while. But you'll have to be really clear that you aren't ready to call the police, okay?" Billy beams when one of the nurses arrives, clipboard in hand.

At least Melina won't think to look for me in a human hospital. It would be like taking a tank to a bicycle repair shop. They want me to write down a lot of details on a piece of paper before they leave us alone, but Billy helps me make up most of that information.

"How far, exactly, is this from the place I'm meeting Roman?" I ask once they're gone.

Ambrosia bites her lip. "It's not close, but you have a while to wait, right? How long will it take him to fly here?"

"He has to take a plane, right?" Billy asks.

I cock my head. "As opposed to what? He doesn't have wings."

Ambrosia laughs. "Well, seeing how our night has gone, I wouldn't rule anything out."

"Luckily, this is all about to be over for you," I say. "Roman should be here pretty early in the morning. I'd say nine at the latest."

"Wait," Ambrosia says. "When he gets here, you're leaving with him? Just like that?"

It didn't occur to me that would upset them. "I'm sure it will be a relief," I say. "And I can explain things to your father, if that helps."

Ambrosia hugs me and I stiffen.

No one hugs me. Ever. I'm not a huggable person in any way. When she pulls away, there are tears in her eyes. "I'll miss you."

No one has ever said that to me, under any circumstance. But what shocks me more than her words is the realization that I'll miss her, too.

Balthasar brings a file with him. "I can't find a single motive for Angel to want your Mother dead."

I close my eyes.

"By all counts, she loved Enora until the day she died."

"Explain."

"Angel stopped multiple attempts to murder your mother in the last two months. Four, actually. We executed an agent from Shenoah, and one from Adora. Two were unidentified."

"If she wanted Mother dead," I say, "she could have simply let one through and never have been implicated herself."

Balthasar nods. "She provided Enora with information on two of her relatives in the past two years that both resulted in banishment, but she never showed one ounce of mercy toward them or any anger toward your mother for her decisions. She turned them in herself, and from what I can tell has had zero contact with them since their banishment."

"Not that we would know if she covered her tracks, by definition."

"And with her skillset and contacts, she could brush over any evidence easily."

She's been Mother's spymaster for over five centuries.

"She was also your mother's chef. Enora trusted her implicitly."

Mother would tell me to keep looking, because she'd never have believed Angel would harm her. But Lyssa kept a secret for almost two decades. How well do we ever know anyone? I drop my face into my hands.

Balthasar puts a hand on my shoulder. "I'm so sorry, J."

"I'm failing her," I whisper.

His fingers tighten. "You aren't. You're bearing up under all this strain admirably. I've been very impressed, honestly, and if she can see us right now, she's impressed too."

I lift my eyes to his. "What would you do?"

"I'd free Angel and use her to find the real killer. As you mentioned, her skillset is impressive."

I tell him about Nihils and Cina.

He brushes the scruff on his face with his hand and breathes in and out slowly. "You're doing great work, you know. There are so many angles on this that it's hard to track them all down. Keep in mind that whoever actually poisoned her is unlikely to have done it *sua sponte*."

On their own. I bob my head. "That's probably true, and getting them to provide me information on whoever gave them the orders. . ."

"Your plan to ask Nihils questions while distracting him physically is a good idea."

"If we release Angel, could we put someone on her to watch who she talks to? Can we tap her phones?"

He compresses his lips. "Spy on the spider herself?"

I shrug. "Maybe."

"I like your enthusiasm, but it's very unlikely she wouldn't recognize all our attempts."

"We can still try." We hammer out a plan involving three layers of surveillance, so that hopefully, even if she finds the first level, or even the second, we'll still have eyes on her.

"I guess I should talk to her again," I say after we finish.

"I'll come along."

"Thanks."

She's sitting in the same exact meditation pose when we reach the holding cells down below. "Has she caused any problems at all?" I ask the guard on duty, Gideon.

He shakes his head. "Not a single complaint or a request. Not even a question."

This time I enter her cell.

Angel unfolds herself gracefully and stands up, then she inclines her head respectfully. "Your Highness."

I flinch at the slight.

"I don't mean to insult you," Angel says. "But your mother named Chancery before she died. Paperwork is a formality. Even you acknowledged that, which leaves you the Heir."

"Correct."

"Don't be petulant when I honor the reality of our situation. I wouldn't chafe at you mentioning that I'm incarcerated."

She sounds so much like Mother. I close my eyes.

"Speaking of the present circumstances, where is Chancery? I expected her to interrogate me next."

I open them again and breathe in deeply. "I haven't killed her, if that's what you're asking. I have no idea where she is, but probably New York. She left with Alora. She'll be back in a few days and we'll settle things then."

"Interesting."

"What is?"

"You could have insisted on fighting her immediately, yet you gave her time to prepare. She was far more distraught than you over your mother's death."

"I mourn my mother."

"Of course you do, child, but you weren't incapacitated by it like she was. I'm surprised you didn't press your advantage."

Why wouldn't I? Judica the monster, who would stab her sister in the heart while she stood over their mother's dead body. When the rage flooding my chest has nowhere to go, my hands begin to shake. "I'm not here to discuss my sister."

Angel shrugs. She either can't sense my anger, or she doesn't fear it. I wonder which. "Why are you here?" she asks.

"If you decided to kill my mother, how would you do it?"

Angel smiles. "That's a very good question. Well done."

"Answer it."

"I suppose it would depend on my motive."

"Explain."

"If I were angry and I wanted retribution, I would probably approach her when she'd be distracted and behead her."

"You'd immediately be killed," I say.

"I would, but I respected your mother a great deal, and if I felt I had no choice but to eliminate her, either out of revenge or duty, I wouldn't hide my actions."

"Convenient."

She shakes her head. "If I felt she was making a grave mistake, I might do it covertly. I might have cut her life short through more devious means, so that I wouldn't be harmed by the fallout. If I had more confidence in the next person in line for the throne, I could take no further action."

"In that case, you could use poison to eliminate her."

Angel inclines her head. "Even so. But since I'm the head chef, I'd probably find another delivery mechanism, one that didn't shine a neon light in my face."

"What if you poisoned her via her soap," I say. "Or her shampoo."

Angel shrugs. "Not the case here. I'm sure Chancery was right and you'll find the poison was administered via her eggs."

"What makes you so positive of that?" I put a hand on my hip.

"Cookie died as well, and both Chancery and Duchess eschew eggs. Common knowledge in the kitchen. So someone who wanted one of them dead and not the other would have targeted that fact. The effectiveness of any other food would have been prevented by her dog. I told her a dozen times or more to divest herself of Duchess and find a dog that eats anything and everything. She ignored my admonitions.

"If I had decided positively on poison, I'd choose one I could place in her cosmetics, or through a tack on her shoe. I would likely vary the delivery mechanisms, honestly, if it was a slow acting poison as I assume this was. That would make tracking me down exceptionally difficult. And I'd employ the use of several helpers, who individually had no idea what they were doing."

I sigh.

"But Judica, I had no reason to kill Enora. Now that she's gone, I stand to lose my position, my joy, and my life, in that order."

Her position is likely as Intelligence Officer. Her joy has

to be cooking. And Balthasar found nothing to contradict her statement.

"I won't lie and tell you that I haven't made mistakes over the past few centuries, but your mother knew about every single one. The one mistake I never made was lying to her, and I won't lie to you now. In fact, I made a solemn promise to her during her last breaths. I told her I'd do whatever it took to ensure that Alamecha stayed safe and strong in the coming years. I told her I'd sacrifice every-thing I have, if it comes to that. I meant that promise."

"I'm going to free you today, Angel."

Her eyes widen.

"And if I hear anything that contradicts what you've told me, if I see any evidence that you've lied to me, I'll execute you myself."

She inclines her head. "I'd expect no less from Enora's daughter."

"But I am not my mother." My lips curl up into a half smile. "So I won't stop there."

"Excuse me?"

"After I kill you, I'll kill your sons, all forty-one of them."

She swallows.

"I'll kill their one-hundred and seventy-nine children, and I'll kill your twenty-six daughters and their two-hundred and eleven children."

"You wouldn't."

My eyes flash. "You can save them by confessing your guilt to me now. Because if I find out you lied to me, and that you killed my mother, you will wish you'd killed me too. I will end your entire line. Forget deletions to your DNA, you will be eradicated from this earth along with every single person you ever touched."

Angel's smile surprises me. "You are what your mother

made you, and she's never fashioned a weapon quite as glorious. With anyone else, this would be a threat meant to intimidate. With you, it's a fact. You'll kill hundreds of innocents if I dealt you harm and don't confess it freely."

Something inside of me trembles, because I think she's right. I might actually do it, if I find out she betrayed my mother. But I won't only do it because she took my mother from me. In part I'll do it because she fooled me, and I do not like being made to feel imbecilic.

Luckily that doesn't happen often. "I trust that won't be an issue."

Angel clasps her hands in front of her. "I would sacrifice my entire family if it was necessary to honor the vow I made to your mother, but as it turns out." She shakes her head. "You won't need to harm me or mine. I've been entirely loyal to both her and you."

I open the cell door and gesture for her to precede me. She walks through right away, which means she won't notice that my hands are shaking.

An hour later, when I walk into the arena for my training session, I've regained my serenity, at least temporarily. Confronting former mentors and possible assassins isn't something I enjoy.

Five evians wait for me. Roman, Barrett, Agate, Agamemnon, and Nihils. They all meet my eye, except for Nihils. Good. He's nervous. But at least he hasn't been summoned or confronted head on. I didn't even shift the schedule.

Roman sets us all to stretching, a mostly fruitless endeavor for anyone above tenth gen, but I comply. Barrett and Agamemnon were both purchased by Mother so I'd have options, and they're as perfect as you'd expect. Both are eighth gen, and both are tall. Barrett's skin and hair are dark brown, and his eyes are grey. He's well-muscled and keeps his hair short, as prudence dictates. Agamemnon has pale, pale skin, with black hair and eyes so dark they're almost black. He's lean, but his muscle is corded like a whip. His features are sharp and pointed, like someone drew him when they were angry.

Nihils looks almost smudgy by comparison with his button nose and curved jaw, but then again, he's fifteenth generation. It's respectable, but it's not overly impressive. Agate's hair is fifteen different colors, as though she couldn't quite decide. Black strands mix with dark, deep brown, and light brown, and red, and orange and tawny gold, and even locks of white shot through the mix. Her eyes dart from me to the boys nervously. She's fourteenth generation and probably dreads these trainings as much as Nihils. But I need to practice with a variety of opponents, so everyone is recruited to help occasionally.

Both Agate and Nihils are respectable fighters with good bloodlines, but I'd decimate either of them in a solo fight in under a minute. There's a reason I mostly train with the men Mother bought. They're the closest to my skillset.

"We're going to do something different today," Roman says. "Instead of attacking in pairs or engaging in preset sequences, you're going to attack all at once."

Sure they will. Someone always lags, and I'm pretty sure I know who that will be.

"Are we using weapons?" I ask.

Roman grins. "Up to you, Your Majesty."

I bob my head. "Let's do this the hard way then, hand-to-hand." I said hard, but I meant slow. I need time to work on Nihils. Time to press him, to scare him into talking.

"Zanshin," Roman says with a half-smile. "Who can tell me what that word means?"

Barrett snorts.

"Some of the people present haven't had the benefit of the same training as you, Barrett," Roman snaps.

"It's a state of awareness," I say. "You can only achieve it once you've moved beyond the need to think about attacking or defending and you're able to be proactive about what and who is near. Your body needs to move through patterns of sladius without conscious thought, naturally knowing what moves and countermoves to use to accomplish your goal."

"You should all be watching Judica during this fight to learn from her," Roman says. "Balthasar always says she has an aptitude for multi-opponent work, and she naturally understands the rules of facing more than one enemy."

Blah blah blah. "Let's go." He's making me nervous, and the last thing I need is to actually lose when I should be interrogating Nihils.

Luckily Roman steps out of the ring and leaves me with only four opponents to face. When he starts us, I'm standing as I was bidden to do, in the center of the ring. But the second we start, I pivot and back toward Nihils. The first rule of fighting multiple opponents is to keep them all in front of you, but with four attackers and me in the middle, I've got to reach the edge somehow. My only hope at doing that while not eliminating Nihils right away is to let him get behind me. Plus, you always put the weakest danger at your back.

Barrett and Agamemnon advance together, coming at me from forty-five degree angles while Agate rushes me from the front. Nihils' arm wraps around my neck from behind and he uses his other arm to shove my head down and solidify the headlock. I have a cool five seconds before my brain becomes blood deprived and shuts down. Plenty of time. I step backward hard and fast, to throw him off balance, and then I bend my knees and lunge forward, tossing Nihils over my shoulder and slamming him into Agate's advancing form. They both go down like bowling pins, leaving me with ten seconds while they regroup to face the two main threats.

I'd rather not take them out together. One at a time is so much simpler.

I circle back and around, putting them both in front of me, and Nihils and Agate behind me. Agamemnon swings at my face and I let his fist connect to draw him in. I can heal the damage from a half-baked hook quickly. Now he's close enough for me to hammer quick blows into his ribs.

Roman calls out from below. "Step it up, guys. This is pathetic."

Barrett kicks at my knee, and I leap out of the way, putting space between me and Agamemnon. I'm circling back around though, edging ever closer to Agate and Nihils who are recovering quicker than I hoped. They're back up on their feet and I'm back to square one.

"Let's step this up a bit," I yell. "Toss us some blades."

Roman grins. He likes blood spray. But he's a punk, so he tosses a blade to Barrett first, and then to Agamemnon.

I'm stuck ducking and using my forearms to block their slices, and my blood makes the mat slick beneath me. My blade finally sails through the air. I snag the hilt and continue its arc, slicing toward Agate. She tries to leap out of the way but slips and falls in the process.

I'm about to hit her in the waist with a clean shot that ought to sever her spine when another blade blocks me.

Nihils.

I can't quite stop my smile then, but my training kicks in full force. I pivot, slice and jab at intervals, almost losing sight of my goal. I slide my blade across Barrett's hamstring and kick him in the chest. He flies into the edge of the ring and I point. He's out. Roman drags him over the barrier and to the ground outside.

Then there were three.

Agamemnon's shock at Barrett going down makes him sloppy. He thinks I'm distracted by Agate's frontal assault, so I pull a small dagger from my thigh sheath and throw it at him. It sinks into his chest until it hits his sternum. If my aim wasn't off, I'd have hit his heart. I swear under my breath.

I slam my free hand into the pommel of Agate's sword, knocking it out of her hand, and rush toward Agamemnon. He's pulling the blade out when I bring my sword down into his chest, severing his subclavian, brachiocephalic, and carotid arteries.

I kick him over to the edge of the arena so Roman can drag him out to heal. Two to go.

Nihils' sword arcs downward and I let it slice into my shoulder before I jump back. Agate has retrieved her sword and approaches from my left. Time to dispatch her so I can apply some pressure to Nihils.

"Have you two ever dated?" I ask.

Nihils eyes widen. "Agate and me?"

"That's what I'm asking."

Agate shakes her head, the tip of her sword drooping. "No, Your Highness."

I take my opening and knock her blade wide, and then I strike her in the throat with my free hand, collapsing her windpipe. Then I stab her through the stomach with my blade, the impact shoving her back against the rope. It's simple to flip her over from there. Her head cracks when it hits the floor below. Should take a big chunk of time to heal all that.

"So you haven't made out with *her*?" I ask quietly.

Nihils swallows nervously.

"Not like you did with Cina. Repeatedly."

He shakes his head tightly and swings at me.

I parry easily. "What I find curious," I say, "is that Cina insists she never kissed you at all."

"She's lying," Nihils says. "I told you she was upset."

I knock his feet out from under him and leap on top, my blade at his throat. "She didn't pause, or look away. Her heart didn't race, or her pulse spike. In fact, she was convincing enough in her protests that I believed her, one woman to another. The problem is that, if she's telling the truth, that makes you a liar, Nihils."

His heart rate accelerates. "Why do you believe her over me?"

"She's gay, Nihils," I whisper.

The blood drains from his face. I let him up and he scrambles to his feet. "Then you know."

Now I do. "Why would you do it?" Pain tears through me at the thought of this little worm poisoning my mother, injecting her soap with an agent that weakened her bit-by-bit.

"I'm not telling you a thing."

Fury unlocks the demon inside of me and I play with him. Slicing his left side and then his right. He can't hope to block as fast as I can carve. Lacerations climb his legs, his arms, and his chest as I circle him patiently. Pain is my oldest friend, but Nihils doesn't seem to know him. He seems unduly agitated by my tender ministrations.

"Who made you do it?" I ask. "Who gave you the poison?"

"Judica," Roman says behind me. "Enough."

"Back off," I say sharply.

"I can't tell you what you want to know." Nihils' shirt and pants are so shredded they could fall off at any moment. "Because I don't know anything else."

"Try," I say.

"It's not as simple as you think. Your mother has a lot of enemies, but my master is organized, and not alone."

"Who do you report to?"

He shakes his head. "No way. You're scary, but not the scariest person on this island."

I slow my blows, stepping back. "What about Balthasar? He works for me, you know."

"I was worried you'd threaten that." Nihils pops something in his mouth and grins at me. It's macabre to be sure, his face bloody, his teeth white. "At least I'm dying with the knowledge that I've done my part. Before this year ends, Ni'ihau will burn."

He has a kill pill. Rage bubbles over inside of me. "No!" I scream, acting without thinking. He can't die by his own hand. He deserves worse, so much worse. Torture, punishment, and untold agony before he dies. But now there's no time for that. Now the best I can hope is to cause his death myself, to deny him the control over the timing. And if I kill him in training, word won't spread that he took his own life. That would signal his master he'd been found.

Without any more thought, I bring my sword out and around, separating his head from his body. The body collapses, but the head flies through the air and lands on the ground of the arena.

Only then do I recall that I'm not alone, not by a long shot. Agate, Barrett, Agamemnon, and Roman I expect. But dozens of faces watch with horror. Not only did I get nothing from Nihils about my mother, but all of these people watched me kill him.

I don't care about my reputation, but I can't have his master go to ground. I can't lose the one lead I found. How can I fix this mess?

Roman stares at me like he doesn't even know me, but

the other faces don't look shocked. They're vaguely disgusted, but it's almost like they expected me to behead a random member of the family while training. Because I'm the vicious twin. The insane berserker, some of them call me.

Fine. If that's what they think, then that's my cover. "He supported my sister's claim to the throne."

I hop out of the ring, toss my sword to Roman to clean and stomp from the room. If they want a monster, I'll give them a bloody monster. Besides, fear is better than pity every day of the week.

I wasn't lying when I said I'd do whatever it takes to find justice for my mother. Even if it means that Ni'ihau actually burns.

13

THE PRESENT

The nurses flutter around me like mosquitos at first, but I refuse to let them call the cops and I won't provide any details. Eventually they move along to other patients and leave me here to consider my options.

Which is exactly what I should be doing.

"How do we pinpoint exactly where my sister's compound is located?" I ask.

Billy borrowed his father's laptop, thankfully. "Here's our house." He points. "And if you look on Google earth, you can follow satellite images north to where you said you came from." He hands me the laptop. "Now, you can scroll around like this until you find the spot that looks right. Here's how you zoom in and out. It's on satellite view so you can see actual photos."

It doesn't take long to work out where her compound is, thanks to these disturbing images of the buildings. It's bigger than I expected. Besides the main house I saw, she has about five other houses circling it. Presumably her people live in them, and who knows how many live in the neighborhood on the other side of the high fence.

"I can't go back," I say. "Not until I've avenged my mother."

"I thought you said your twin is the queen now." Billy says.

I nod.

"Shouldn't you ask her what she wants you to do?"

"Chancery would want me to kill Melina before returning home, trust me on that. She was even more upset by Mother's death than I was."

"Then what would it hurt to call her and check in? Maybe she'll send you some help."

Billy is trying to be helpful, but he doesn't know me at all. Now that Roman's coming, I really won't need help. And I'm not even one-hundred percent sure that I should go back at all. She set me free, so she shouldn't be surprised or upset if I don't sit in her shadow like a dog, waiting for orders.

Maybe I should leave court entirely and live among humans. Chancery considered it, and now that I've met some humans, I can see why. They aren't so bad after all. Not geniuses, by any means, but good in some ways, and insightful too.

But before I can make that decision, I need to right this wrong. I couldn't kill Chancery, but I can kill the sadistic, kidnapping, delusional Melina. My father's shining star who betrayed our mother and then killed her. It's time for her to go down.

I spend the next few hours assessing what route I could take inside. I make a list of supplies, and then I develop the first draft of a plan. It's risky, it's dangerous, and it's not a sure thing. But I think I can pull it off. By my calculations, Melina probably has around a hundred and twenty evian guards. I can't take out that many, even with Roman's help. But they won't all be facing me at once.

I look at this as a multi-opponent fight. I'll need to circle and attack. Pivot and attack again, keeping them in front of me, keeping my back against the wall. Then I need to get in, eliminate Melina, and get back out.

"You need a bomb?" Billy's eyebrows rise. "For what?"

"You're reading it wrong," I say. "I need a flash bomb. I don't need to destroy anything, but I'll need a distraction. Several, in fact."

He shakes his head. "I don't want to be involved with that. It sounds like a terrorist attack."

"Oh, for the love. I'm not trying to kill anyone other than my sister."

"Oh good, only one planned murder," Billy says. "That sounds way better." He doesn't sound sincere.

"No matter your intention, there may be other casualties," Ambrosia says.

"There's always collateral damage," I say, "but it's worth it in this instance, trust me. The amount of destruction one Alamecha woman can cause is. . . practically catastrophic."

"Aren't you an Alamecha woman?" Billy asks.

I grin. "Precisely."

Eventually Ambrosia falls asleep, and Billy passes out right after her.

This is my window. It's been almost six hours since I called Roman. A flight to Austin takes roughly eight hours. Assuming he left as soon as he possibly could, and that our jets are slightly faster than a commercial aircraft, he could be at Maxine's in the next ninety minutes.

It's time for me to ditch my sweet, big-hearted humans. They're with their dad now, and I don't want them getting hurt. I'll send them some kind of note with compensation for their aid when I return home. Even though I know it's the right thing to do, I struggle with leaving.

I tiptoe outside the room, and nearly run into a stretcher outside the door where their dad is sleeping. He's not a bad man, either. Misguided maybe, and too optimistic about his own capabilities, but he means well. I wish my own father had loved me enough to give up his insane causes and be a father, but we don't always get what we want. In fact, in my experience, we almost never do.

The sun is just coming up when I walk out of the hospital. No one stops me, or even says a word. Probably because the nurses have changed shifts and the new ones haven't come to check in with me yet. Ambrosia mentioned the night nurses would be off about half an hour ago.

I do swipe a Snickers bar and two granola bars from the nurses' station, as well as a bottle of Gatorade. I need food. More than this, but it'll hold me over.

I walk casually down to the parking lot before I start running. It's a solid ten miles to the restaurant based on the map I looked up on the laptop. It won't take me long, but I want to be waiting for him when Roman finally arrives, even though it won't be open for hours yet.

I reach the restaurant and sit down on a bench just outside. I can't think of any way Melina would know to track me here, but I remain vigilant just in case. The first few moments I look back and forth frenetically, but after that I get bored.

I've never had so little to do in my life.

My mind wanders, circling back to my human experience. Billy and Ambrosia baffle me. Their father has a job that's high powered, for a human. He cuts up other humans who are sick—slicing their hearts into pieces and sewing them back together. It must be an agonizing job and a scary one too. He holds people's lives in his hands every day.

But he couldn't save the life of his own wife. She died in spite of everything he could do.

I've only felt a sense of helplessness like that once. When my mother died. Which makes it natural for me to want to right that wrong. Killing Melina will avenge Mother's death, and then I'll feel better about all of it.

Right?

I shake my head. Of course I will.

I review my plan backward and forward. With Roman's help, it should work. I'll dig under the wall at the weak spot between houses three and four and then follow the line of shrubs they failed to keep properly trimmed. I should only have to kill two, maybe three, guards in order to reach the main house where Melina must be located. The guards will likely be much heavier there, but perhaps not. I'm not sure how well Melina knows me. Will she expect retaliation? Is she expending her resources trying to recover me?

I don't know her well enough to have any idea.

But even if there are twice as many guards as she had the other day, we should be fine. Roman will set the charge out front, just on the outside of her gate. The blast will be large enough to destroy the huge live oak, but mostly it will make a lot of noise and bright flashes. That should draw Melina's attention to the front of the house, allowing me to sneak into the back with minimal collateral damage.

Then I just need to find my treacherous sister and end her. Basically my entire life has trained me for that part.

Getting out afterward will be the true difficulty. Roman will probably offer to create another distraction out front, but any way you slice it, someone will likely notice Melina has died. Escape can't be planned with my limited knowledge of the setup or personnel. At least I work well on the fly.

The one thing I won't do is track back down through

the same neighborhood. Ambrosia and Billy have been through enough.

A red Honda CRV parks on the far side of the empty parking lot. A woman in a dark leather jacket climbs out and eyes me warily. "Ma'am, can I help you with something?"

"I hope I didn't alarm you." *Don't mind me. I'm just a lady with a sword poking out of the back of my shirt.* "I'm supposed to be meeting a friend, and I know it's early, but this is one of his favorite restaurants, so he suggested we meet here."

"Oh, that's fine. But it's pretty chilly. I need to take inventory, so you're welcome to wait inside."

Why are all these humans so gullible and kind? No evian would buy that story, and none of them would invite an armed person to sit inside with them. "Thank you so much, but I enjoy the brisk air. I'm great. If it doesn't bother you, I'll just wait out here."

The lady tilts her head but doesn't argue. "Alright, but if you change your mind, just tap on the front door, okay?"

"Absolutely," I say. "I'll only be here until my friend shows up."

Fifteen minutes later, the woman comes back outside with a plate in one hand and a plastic cup in the other. "I made you some beignets and coffee. I thought you might be hungry out here, all alone."

"Thank you," I say. "But you really didn't need to do that."

"I insist." She thrusts the plate and cup at me.

She's bringing a complete stranger food. . . because she's worried I'm hungry. The more time I spend around humans, the worse I feel about my attack on China. Are all humans this good? I'm beginning to worry that they aren't the inferior beings I believed them to be.

"Do you need to call anyone?" the woman asks.

I shake my head. "I really am fine, I swear."

"Alright, sweetheart. I have a daughter about your age, and I feel terrible about you sitting out here all alone."

"Oh," I say. "I'll come sit inside if it will make you feel better."

"It really would at that," she says. "I'm Miss Mason, and I own this restaurant. I'll rest much easier knowing you're inside where it's warm and no one can walk right up and snatch you." I carry my beignets inside, and the coffee too. I eat them all quickly, and my stomach finally stops feeling quite so empty.

Beignets are delicious.

"Who's this friend you're waiting for?" Miss Mason asks from the other room.

"Oh, he's an old family friend. I wasn't supposed to be here, in Austin, I mean."

"You wound up in a city by accident?"

Hm. It does sound a little strange. "It's a long story," I say, "but it was a bizarre set of circumstances that won't ever be repeated."

"Either family drama or a boy." Miss Mason cocks her hip.

"Family drama," I say. "Definitely. My friend who is coming to pick me up is very reliable and never creates drama."

"What's this white knight's name?" she asks.

"He's not a knight," I say. "He's a normal guy. But his name is Roman."

A black sedan pulls up outside, and Roman steps out. He hands a few bills to the driver and turns toward the restaurant.

"Actually, that's him now."

Miss Mason sprints into the front room.

"Thank you so much for letting me sit inside and for

bringing me food." I walk toward the front door, passing her where she's looking out the window.

She grabs my arm and squeezes me tightly. "That." She points. "That is not a normal guy!" She gawks at him, her lips parted, her eyes glazed.

"He's not bad looking," I admit.

"Is he a lot older than you?" she asks.

"Three years," I say. "But I like older guys."

She whistles. "I can see why. What a hunk."

A what?

Roman reaches the front doors and leans close, with one hand over his eyes, to peer in through the glass. When his eyes meet mine, an electric pulse shoots through me. He came all the way here, alone, because I called. I mean, it's his job. Or I think it's still his job. That's probably why he came. But his words from the moments before Angel knocked me out echo in my mind. *I'm in love with you, Judica. I've loved you for years and years.*

I shut him down. I told him—what did I tell him? I cast back in my mind and realize I didn't say anything at all. He took my lack of a response as a refusal. He left while I stood, dazed, unsure what to say. He probably won't ever say anything like that again. He has probably changed his mind.

Maybe he's even met someone since I disappeared. Noticed how much happier he is when I'm not around.

He taps again and I jump. "Well, I'd better. . ."

"Yes, of course, dear. Be safe, okay? Don't let that family drama ruin your future." She winks and bobs her head in Roman's direction. "It looks to be a pretty bright one."

"I'll do my very best to avoid any future family drama." I flip the lock on the door and yank it open. Then, before Miss Mason can introduce herself and suck me back inside,

I wave and duck outside. Roman steps back so I have room to walk past.

I start to do just that, behaving around him exactly as I always have, but it feels wrong somehow. Seeing Roman through Miss Mason's eyes, I've realized how lucky I am to have someone like him hop on a plane the second I ask.

I change course and barrel into him, my arms circling his torso and squeezing tightly. "You came."

He exhales loudly, his hands frozen away from his body. "Of course I did."

"I can't believe you're here." I escaped my holding cell in my underwear. I fought off Melina's armed assailants. I wasn't afraid on a restaurant bench alone. I was completely fine, waiting inside the restaurant with a total stranger. But now that Roman's here, tall, warm, and capable, something inside of me splits open, like I've barely been hanging on all this time. Like I want to collapse and surrender to someone else.

His hands stroke my hair. "Of course I came."

I want to fall into him forever and never have to slice or shoot or attack anyone ever again. I want Roman to take me away, but not back to Ni'ihau. Somewhere else, somewhere safe, somewhere not haunted by my mother, my sisters, the throne that isn't mine anymore.

"Was it hard to get away?" I ask.

Roman grunts. "I should be asking you that. How did you escape, if they took you and Melina wanted to kill you?"

If I get in to that right now, I'll completely lose it. I need some space, between being taken, and between me and Roman. I stumble back a step, outside of the circle of his arms. "I don't want to talk about it here."

"Understood. From my end, I called in a few major favors to leave, but you'll be pleased to know that Chancery doesn't know where we are. I doubt she even knows why I left."

"Oh Roman, you could have told her. I don't want to get you into trouble."

"That's your middle name," he says. "Judica Trouble Alamecha."

He's mocking me. That's a clear sign that he's not feeling the same thing that I am. He might not have missed me at all. In fact, his life might have been better if I hadn't called him and never returned home. I can't swallow past the lump in my throat. "I'll make things right, I swear. But first I need your help with something here. Something big."

"Why are you here?" he asks.

"At this restaurant, you mean?"

"You said Melina kidnapped you and brought you here. What did she want?"

"She wanted me to tell her why Mother changed her mind and named Chancery."

"Do you even know the answer to that?" Roman's brow furrows. "Isn't that what everyone wants to know, including you?"

"Exactly," I say.

He frowns. "Why would she think you knew?"

Mother said I couldn't tell a soul, which certainly includes Roman. But she's gone, and I'm here. "Is that driver waiting for us?"

Roman nods. "He'll wait however long we need."

I walk over to the bench I was warming earlier and sit down. Roman sits next to me. Mother didn't approve of Roman. Mother told me not to pick him for my Consort. Well, Mother's not here. And she promised me that she'd make me her heir, and she didn't. Maybe she wasn't infallible after all.

"Here's the thing," I say quietly. "No one else knows

this, just me, Chancery, and Inara. But Chancery tried on Mother's staridium ring, and something happened when she did. It set off an electromagnetic pulse of some kind, wiping out the island. Twice."

Roman frowns. "Chancery did that? On accident?" He scratches his cheek and then folds his hands in his lap. "That makes sense."

"Does it? When Mother had me and Inara try it on, nothing happened. Not a single thing."

"How would Melina know anything about that?" he asks.

"I don't think she did, or not any details. Angel told her about the EMP, because she asked me about it. They both knew that Mother changed her mind shortly after that bizarre occurrence. But Melina thinks the whole heir changeup has more significance than that, even. She has this wacky prophecy tattooed on her arms, and she thought Mother changed tracks because she discovered Chancery was the queen it talks about, sent to unite the families and save the world. If I'd told her what I just told you, she'd have executed me on the spot, I guarantee it. The only reason I'm still alive is that she was waiting for confirmation from one of her spies in court that Chancery was chosen to replace me for a reason."

"She's really nuts, huh?"

I think about how I let Angel go. How she took me to Melina and had clearly been working for her all along. Angel lied to my face, and I believed her. When she told me about the promise she made to Mother. Tears threaten and I blink them back. "I'm virtually positive Melina and Angel killed Mother. As we all know, Angel had means, but no motive. Somehow, her connection to Melina gave her the motive."

"Wait, Melina didn't tell you that she killed Enora?"

"I accused her and Melina never denied it."

Roman slings an arm around me and pulls me close. I lean my head on his shoulder. "It's been a really hard couple of days for you. I'm sorry."

I listen to the smooth rhythm of his heart. "I've been thinking about running away from everything."

Roman tenses. "That's not like you."

It sure isn't. "I can't do it," I say. "Don't worry. But that it even occurred to me gives me some insight into my sister."

He squeezes my shoulder. "You're more like Chancery than you realized?"

"Maybe," I admit. "But Alamecha is everything to me."

"So we're headed back to Ni'ihau?"

"Maybe not quite yet."

"What do you need to do first?" he asks.

Roman knows me. "I can't just leave her." I look up at his face.

He closes his eyes. "You want to kill Melina."

"She's unhinged, Roman. I have no idea what she'll do next. She could come after me again—we know she has people at court—or she could target Chancery instead. What if Melina decides *she's* the 'Eldest' in her weird prophecy who is supposed to lead Alamecha to save the whole world? Or what if she thinks Chancery's off the path and kidnaps her to pull her puppety strings?"

"Is this about any of that?" Roman peers down at me.

"What does that mean?"

"It means, you finally found out who killed your mother."

My voice is flat. "Would it be wrong, if that was my only reason to do it?" Am I really a monster?

"We'll make her pay," Roman says, "and then we'll go home."

He doesn't answer the question I didn't ask, but how can I expect him to? Immediately, though, he's on my side. I quickly outline my plan.

"That's quite a list of materials we need," he says. "From weapons to flash bombs to ammunition. How exactly did you plan to procure all of those things?"

"You have money, right?" I ask.

Roman bobs his head. "It makes the human world go round, but they don't just have a store where you can go and buy whatever weapons you want."

"We're in Texas. I heard they do." I shrug. "Well, if they don't, then we need to figure out how to find them here."

When a red Porsche Cayenne rolls up in the parking lot, Roman and I both sit up, identically alert. When Ambrosia and Billy hop out, I curse under my breath.

Roman unsheathes his sword and pulls out his 1911. I put a hand on his arm. "Stand down. They're friends."

"They're human," Roman says as though I don't have eyes or ears of my own.

My mouth turns up on one side. "I'm aware. They're still friends." Friends I meant to leave behind. But then I sat here, at the place Billy suggested, for far too long. I'm an idiot. Or maybe I wanted them to find me.

"I can't believe you ditched us!" they say in unison.

"I'm bad for your health," I protest. "I wanted to keep you safe."

"OMG, is that him?" Ambrosia asks. "You did *not* mention how hot he is."

I suppress a grin. "Roman, this is Ambrosia and her older brother Billy. They sheltered me from Melina and gave me food after my escape. They also helped me disarm and incapacitate Melina's people and make it here."

"And then you bailed on us while we were sleeping," Billy says. "Which was pretty lame. Humans need sleep."

"Evians need sleep as well." Roman smiles. "Less than a human, but we do sleep. In any case, we greatly appreciate your service." Roman sheaths his sword and tucks his gun into his back holster. He reaches into his pocket and pulls out a wad of bills. "I hope this adequately conveys my gratitude."

"We don't want your money," Ambrosia says, one eyebrow lifted.

"Speak for yourself," Billy says. "That was one rough night." He snatches the wad of cash from Roman and stuffs it in his pocket.

"Give that back to him," Ambrosia says. "Right now."

"Hey, look. When we woke up, we had to drive home and clean up the mess before Dad got off and freaked out. I think we may have to throw that steam cleaner away. They are just not meant to clean up dried blood. But then we had to drive over here in Dad's car. He's going to be pissed if he realizes that, and he might even take my keys. In which case, this money will really help me out. And if they're telling the truth, they have like a gazillion dollars."

Ambrosia shakes her head. "Dad's back in surgery. He'll never even notice we took the car, and I doubt he knew we had a steam cleaner in the first place."

"Keep the cash," I say. "But share some with your sister."

"Are you going to do it?" Billy asks. "Are we going after your sister?"

I nod. "I'm doing it, but you two are not helping. It's far too dangerous."

"But I bet you need some help getting the items on that list we made. Even if you have money, which clearly you do," Billy says, "you probably have no idea where to buy it all."

Roman whispers, "He's got a point."

"Fine," I say. "But you help us find the supplies I need, and then you're done. You go stay with a friend until all of this is past. Promise?"

Ambrosia smiles and Billy nods.

"It's a deal," Ambrosia says. "Now let's go put a stop to your homicidal sister, once and for all."

❧ 14 ❦

THE PAST

Nihils was going to die. I know that; I do. I killed him before his kill pill could, that's all. But walking away from him is still much harder than I expected it would be. Especially since everyone else thinks I killed him for supporting my sister.

I didn't think I cared what people think of me. Maybe I don't, to a certain extent. But I care what Roman thinks, and he's looking at me with searching eyes. He wants answers. And I can't give him any.

After I storm past him, he follows me to my room doggedly.

"Umm, I need a shower," I say. "Ridding the world of the people who support my sister is exhausting, so I'm going to go inside and close the door now." When I open the door, Death is waiting patiently on the other side. He licks my hand eagerly. He doesn't believe I'm a monster, at least. I try to slip into my room and close the door, but Roman shoves past me, closing it behind him.

"You need to tell me the truth about what is going on," Roman says. "Everyone else may believe you threw a tantrum back there that killed someone, but you'll never convince me that's what happened. You're not a psychopath."

"All evidence to the contrary." I sigh and cross my arms. "What if I am?"

He shakes his head. "You aren't."

Tears well up in my eyes. Why does he have faith in me when every piece of evidence is stacked against me?

"Don't cry," he whispers. "But you need someone on your side, someone you can trust. You're not in this all alone."

I wipe the tears away with bloody hands. I probably look like a hunk of aging meat hanging from a hook. "Nihils poisoned my mother."

Roman's mouth drops open. "No."

I nod slowly.

"No wonder you killed him." Roman pulls me toward him for a hug, apparently unconcerned about me needing a shower.

I resist at first, but it hurts too much to be strong. When his arms wrap around me, a tightness in my chest eases and I can breathe again, freely. I should tell him how I feel. My body heals in seconds, but my heart? It hurts so badly every day that small things fall away. Nothing else matters, and so I'm numb all the time. I want to tell him all of that, but I can't. Saying those words would destroy me. "It hurts," I finally say. Even those two little words leave me bare, vulnerable. I want to laugh them off. Make a joke about some wound or another.

But that would be cowardly. I am many things, but I am not a coward, so I let them stand.

"I know," Roman says. "That pain probably won't ever go away, but you'll handle it better with time." He should let me go. He should step away and look anywhere but my face. I need to scrounge up some kind of pride, some semblance of normalcy again, but I can't do it. He releases me a little, and then he gathers me closer, but shifts me so my face is against his chest. "It will get easier, I promise."

"Mother deserved better," I say. "I ruined everything."

"You killed him," he says. "Which is exactly what would have happened after a trial, or days and days of torture. You have always been efficient. Your mother knows you, and if she can see any of this now, she knows what you're up against. She is proud of you."

For challenging Chancery? For running my sister away? For fumbling this investigation so horribly? I shake my head against his chest. "No, you don't understand. Nihils was working for someone. There's a bigger group that orchestrated this. He has a boss, at least one, and he died before I could find out anything useful."

Roman's voice is clearly set to 'soothing' when he asks, "I don't mean to upset you, but if he had information on whoever he reported to, why did you kill him?"

I clench my hands and shove away from the comfort I don't deserve. "He took a poison pill," I say. "He was going to die without telling us anything either way."

"So we explain that. No one will think ill of you for doing what you did."

"But if everyone knows why I beheaded him, the real reason-"

Roman closes his eyes. "His boss will know, too."

"It was my only play to try and salvage something, anything, I don't know. I had a split second and I panicked."

"If you'd done nothing, his boss would surely have heard that he died of poison."

"And given what people think of me." I shake my head. "His boss might not know why I did it, or even realize I was on to him. No one knows I went to his room, since I did it alone, and he has been slated to fight me for weeks on the schedule."

"We need to search his room and belongings immediately," Roman says, "but without alerting anyone that we're doing it. I can send someone to officially prepare his belongings to be sent to his family."

"Clean-up crew," I say. "Wait." I bite my lip. "What if we put the word out that we found something. A journal, or a notebook."

"I'm listening," Roman says.

"His boss would be nervous, right?" I begin pacing from one end of the room to the other. Death is so accustomed to my pacing that he lays down against the wall with a huff. "He or she might show up to grab it, if we put out that we had it. But where would we take it that they might ambush us?"

Roman smiles. "If I 'find' it during the search, I could read a page or two, and see who contacts me. Then, instead of rushing it to you, I could tuck it in my bag. I could ask the other members of the crew not to say anything."

"Why would you be conducting the search?" I ask. "You're my captain of the guard."

"Not me, then," he says. "Someone else. Who else do we trust?"

"Balthasar, you, Chancery. That's my list of people I know wouldn't have killed Mother, absolutely."

"What about Angel?" he asks.

I shake my head. "I let her go because she's too obvious. It doesn't mean I believe she's innocent. I just don't know." I growl.

"Let's think this through," Roman says. "I'm not very clever, so I always take things one step at a time. We want to make up a notebook so that whoever was Nihils' leader thinks he took notes. And, honestly, maybe he did. We don't know. But let's assume there's nothing to find. We need to make someone think there *is* something to find. And we can assume that the person who was directing him isn't sure whether we were on to him."

"I'm with you so far," I say. "We have a typical pack and clean for his room that someone will be assigned to do. Did my mother ever direct that? Or is it a simple Larena task?"

Roman shrugs. "Probably Larena. But what if you stepped in because you felt guilty? You can tell Larena you're remorseful and you want someone important to gather his belongings and extend an apology to his family."

I lift one eyebrow.

"Maybe 'apology' is taking things too far. But to provide the news to his family."

I shrug. "But then you go to collect things and, what? You find the notebook. There's no way that you can broadcast what you find."

"We ask for volunteers to clean the room," Roman says. "I promise you that his boss will either volunteer or send someone to monitor it. If I were him, I would. I mean, you know your agent died in a freak way. You know there's an ongoing investigation. So if I show up in the middle of the cleanup and find something, then I don't put it in the box, they'll send someone after me. They would have to."

"It's the best chance we have," I say. "But that's a lot of risk for you."

"It can't be something you find. It's getting the information *to you* that gives them a window to strike."

But it makes Roman the target. For people who recently killed my mother, and effectively, Nihils, too. I don't like it. In fact, I hate it all the way down to my toenails. "It's too dangerous."

Roman's face blanks, a lack of expression in his eyes I've never seen.

"You don't trust me to do it," Roman says. "But would you trust Balthasar?"

"He's too high profile," I say.

"What about Edam?" he asks. "Would you have allowed him to do it?"

He's hurt. He thinks I doubt his ability and that's why I don't like the plan. "The worm gets eaten, Roman, every time. That's what happens when you go fishing. Whether you catch the fish or not, the worm is a goner."

"I'm not a worm." His eyes flash.

"No, I mean, I know that," I say. "Obviously."

"If you want to catch your mother's killer, this is your play." He crosses his arms, the muscle in his forearms rippling.

My mouth turns to sand. "Of course I want to catch her killer." But she's already dead. I don't want to catch her if it means losing one of the only people I care about. My only friend. I open my mouth to tell him that he matters too much.

But it's too late. He's walking toward the door. "Great, then I'll set things in motion. The boss will have from the time I find the fake notebook until I meet you at five to contact me. I will be ready," he says.

If I tell him no, he'll take it as a lack of faith in his ability. If I go through with it, he'll probably die. I reach for him, and stop. I clench my fists and stumble backward, bumping up against Death. His furry head rubs against the back of my leg, then he starts to lick the blood from the area behind my knee.

Roman grabs the handle of the door, and I open my mouth. I don't know what to say, but I need to stop him. I can't lose him too. Before I can think of anything, he releases the doorknob and spins on his heel.

"What?" I ask, my eyes wide, my heart hammering.

He glances at my heart and back to my face, clearly wondering why I'm upset. "I had a thought. I don't want to upset you, but I felt I ought to share it. Pardon me if this is the wrong thing to say."

"Go ahead." I won't fault him for anything right now, truly.

"Your sister."

"Chancery." I can't help the scowl.

"She left with Edam."

"Mm."

"I know he was your—ahem—boyfriend for a while, and that you aren't on good terms now."

"What's your point, Roman?"

"Has it occurred to you that she might take him as a Consort?"

It should have occurred to me. How hasn't it? "Yes. Of course it has." My mind isn't racing a million miles a minute right now. I'm totally not terrified at the idea of dying by my ex-boyfriend's sword.

"Right," he says. "Of course." He turns around again, but he pauses. His voice is small and his eyes are still facing the door when he asks, "Are you at all worried about that?"

I shake my head a little too vehemently, not that he can see me. "No, not at all."

Roman knows the same thing I do. Edam can defeat me. Edam could kill me. Which means Chancery could defeat me when she returns.

"What are you suggesting?"

He shrugs. "Nothing, Your Majesty. I wanted to make sure you were prepared, that's all."

I wasn't prepared. The idea hits me like a delivery truck, but I won't send a hit team. I can't do that, not to Chancery. "I won't assassinate her," I say. "It's beneath me. If Chancery won't face me herself, then so be it. I'll take what comes."

He bobs his head, turns, and leaves.

I sink onto my bed, dropping my face into my hands. Would my sister use my ex-boyfriend to kill me? I close my eyes and imagine her face, her doe eyes, and her care for everything. She spent the past seventeen years protecting one weak thing after another. A bird with a broken wing pooping all over the patio. Half-humans, full humans, dogs, horses, political opponents, traitors. Can the person who champions everyone in the world really kill her sister?

If someone like her can bring herself to kill something, I must really deserve to die.

I think about Nihils. Killing him was the first time I've killed anything myself. I didn't think I would care. After all, he deserved it. He killed my mother, or at least had a hand in it. He was dying anyway. And yet, I still see his eyes, full of fear, his hands, shaking. I can still see his shock when my sword connected with his throat. I relive that second over and over, the utter revulsion I felt when my sword cleaved his head from his body.

I suddenly feel awful, a hot wash of liquid flooding my mouth. I rush into the bathroom to look in the mirror. Have I been poisoned? My cheeks are flushed, my stomach aches. Just in time, I turn to the side and retch in the toilet, expelling the tail end of my breakfast into the pristine white porcelain bowl. I've never thrown up in my life, but I've heard of it. The mostly digested food tastes awful, acidic and bitter. I look at the orangey liquid and half a grape in the toilet bowl and turn away to wipe my mouth on a bloody sleeve.

For the first time since Mother died, I wonder whether

I can really kill Chancery. She makes my blood boil on the regular. She disagrees with everything. She's always demanding things. She never fully comprehends the darkness in the world or the duty we have to maintain the strength of our family. She's a clueless, pampered, spoiled, entitled brat.

I have thought about strangling her often. I would enjoy following through on that, but she'd heal when I was done, and hey, she'd understand a little more of what I've endured for the last sixteen years. But the thought of doing to her what I did to Nihils leaves me hugging the toilet bowl again. This time there's nothing left in my stomach to regurgitate.

Eventually I force myself into the shower, banishing thoughts of Nihils, Edam, and Chancery. I'll face things as they come and not a minute sooner. It's too much otherwise. Which makes me think of Roman, who even this very moment might be attacked. Or killed. I close my eyes.

I face things as they come, and there's nothing I can do to stop Roman now. I finish my shower and dress myself. I toss my destroyed clothing into the incinerator and press the button to burn. Mother had it installed in my room a few years back. I go through a lot of clothing, which is why it's easier to wear mostly black. Blood stains don't show on black, and I only have to trash things when they're sliced up.

A tap at the door is probably my lunch, but my stupidly nervous stomach executes a backflip anyway. What if it's someone else, coming to tell me that Roman is dead. What if it's Roman, with enemies giving chase? I might need my sword. I grab it on the way to the door and swing it open.

"Oh, hello." Inara's eyes widen and she backs up a step. "Everything alright?"

"Yes, absolutely." I poke my head around the corner of

the door and check. Both my door guards seem calm. Their heart rates are steady. No word from Roman, then. Not yet.

"Umm, okay. Well, Angel asked me to bring you this." Inara's holding a tray full of several of my favorite things: quiche, stew, and steamed broccoli doused in cheese. There's even a strawberry malt in a tall, frosted glass.

"Thanks." I sit down at the small table in front of the window in my room. Inara drops the tray in front of me and sits across from me. I pinch pieces off to feed to Death. He snaps them up one at a time. I dump a little of the malt into his food bowl at my feet and he laps it up.

"You released Angel," Inara says.

I nod. "Do you think it was a mistake?" I bob my head at my tray. "Should I be nervous?"

Inara shrugs. "I haven't talked to her. You're the one who has to decide that. She certainly had the means, but I've never thought she had any kind of motive. By all evidence, she loved Mother."

"Still, someone who loved her might have killed her. It happens."

Inara sinks into a chair in the corner. "Our world is a twisted place. The ones we love have the greatest capacity to injure us, in more ways than one."

"Do you think I'm safe?" I ask.

"None of us are really ever safe." Inara looks out the window. "Sometimes I wish I was born human, so I could have lived without worrying about everything incessantly."

"But you'd already be dead," I say. "And I'm glad you're here."

"Are you?" Inara meets my eye.

"I am," I say. "I'm surprised you stayed, honestly. I thought you'd go with Chancery." It hurts to be so honest, but thinking of killing Chancery and losing Mother has made me acutely conscious of our lack of control, of the finite nature of time, even for us.

"I was going with her," she admits, "but she told me to stay."

I don't blink or cry or frown. I'm proud of that. "So you're here to spy on me?"

"I hope not, or I'd be a pretty terrible spy, wouldn't I?"

"I suppose so." Death is still fine, so I think I'm okay to eat. I pick up a spoon. "Then why did you stay?"

"Because I love you too, Judica."

But she supports Chancery.

"You think because I love her, I'm on her side." Inara's voice is flat.

"Are you?"

"There's a reason twins are usually not both allowed to live." Inara stands up and begins to walk back and forth in front of the window. "The family struggles in these cases. I think you'd make a better ruler, but I respect Mother. I wanted to support her, and I tried to do that immediately after her death. That doesn't mean I won't change my mind, and you've been doing an admirable job holding things down in her absence, whereas your sister fled at the first chance."

She's telling me that she's shifting. Or that she might. "But she wasn't prepared for this like I was."

Inara's brow furrows. "Are you making excuses for her?"

I shake my head. "Absolutely not."

"Look," she says. "I want you to know that Chancery is asking for video footage of you fighting."

I lift my chin. "She's training?"

Inara nods.

Which means she's not relying on Edam to do her dirty work, at least, she hasn't decided to yet. "Send them."

"Yes?"

"She should be doing her due diligence. It's prudent. She's almost eighteen years late on that, but better late than never."

"You think she might defeat you?"

I might not be the heartless killer everyone sees. I might not be able to do what needs to be done, especially when it involves mowing down one of the kindest people I've ever known, one of the most selfless. "Not even I know what the future holds."

Inara walks toward the door. "If you ever want counsel or just someone to talk to, I'm here."

"Thank you."

She reaches for the door handle and stops. "For what it's worth, I think Chancery knows where the ring is. She may not realize it yet, but if Mother made the switch, she would have signaled her plans to Chancery somehow."

"Duly noted, but we're going to search every nook and cranny for it anyway."

"Understood."

Half an hour of delays and still no word from Roman.

I decide to proceed with my afternoon as though nothing is wrong, but it's hard. Horribly hard. I meet with Larena, and then I hear petitions. I have no patience for the minor disputes, squabbles, accounting issues, posting requests, and on and on. I handle a call with the Prime Minister, and then with several key US senators after that, and at no point do I ask about Roman. But it's on the tip of my tongue the entire time.

I leave the throne room and stride for my room, my long steps eating up the distance between me and my destination. If Roman's not there, I am carving my way to his side. Every time I blink, I see him lying on the ground, surrounded in a pool of red. Roman should have returned to me by now. Something is wrong.

When I reach my room, he's not one of the guards at the door. My heart contracts painfully and I pull my sword from its sheath. My guards, Dante and Rochefort, blanch. "Where is Roman?" I ask.

Before they can answer, my door opens. Roman's head pokes out and something inside of me gives out. My knees wobble, but I force them to hold steady. I practically rush through the doorway and toss my sword on the bed.

"I'm so sorry," he says.

My mouth drops open.

"I know you're hoping I have news. I know you were wishing I'd been contacted, or attacked, or anything."

He's such an idiot. After losing my mother, the one thing I want more than finding her killer is not to lose anyone else.

"But the worst happened."

He's alive, so that's not true.

"No one took the bait." He pulls a notebook from his pocket and tosses it onto the bed.

"Oh, right." I scratch my chin. "That's terrible news. Really awful."

Roman beams at me. He must know that I was in agony. He knows how I feel, how I've always felt. He pulls a scrap of paper from his pocket. "But I do have a consolation prize."

"Excuse me?"

He lifts his other hand and I realize he's holding a book. *Lolita*, by Vladimir Nabokov.

"Uh, I'm sorry. What?"

I take the paper when he offers it and realize it's toilet paper. A handful of symbols are scrawled on it hastily.

"This was stuck in the bottom of his trash bin. You don't want to know what it was under." Roman shudders.

"Why do you have *Lolita*?" I ask calmly, holding the

toilet paper gingerly away from my body. I don't recognize the smell, but it's nothing good.

"It took me a few minutes, but I cracked his cipher."

"He had the book in his room?" That's just sloppy.

"He was fifteenth gen. Maybe he didn't have a photographic memory. Who knows?"

"What does this say, then?"

"Bluff," Roman says, "at midnight. Extraction."

"He was leaving," I say. "He knew I would figure him out."

"Or he feared it enough to demand that they come and get him."

"It had to be for tonight," I say. "Do you think there's any chance they'll still come?"

"Everyone knows he's dead, but what if he wasn't the only one who wanted out. If he was working with anyone else, they might want out, too. They might not have taken my bait, but we might have a second bite at the apple."

I swear, and then I feel guilty about it. The crutch of the uneducated, I know, Mother. But sometimes swear words are the only thing that fit how I feel.

"It can't hurt to try," Roman says. "Since it's our only lead."

"Are you suggesting we head up to the bluff tonight at midnight?"

Heat rushes to his cheeks. "Only if you want me to accompany you."

"Who else would I take?"

Roman ducks his head a little, and walks toward the door. "I'll meet you here at half past eleven. We can sneak out your window."

I'm more excited to see him tonight than I should be. My rendezvous later comes to mind when I'm reviewing placements with Larena, and staff lists with Inara, and menus with Angel. Roman's face pops into my head when I'm talking to the President of the United States about the new tax plan. I'm sure it's just excitement or hope that I'll find Nihils' conspirator, but it's insistent, this unsettling feeling of nervous shakiness.

I ought to sleep for an hour or so before we head for the bluff, but instead I change my clothes. Four times. What is my problem? It's not like the various shades of black will make any difference in whether we're able to hide from anyone who actually comes for the extraction.

I nearly jump out of my skin when I hear Roman's tap on my door, one minute early. It makes no sense, because I knew he was coming. Death can sense my anxiety and circles my feet frenetically. I nearly trip over him when I walk across the room.

Roman lifts one eyebrow when I open the door. "You could have told me to come in."

I glance from side to side, taking in the door guards posted.

"I needed to move," I say. "Come in. We have a lot to talk about."

Roman's wearing a black tank top that exposes his sculpted shoulders. He closes the door behind him and smiles at me. "We do?"

I step backward involuntarily. "No, but they need to think we do, because otherwise, what will they think we're doing in here for so long?"

Roman's smile shifts a hair and becomes a cocky grin. "Yes, what could they possibly think we're doing this late at night, in your bedroom?"

Do not react, do not blush, and do not freak out. He's just being goofy. "Let's go, just in case they come early."

"You know it's imperative that they not see us."

I bob my head. "We'll figure it out."

Roman's eyes rake down my body and then back up. "You're wearing all black. That's good. It's so dark out tonight, we should be able to move close to undetected."

"That's the plan."

He crosses the room and opens the window, the muscles in his back rippling from the strain. I look down just in time.

He turns toward me and asks, "Coming?"

I answer by jogging over to the window. He's already through and offers me a hand. When I take it, a strange tingling starts in my fingertips. I snatch my fingers back the second my feet hit the ground outside, and we both head across the rear pavilion and toward the bluff.

The first guard, Günter, stops us.

"We're going for a jog," I say. "Roman's with me for safety, but please keep it off the radio and your record. If we decide to do more under-the-radar training, I don't want our routine to become predictable."

Günter bows. "Yes, Your Highness."

Roman's shoulders stiffen at the slight. Most people are saying Your Highness, which is fine. I'm Heir, not Empress, but it's nice to know that Roman's annoyed too.

I put my hand on his. "It's fine," I whisper. I set out at a jog again.

"Your mother is gone, your sister fled, and they're still acting like you're not Empress," Roman says. "Why doesn't that bother you?"

It does, but it's a fight for another day. It still makes me smile that Roman cares, not that anyone will notice my grin in the darkness. There's just enough light to avoid twisting my ankle. By the time we reach the bluff, I'm actually sweating a little, the humid air making my shirt stick to my clavicle.

"There." I point at a rocky outcropping. "We can both

hide under there, and if anyone else is coming, we should be able to see them."

"Good idea, but we'll have to sit pretty close, facing opposite directions, or we won't see everything."

The bluff is the highest point in Ni'ihau, and it can be seen from all around if you aren't sheltered. But you also have an amazing view from here. I scramble up to the top and then duck under the grassy ledge. The ground is full of scree that I kick away and then smooth out with my hand before taking a seat.

Roman slides over next to me, shifting me over a little to make room for himself.

"Keep your eyes open for any signals or signs," I say. "They can't possibly be sending a helicopter or something here, or we'd see that. It's not that dark. Which must mean they were planning for Nihils to see whatever they had planned from here."

Roman bobs his head. "I'm watching my side, you watch yours."

His heart beats slowly next to me. Buh-bump. Buh-bump. I could set my clock by it.

"Are you happy here?" Roman asks.

"My mother just died."

"I'm sorry," he says. "That was a dumb thing to ask."

"Did you mean, before Mother died?"

He nods. "Yes, I shouldn't have asked."

"It's been a hard couple of days," I say.

"Because of Edam."

For some reason, I'm uncomfortable with Roman bringing up his name. I force myself to respond so he doesn't realize that. "I guess you're glad he's gone."

"I guess so."

"It does mean a promotion for you."

"I don't care much about titles or jobs," Roman says.

I didn't realize he hadn't liked Edam. Everyone loved Edam. Clearly Mother did, and Chancery has for years. "But speaking of jobs, I think he did his pretty well. Did you find everything in order when you took over?"

Roman's mouth turns down on both sides. "Yes."

The silence is deafening after that, and I become acutely aware of the nearness of Roman's body. Heat radiates from him, but it's not uncomfortable. The air has cooled off quite a bit now that the sun has been down for so long. The minutes creep by with no conversation.

But no one comes, and no one shines a light, and no one makes a single solitary peep.

"They know Nihils is gone," I finally say at one a.m. "And no one else is coming. This is a dead end. Sorry I wasted even more of your time."

"I suppose it was a waste of time." Roman's eyes search mine for something with an intensity I have rarely seen, but I can't figure out what. Is he looking for disappointment? Sorrow? Anger?

"Well, we better get back then."

He grunts. "We better." He reaches his hand toward my face and I freeze. No muscles work, my lungs shut down, and my heart picks up speed. What's he doing?

He flicks a spider out of my hair.

I'm an idiot. What did I think he was about to do? He's not the right guy for me, and even if he were, he wouldn't want to date me. I'm the insane berserker. No one wants that.

I trudge back down slowly, Roman at my side. Memories flood my mind. Mother's face, Mother's words, Mother's lessons. She worked so hard to mold me into the perfect ruler, but it wasn't enough. I'm not enough. Mother might have been right to choose Chancery, because I've lost my last lead on catching her killer. I'm a failure at this, just as I failed at everything else.

My arms and legs still work when I climb through my own window, Roman at my back, protecting me as always. "Thanks," I tell him when he climbs back inside.

"Of course." He shuts the window and turns toward me. He steps closer, too close, but I'm powerless to pull away.

Probably a bug on my nose.

"I need to tell you something," he says. "And I'm aware it's not good timing, but it feels like there will never be a great time."

My breathing hitches. I want to stop him, but I can't do it. I can't even force out a single word.

"Edam's the best fighter. He's better at theory. He's better looking. He's scarier and has a better pedigree."

Edam's perfect. My mother loved him, but Edam dumped me for *her*. As if that isn't bad enough, he did that before he even knew I wasn't going to be Heir.

"But Edam never looked at you the way he should have. He never burned for you. In fact, Edam was always wrong for you."

Roman's hands circle my waist. His face lowers to mine slowly. I have a lifetime to stop him. I could shove him away. I could laugh. I could shake my head, or say a two letter word and he'd disappear forever. I can feel it all the way down to my cells.

I don't stop him.

Roman's full lips meet mine and something breaks inside of me. Bands around my heart disintegrate. The anger that has become my constant companion evaporates in the heat between us. Hope soars inside of me as his mouth meets mine, his broad chest pressed against me. His hands tighten around my waist and for the first time in days and days, I'm not afraid.

Roman is the bite of my blade against an enemy, the regrowth of skin over a healing wound, the bunch of my muscles before I strike. I could kiss him all night.

I shouldn't be kissing him at all.

Mother hated the idea of me dating Roman, because he's not good enough. He's not strong enough, or ambitious enough, or strategic enough. Which is probably why I was so terrified when he tried to help. He can't survive in my world, at my level. I will kill him, just by being who I am.

Pulling away from him hurts more than a shattered femur. It stings more than hot coals. It steals my breath and my joy and even my pain. It leaves me bereft and numb and broken. But none of that is as hard as seeing the hurt in his eyes. In his beautiful, velvety eyes. In the eyes that always support me, always uplift me, always worship me.

"I can't," I say.

Roman stares into my eyes for a moment, checking whether I mean it. Whatever he sees is enough. He salutes before he leaves, and I crumple in a heap once he's gone. For the second time in my life, I go to sleep on a pillow wet with tears.

THE PRESENT

Roman dismisses his driver and we all climb into Billy's dad's car.

"Here, you can sit back here with me," Ambrosia says.

Roman scowls, but doesn't argue. He climbs into the passenger seat and lets Billy, who knows the area better, drive. But when the car turns on and the music blasts into the cabin, Roman clears his throat politely. When that doesn't work, he looks back at me.

I shrug. A little loud music won't hurt us.

We spend half the day looking for the list of items, including a burner cell phone for me. It would have taken us far longer without Ambrosia and Billy's help, but even so, we spend more time waiting on incompetent people than we do actually purchasing what we need. Navigating the world of the humans is more obnoxious than I'd have expected. Eventually, though, we locate everything, and I'm ready to assemble it all.

"Where should we go to make the flash bombs?" I ask. "I assume these aren't legal."

Billy shakes his head. "I'm not sure, so maybe it's best to pick somewhere out of the way."

"You're thinking grandpa's old place?" Ambrosia asks.

Billy shrugs. "Our grandpa died almost ten years ago, but Dad can't bring himself to sell his house. It's a ways off, but it's on a few acres and no one would be watching what we're doing."

"Perfect," I say.

It's a drive to get there, but it turns out to be the perfect spot. It is a small, ranch style home, surrounded by big trees and shaggy weeds. Once we set up to make everything, Billy's a little too interested in making the flash powder. "So it's forty percent potassium?" he asks.

Roman's jaw muscle twitches. "Potassium perchlorate."

"And thirty percent magnesium?"

"Thirty-four percent," I say. "And twenty-six percent aluminum."

"This part is dangerous," Roman says. "Maybe you better give me some space."

Billy takes a step back.

Roman scowls. "All of you go outside. The last thing we need is for this to blow up because you're distracting me."

"Your concern for their lives is very touching," I say.

"I'm more concerned about how long it would take us to replace all of this." Roman winks at me to soften the growl in his voice.

I walk onto the front porch, and Billy and Ambrosia follow.

"Usually the front porch is dusty and the inside of the house is clean," Ambrosia says. "But it's the opposite here. The outside is cleaner than the inside, thanks to the wind."

I brush off the bench out front and sit down. "It's still pretty dirty."

"At least there are less spiders." Billy shudders. He whips out his phone and starts poking buttons.

"What's he doing?" I ask.

"Nervous he's telling someone where you are?" Ambrosia asks.

"Maybe."

She shakes her head. "He's addicted to this game called Clash of Clans. Basically, you fight people and steal their stuff and then you use what you stole to make your city bigger. Then bigger people attack you and steal your stuff. It's this whole, pointless, boring, never-ending thing, but." She sighs. "He's always playing it. Trust me, he's smart enough not to tell anyone where we are, even his dumb gamer friends."

I hope she's right.

"So. . ." Ambrosia says, drawing out the 'oooo' sound. "You didn't tell me the friend you were calling was your *boy*friend." Her voice drops to a whisper. "Billy's a little bummed out, actually."

"About?"

"That you're taken."

"Ah." It hadn't occurred to me that the human kid might have a crush on me, although it makes sense. I've always heard humans put a disproportionate level of importance on a mate with an aesthetically pleasing face and body. "Well, your brother was mistaken. Roman's not my boyfriend."

"He's not." Ambrosia's words indicate she understands, but her tone implies I'm lying. Or delusional.

"Believe me, I wouldn't become romantically involved with Roman."

"That man is über hot, and all muscly, and smart, and he rushed out here the second you called him."

I shake my head. "I'm telling you. We're evian. Every

single member of my community back home is hot, muscly, and smart. And most any member of my guard would have rushed out to help me for a text, much less a phone call."

"Okay," she says, "but you didn't call anyone else. You called him."

She's right about that. "I trust him to keep his mouth shut."

"You trust him, and he's all those things I said, and he looks at you like a fat kid eyes a caramel apple in the candy shop window."

"Just stop, okay? As my twin's heir to the throne and as a member of the royal family, I need someone who can destroy anything in his path. I need someone who finds solutions when there aren't any. I need my partner to be capable of taking on the entire world."

Ambrosia crosses her arms. "You just described yourself, and in my experience, relationships between clones are fraught with problems."

"What does that mean?"

"Look. My aunt married this guy, okay? She was career-obsessed, and driven, and dominant at just about every-thing. She went to Harvard Business School and she's now CEO of her third start up. The lady is worth tens of millions. Let's call her the human equivalent of you."

"You're comparing Wonder Woman to a successful busi-nesswoman?"

"Don't get hung up on labels, alright? Seriously, Aunt Cassidy's epic. Anyhow, she married this guy who was first in his class at Harvard Law. Everyone gushed about what a phenomenal couple they made. They stayed married for less than two years."

"They split up?"

Ambrosia nods. "She was absolutely miserable. They fought all the time. She's been married to a new guy now, a guy named Bo, for almost ten years. Dad says they were made for each other, and guess what Bo does?"

"You're going to tell me either way."

Ambrosia grins. "Yes, yes I am. He was a food critic. But he quit that job and now he takes care of their two kids. He's laid back, he's excited about most everything, and he softens all her sharp edges. They're still just as happy now as they were when they first met."

"So you think I should marry a dud."

Ambrosia's eye roll practically makes noise, it's so dramatic. "OMG. Bo is not a dud, and Roman is *not* a dud, and you're totally missing the point. Have you ever heard the word vulnerable, Miss Empress of the World?"

That's an ironic question coming from a human. "Yes. I've heard of it. It means you're not safe, you're open to damage or destruction."

Ambrosia laughs. "What a classic Queen of the World answer. You're wrong, though. It means you're exposed, and if you're ever going to have a happy relationship, you'll need to try it. You need someone you *trust,* like you just said you trust Roman, who you can rely on, who can bring things to the table you don't already have. Which means you don't need a crazy, overbearing warrior who can slice people to bits. You can do that already. You need someone else, someone different than you. But you'll need to be brave enough to handle that kind of person." She leans a little closer. "You'll have to be vulnerable, or you'll never truly find a partner."

"Ambrosia is obsessed with Brené Brown," Billy says. "She thinks reading a few of her books has made a psychologist out of her. Just ignore it and she'll shut up."

Except, I wonder whether I should be ignoring her, because what she said just made a lot of sense.

When Roman walks out of the front door, I try to look

at him with fresh eyes. He's hot, yes. He's smart, also true. He's skilled at what he does. He's not Edam, but maybe there's a reason things between Edam and me were always so miserable. Maybe Ambrosia isn't wrong.

Roman realizes I'm staring and his eyebrows knit together in puzzlement. "Everything okay?"

He's looking at me like he did at that party on New Year's, and I remember that I have no idea who Brené Brown is, and I should not take the word of a few humans over my own mother. "Oh yeah, everything's fine. Are we ready to go?"

"It's all ready to load up, yes." Roman glances back at the front door.

"Coming," I say.

Ambrosia tries to make small talk in the car, but I don't have anything to say. Now that the attack is happening, I'm uneasy, maybe even nervous. I close my eyes and run through complicated math problems, and then I move on to chess moves to occupy my mind. I can do this. I can fix my mistake in not killing Melina the first time around. I can avenge Mother, pay her back for kidnapping me, and then I'll be able to go back home with my head held high.

It'll be hard, but I need to fix my mistake. Angel and Melina will pay.

We drop Ambrosia and Billy off at the home of one of her friends, Paige. Melina's people will be watching their house for sure.

Roman only drives a few blocks before he pulls the car over to the side of the road. "What's going on?"

"Huh?"

"You're quiet, and you seem borderline depressed. It's not like you."

"I made a mistake," I say. "And I'm fixing it. That's all."

Roman looks up at the ceiling of the car, and then back at me. "You're kidding, right?"

"About what?"

"You made a mistake. . . how exactly?"

I set my jaw.

"You think getting kidnapped by your mother's chef was a mistake? Or do you mean that you never should have set Angel free?"

I sigh. "All of it, okay? But please do continue with this highlight reel of the many things I've done wrong. It's super helpful."

Roman leans across the center console so his face is inches from mine. "You are magnificent, Judica, and much kinder than you let anyone realize. But I've seen it. You didn't make any mistakes. You interrogated Angel, and we searched her belongings, and we found zero evidence of her involvement with your mother's murder. Letting her go was the right call at the time."

"A good ruler sees more than one move ahead, Roman."

He slams his hand down on the console. "You are the best leader I've ever seen."

"So good my mother fired me, and Chancery defeated me, and I was kidnapped. In that order."

Roman snorts. "You care about your people, and you evaluate every option, and you show mercy when it's truly merited, and otherwise you uphold justice. And most of all, you are willing to be the bad guy when necessary. That's an underrated value, you know. Right is always more important to you than popular. Don't let your mother's bizarre reversal get into your head."

"Chancery is the—"

Roman swears loudly. "Don't throw that up as a barrier. She's the Empress now, fine. Only because you *let* her be the Empress. Which was you showing mercy, prudence, and foresight. But if you hadn't done those things, Melina would have kidnapped her instead of you. Do you think Chancery would have survived and escaped? Do you think she'd have been able to do what you did?"

Probably not.

"You don't need to answer, because you know I'm right. All we can do in this world is try our very best. Sometimes it's enough, and sometimes it's not. But if we drag around the weight of everything that ever went wrong, we'd be anchored in place at the bottom of the sea."

"Can you just drive, please?"

"Fine." Roman slams the car into gear and tears down the road.

We reach the spot we agreed upon, a mile and a half away from Melina's compound. We're unloading the stuff when we see him.

A sentry.

Melina has a sentry more than a mile and a half away from her base.

Roman pulls his rifle out and shoots the sentry. Three times. We sprint over to where he is, incapacitated by the three gunshots, but not dead.

"Secure him," I say. "As well as you possibly can, and then deal some slow-healing damage."

I close my eyes and think. Melina knows more about me than I hoped she did. She's expecting an attack. Which explains why her search was so lackluster. She knew I'd come running back to her, and now I've done exactly what she expected. I'm like a windup toy. Everyone knows how I'll react.

Roman shoulders his bag and says, "What now?"

"We proceed. So what if she's ready for us?"

"I'm not balking," Roman says. "I'll do whatever you

demand, but consider our odds. Your sister has home advantage—"

"Do not call her my sister."

Roman sighs. "Fine. Melina has the geographic advantage, and on top of that, she's got who knows how many guards and we have. . .two people."

"I can take out every single one of her guards with my eyes closed."

"Maybe so, but all it takes is a few good shots and you'll be on the ground. You can't do anything from the ground."

I'm asking Roman to set the flash grenades and then run like hell from the melee that causes. The risk to him hadn't really clicked for me before now. "Are you scared?"

"Scared isn't the right word," he says. "I'll do anything you ask, but it doesn't seem very prudent." He opens his mouth as if he's going to say something else, and then shuts it.

"Say what you want to say."

"Why don't you contact Chancery? You can use Alamecha resources to do this the right way. If she killed your mother, Chancery would be the first one in line with a pitchfork."

I don't need her help. I can do it myself. Even Ambrosia could see I was a warrior. I shake my head. "No, we do this now. Today. Who knows what Melina will do if we give her time? She could run, never to be found, or assassinate someone else, including Chancery."

Roman's voice is low, urgent. "Or you."

"I'd like to see her try again." That's a lie. I don't want someone out there, secretly planning to kill me. General awareness is one thing, but I don't relish the idea of a target on my back.

"Fine," Roman says. "But use your radio."

I click my radio on and slide the earbud in place. "Ready."

Roman straightens his shoulders and turns to head for the front of the compound. He takes two steps and then pivots back.

"What's wrong?" I ask.

His eyes remind me of storm-tossed waves when they meet mine. He steps closer, and his face is inches away from mine. "We may not pull this off."

I put a finger to his lips. "We will."

He reaches up, takes my hand in his, and presses a kiss to my palm. My heart shudders. For the first time since I woke up in that van, my resolve wavers.

"I hope you're right, but just in case you're not." Roman sets his bag down, and grabs my hips with both hands. He pulls me against him and lowers his lips to mine slowly. But this time, it doesn't feel like he's giving me time to stop him. He's daring me to do it.

And I can't.

Now that he's mentioned that I might never see him again, I can't bear the thought. His broad, calm strength. His quiet support. His unfailing confidence. Roman has seen me since I was small. Not the relentless, perfect statue, not the insane berserker, but me. The scared, confused, desperate little girl pretending not to care.

And he wants me in a way none of the power-hungry, accomplished, genetically superior men do. He wants me no matter what my role is within Alamecha. Mother was wrong about him, and now that I know it, the idea of letting him go slays me. His lips against mine are urgent, and when his hands move into my hair, I whimper.

He releases me abruptly and steps backward.

I growl.

He grins and wiggles his eyebrows. "Now let's do this thing."

I nod my head dumbly. What thing? Oh. Right. He's referring to killing Melina. Yes. We should do it, and just as soon as my knees start working again, I will.

When Roman jogs off, he's still smiling from ear to ear. There's a matching smile on my face as I move silently through the thorny underbrush, sticker bushes, and tumbleweed. Why would anyone choose to live here? I notice two other sentries, and I evade them easily. But when I reach the wall, I stop cold.

Instead of the simple wall that I left yesterday, I'm looking at a razor-wire topped, electrified perimeter. Every forty feet, a guard with a fifty-caliber gun stands on top of what looks like a hunting blind.

I'm screwed.

"Caesar, it's me, over."

"I hear you, Peacekeeper, over."

"They've got fifty-cals and triple the guards. Plus electric and razor upgrades, over."

"Orders? Over."

What are my orders? I might be able to squeak through and kill Melina, but I doubt I can make it out alive afterward. And I'm pretty sure Roman will figure that out. He won't be willing to simply lead people away. He'll come back for me, and he'll die doing it. The idea arrests my heart. I shouldn't care what happens to me after I die, but I do. There are things worse than leaving this world. I didn't realize that until this very moment, but there are. I know, and the reason I understand that fact scares me.

Because I love Roman.

I'm not the perfect person Mother raised me to be, and I wasn't good enough to rule Alamecha. I'm not strong enough to do this alone, either. I can't fix my mistakes, not if I want to survive, and when I think about Roman, I do. I want to survive.

That thought scares me more than the prospect of fighting my way through Melina's guards. At least attacking is something I know how to do. Loving someone is not something I ever planned. It's not something I'm even remotely prepared for. I can't be someone I'm not, and I can't let Mother down, not again, and if I go down swinging, well, I'll take Melina with me. That can be my legacy. I cleared the path for the Eldest, or whatever nonsense Melina was spouting.

Balthasar trained me too well for my feelings to override my head.

"Light them, over," I say.

"Will do, over." Roman says.

I close my eyes. I will likely die today, avenging Mother. Then Roman will return, and he might die too, avenging me.

When will it end?

"Wait," I practically shout. "Don't."

"Don't? Hello?"

"Don't light it, Roman. I love you."

No response. Did he hear me? "Roman! I know I said to do it. I don't want her after me forever. I don't want to live with a target on my back, but Roman, don't light the flares. I don't want to risk it, I don't want to risk us."

Still static.

I start back for the car at a dead sprint. I shoot two sentries and keep running. Did someone catch him? Is he alive? What have I done? Why didn't I realize this sooner? Why am I so stupid?

I slam into something, a very hard thing, and fall on my butt. I heave in a breath to replace the air that was just knocked out of me, and leap to my feet, unsheathing my sword.

"Relax," a familiar voice says. "It's only me."

I turn slowly toward Roman.

"You scared me!" I say. "Why didn't you respond? I thought you'd died."

The corner of his mouth turns up. "You were worried about me."

A tear forms at the corner of my eye and rolls down my cheek.

He rushes to my side and wipes it gently away. "I'm sorry. I wanted to hear you say it in person. It was selfish, and I'm sorry. It didn't occur to me that you'd panic. I should have known."

My swing goes wide, but I still land a solid punch on his shoulder.

"Ouch," he says.

"That's for freaking me out, you jerk."

"Should I punch you, too?" he asks.

"For what?"

"For being so goofy you don't realize how you feel until we're standing in front of your maniacal family member's house?"

I roll my eyes.

"Or maybe because you're insisting we have this whole discussion while the woman who wants you dead is only a mile away."

"We could be so lucky for her to come strolling out here. I'd take her down so fast—"

Roman kisses me then and every thought in my head dissolves like cotton candy in rain. My heart races. My chest aches. A shiver shoots up my spine.

"That should hold us over," he says. "Until we can do this more properly."

Properly. A word I never thought anyone would use to describe me.

I close my eyes and lean my head against his. He's here, and I'm here, and we're both alive. His hand reaches under my chin and tilts my face upward. "But I can't let another second pass without telling you something. Judica Alamecha, I adore your spirit. I love the spark in your eye when you're cranky. I forget to breathe when I watch you fight. It's truly a glorious thing. But none of that compares to your bravery in the face of danger, and your righteous fury when someone you love is harmed. You're the best part of every single day, and when you disappeared a few days ago..." He chokes, and his eyes well with tears. "I know I don't deserve you. I'm not enough for you, but I swear I will try every single day to improve. I'll spend every ounce of my strength training, studying, working to be what you need, because I love you. Not a little bit, not most of the time. I love you limitlessly. I love you from the depths of my soul. I love you in the dark and in the light. I love you at your worst, and at your best. I love you from now until forever, with every fiber of my being."

I can't formulate words, not in this moment. "Kiss me again."

And he does. Oh, he does.

❧ 16 ❧

THE PAST

"May I have a word?" Inara asks.

I motion for her to precede me into my room, and I close the door behind us.

"I've gotten another call from Chancery," she says. "I thought you might like to know."

"What now?"

"She heard a rumor about the plans for China."

I clench my fists. "How could she have heard about that?"

"Apparently Mother left her network to her in some kind of letter."

I close my eyes. Every time I turn around, Chancery gets another leg up.

"I'm afraid that's not all the news."

I run my hand through my hair. "What else?"

Inara looks at her feet. "I believe she has chosen a Consort."

I swear, repeatedly. "Edam."

"Even so."

I kick a pillow that fell to the floor and it flies across the room. "I can't defeat him," I say. "I can't."

"You need to focus, and detach yourself from who you're fighting."

I spin to face her. "You think I don't know that?"

"I'm sorry," she says. "I'm not trying to upset you."

I breathe in my nose and out through my mouth. "I know you're trying to help. I do. But there are things you don't know. Edam's not normal, not even for an evian."

"What do you mean?" she asks.

"Balthasar ran some tests on him. He heals about fifty percent again faster than I do, for instance. He also moves faster than should be possible. He's a freak, a fighting freak. No matter how much I train, I'll never be able to defeat him."

Inara's brow furrows. "Why is he like that?"

I throw my hands up in the air. "I have no idea, okay? No one knows. The point is that I'll lose."

"She may not choose him after all. I gathered from her call that she's agonized over this decision for days."

"Perfect," I say. "Well, maybe she'll make the moronic choice so she can *die*. I'm afraid even my twin isn't quite that stupid."

"But if she does name him." Inara pulls a small jar from her pocket. "This might help."

I gulp. "Tell me that's not poison."

She shakes her head. "Of course not. Good heavens. It's an anti-coagulant. If you coat your blade with it, it'll slow his healing dramatically."

Leveling the playing field. "You're brilliant."

"It's illegal, of course. So, don't tell a soul, not even your guards. Do you understand?"

I pretend to zip my lips closed. "I do."

"The other news is that she should be here in a few

hours. Once she discovered your plans, she stepped up her timetable."

"I'm not done with my analysis," I say. "On where I should launch them. I want to do minimal damage, but scare the government badly. I want to foster an environment where they are desperate for allies, not destroy them. I want to leave them no choice but to turn to me."

Inara inclines her head. "I'm not here to tell you what to do. I'm just letting you know that your twin plans to stop you by any method possible. If she has the ring, which we should assume she does, then she'll have a bargaining chip. Having something she wants is a good way to demand the ring in exchange."

I purse my lips. "But this attack will work. After our disastrous start, we really need to begin from a position of strength. Don't you agree?"

"You know that I do."

"But you think I should delay the launch to bargain with her?"

Inara taps her lip. "Or."

"Or what?"

"You could launch it now, before she arrives, and then when she asks you to agree *not* to do it, you can agree, since it's already been done. You can always agree not to do something *again*."

"And even if Edam kills me, I've done Alamecha a favor. Something my weak sister can't undo."

Inara nods. "Precisely."

"Thank you," I say. "Now if you can select the location for the bombs, that would really, really help."

"I think I should have time for that," she says. "But there's something else."

"Yes?"

"Alora."

"What about her?" I ask.

"She's a power, among the family and outside of it. She's level-headed, wise, and quite the warrior. You'll want her on your side after you defeat Chancery."

"She's not going to support me. She adores Chancery."

"But at that point," Inara says, "it will be water under the bridge. One of the reasons Alora is such a powerhouse is that she's pragmatic. She'll understand you were forced into this position."

"If she even agrees to talk to me."

Inara smiles. "That's where I come in. If you make it look like I supported Chancery too, which Alora and Chancery already believe, then after Chancery has passed away, I can credibly go to Alora and tell her why I support you. I can smooth things over."

Yes. "That would be amazing. I want Alamecha united and strong, not fractured and divided."

"But."

"But what?"

"We need to sell it."

Oh no. "What does that mean, exactly?"

"You're going to need to torture me. Convincingly. Cut off some fingers. Something that takes time to heal so Chancery can see that I've been abused."

I shake my head. "No way. I can't do that to you. You're my sister, and your advice has been tremendously helpful." And if she hadn't stayed, I'd have been utterly alone. And she's so much like Mother that it would feel like I was harming Mother.

I can't do it.

Inara pulls out a dagger and holds it in her right hand. She places her left on my end table and saws off her own index finger.

She doesn't even whine.

I close my eyes and look anywhere but at the blood. How? How could she do that to herself?

"That was not even close to being fun." Her heartbeat has escalated, unsurprisingly.

Death circles my feet, picking up on my agitation, and then sniffs the air, smelling Inara's blood. When he starts to walk toward her, I imagine him chewing on her finger.

"Stop, please. Surely that's enough."

"It's not," she says. "Not even close, but I'd really appreciate it if you'd take over from here."

I really don't want to, but it doesn't seem like I have much of a choice.

17

THE PRESENT

"I really want to thank you for all that you've done for me," I tell Ambrosia and Billy. "Truly, I would have had things much harder if I hadn't found you."

Ambrosia is crying, and she rushes over and wraps her arms around my neck. I glance at Roman desperately. He's laughing soundlessly, the jerk. I finally manage to twist out of her embrace and step backward, toward Roman.

He slings an arm around my shoulder.

"I told you he'd be the best boyfriend," Ambrosia says.

"Yes, you did."

Roman beams at her now. "Thanks. I think Judica needed a little push."

"Rosy's great at pushing people," Billy says. "Too bad there's not a major in college for being bossy."

"Oh there are classes, alright," Ambrosia says. "They call them leadership training."

"I almost forgot," I say. "I've got something for the two of you."

Roman places two envelopes in my hand, heavy envelopes. "I know you didn't help me for compensation, but I know humans place a lot of value on this." I pass the envelopes to Billy and Ambrosia.

Ambrosia shakes her head. "I don't want anything."

I hold my hands out, palms facing her. "I must insist. It's the end of what Roman brought in case we needed it."

Billy's busy counting, his mouth already curving into a half-smile. His head whips up. "These bills are all hundreds."

"It's only a hundred and eleven-thousand dollars," Roman says. "Split two ways."

Ambrosia splutters. "Now I really, really can't take it."

"I wasn't kidding," I say. "We run the whole world. Think of this as a tax rebate for your service to the country."

She giggles. I'm going to miss that giggle.

"It's time to go," Roman says. "We need to leave before Melina figures out we aren't coming after her and starts searching airports."

Ambrosia pulls me in for one more hug, and then Billy does too. And then I'm following Roman to the jet.

"Does my sister know we're coming home?"

Roman's face scrunches. "About that."

Oh no.

"I might have stolen this jet."

I close my eyes. "Might have?"

"I tied a few people up and took it."

"Roman."

His voice rises. "You were in trouble. I didn't know what else to do."

"Well, let's hope my twin's bottomless mercy works in our favor this time."

"She was really upset that you were gone."

"As in angry, upset? Or worried?"

Roman touches my nose. "Your face is the one I can

read. I don't know what she was feeling other than agitated, but she loves you. Otherwise, she'd have chopped off your head or locked you up after that fight. To me, that's promising."

I follow Roman up the stairs to the jet, and I'm shocked when I see two humans sitting in the cockpit.

"Umm," I whisper, "I thought you said you flew the jet."

"I did," he says, "but I don't want to fly it home. I hired these guys before I gave you our leftover cash."

Smart. That was smart. Maybe Mother was wrong about him.

The second we take our seats, exhaustion rolls over me like a wave. I haven't slept since Melina held me captive. Roman wraps an arm around me and I lay my head on his shoulder gratefully.

"Let me know if this gets uncomfortable for you," I say.

"Oh, you won't bother me," Roman says. "I promise. Get some sleep."

I do.

Roman's shaking wakes me up. "We're landing."

I bolt upright in my chair and rub my eyes. "I slept for eight hours?"

He looks at me like I looked at Death as a puppy when he chewed on his own tail. "Don't worry. You only drooled a little bit."

My hand flies to my chin.

"Gotcha."

"You jerk," I say. "I knew I didn't drool."

"And yet you checked," he says.

"That's very bad boyfriend behavior," I say, my heart lifting at the word. "I hope this is not how you plan to proceed."

Roman leans over and kisses me right on the mouth.

"How's that for boyfriend behavior?" he asks when he finally pulls back.

The landing gear deploys and the plane touches down. The view out of the window is one of the most staggeringly beautiful I've ever seen. Ni'ihau may not be the lushest of the Hawaiian islands, but it's home. I didn't realize how much I missed it until I returned.

My heart races when I unbuckle my seatbelt. Will Chancery be angry to see me? Happy? Disappointed? My hands are shaking when I stand up.

Roman takes my hand in his. "It's going to be fine."

We walk out of the plane together, the sunlight momentarily blinding me. As soon as my eyes adjust, I see her. Chancery, flanked by Edam and her pet human, standing at the bottom of the runway. It's so like when I met her plane a few days ago, and yet so different. Guards still line the runway, but none of them are holding guns or swords on me.

And she's smiling.

I take the steps one at a time, but before my feet even hit the ground, Chancery rushes toward me. She doesn't hesitate, or chastise, or express disappointment or frustration.

"I'm so glad you're alive." Tears streak her cheeks liberally.

I hadn't considered my absence might cause her pain. I'm actually surprised she would care enough to be upset. It's not like I've been a model sibling.

"I'm here." I release Roman's hand and wrap my arms around her, too. It feels unfamiliar, and awkward, and strange.

Probably because in nearly eighteen years of life, I've never once hugged her.

"I'm sorry you were worried," I whisper. "I didn't mean

to scare you. I should have called you, or had Roman tell you where I was."

She lets me go and straightens, schooling her features into something very near to Mother's regal face. "What exactly did happen?"

"Oh," I say. "I didn't realize that you didn't know."

Chancery stares at me and I feel practically compelled to share.

"Angel knocked me out and took me to Melina."

She gulps. "Melina?"

"This is likely to be a lengthy discussion."

"And you need to get food and clean off." She gestures for me to walk ahead of her. "Don't let me stop you. But as soon as you're ready, I'd love to hear the whole story. And of course, I'd love to include you in the discussions we've been having."

Whoa, that doesn't sound good. "What discussions?"

"Before we can talk about all this, you need to go get cleaned up, and we need Job to evaluate you."

Death's bark sounds from across the empty field. I crouch down and watch as he sprints toward me, and barrels into me, licking my nose, my cheeks, my neck, even my mouth. I finally straighten up, and he sits on my feet as though he's worried I'll disappear on him again.

Roman's fingers interlace with mine and my heart swells. I'll always miss Mother. That won't change, but my heart is more full in this moment than I ever imagined possible. Melina better watch out, because nothing in the world can stop us now that Chancery and I are on the same team.

The End

If you enjoyed unForgiven, I've included the first chapter of the third book, Disillusioned, as a small bonus.

If you'd like a FREE full length novel from me—sign up for my newsletter at www.BridgetEBakerwrites.com! I'll send you a copy of Already Gone FREE!

Also, in case you want something to do while you wait for Disillusioned, check out my other YA series, Marked. It's a complete three book set, available now! You can grab it here.

Finally, if you enjoyed reading *unForgiven*, please, please, please leave me a review on Amazon!!!! It makes a tremendous difference when you do. Thanks in advance!

18

DISILLUSIONED SAMPLE

One week from today, I turn eighteen.

Six months ago, Mom mocked me mercilessly when I insisted I wanted stargazer lilies for the party. But she couldn't change my mind, no matter how many exotic options she suggested. Her disappointment in my pedestrian flower choice was nothing to face she made when I told her I wanted bouncy houses. I thought it would be hilariously ironic to have stuff reserved for little kids at my party when I'm turning eighteen.

She and I spent hours planning this party, and it should be epic. Elegant, posh, delightful for the first two hours, and then the bouncy houses, the snow cone stands, the cotton candy comes out and the ball gowns go in the corner. With all the bad things lately, I should be excited about a party.

I'm not.

Because one week ago, on her nine-hundredth birthday, my mom was murdered. So when my chamberlain, Larena, walks into the conference room with cake samples and dozens of new flower choices in vases, I practice the soothing breath techniques Mom taught me.

I do not want a party for my eighteenth birthday. I *really* don't want the party Mom and I planned. In fact, the idea of celebrating anything right now horrifies me. We haven't even had Mom's funeral. I close my eyes and shake my head.

"Before you throw me out," Larena says, "hear me all the way through. Your mother and I finalized all the details weeks ago. All that remains is the final flower selections and the cake flavor." She clears her throat. "It's not all about you. The people need something to look forward to."

I should be laughing, and telling my mom that I want *stargazers,* still. We should be arguing over whether the cake is orange flavored with chocolate frosting like I love, or vanilla and chocolate like most people prefer. I shouldn't be thinking about my party while I'm planning her funeral. "Cancel all of it."

Larena's lips compress and she sighs slowly. "I think that's a mistake."

"Why not?" I ask. "It's my birthday and if I have nothing to celebrate, why should I?"

Larena purses her lips. "If you're not worried about general morale, consider this. Your mother would be disappointed if you didn't celebrate your existence. Her whole life changed when you came into it."

Yes, it did. Because of me she had to fight a handful of skirmishes and execute her best friend. I've been a failure since day one, and now I'm about to be crowned empress as some kind of cosmic joke. "Fine," I say. "Throw a party and I'll go, but I don't care what you pick for decorations, and I'm not going to dicker over the cake. Chocolate. Because this isn't about me, clearly."

Maybe I should make the entire party black. Judica's

either dead, or she's about to attack me, and I probably won't know which until I'm blown to bits by a nuclear bomb. A wave of exhaustion rolls over me. I'm not sleepy, but I'm so tired of everything.

Noah strolls into the room as if on cue, his eyes taking in the haggard expression on my face. "You don't look so great."

"You should not speak to the queen like that," Larena snaps.

"Oh, sorry. You don't look so hot, *princess*." Noah winks at me. "Not sleeping well?"

I roll my eyes. "Not sleeping enough, probably, but I'm fine, really."

Noah takes a seat near the end of the table. "Are those snacks for this meeting?"

Oblivious Noah doesn't even recognize a cake tasting. "Sure," I say. "That's what they are. Why don't you try that dark one."

"Chocolate? That's a little boring for me," he says.

I shake my head. "See the tiny chili pepper on top? That's chocolate spice." I lift my eyebrows. "Your mouth will burn for an hour."

"Sly, princess, but then you gave up the secret. How will you punk me now?"

"Punk him?" Larena asks.

"You know what?" I ask. "I've got a solution for you both. Noah, I'm putting you in charge of all details for my birthday party next week. You'll work with Larena to hammer out anything else she needs."

"Princess knows I throw a dope shindig."

Larena's nostrils flare. "Perhaps we can begin by not using the words 'dope' or 'shindig' under any circumstances."

"Oh." Noah folds his hands neatly in front of him. "It's one of those kinds of parties."

I shake my head. "If I must have a party, I don't want a fancy one." I think about the ice sculptures, edible helium balloons and chocolate fountains at Mom's party not too long ago. I can't walk into something like that, I just can't.

"Dope it is," Noah says. "Tell me this, boss lady. Do you have any connections for electric bulls?"

I snort. "Not quite that wild. More like if one of your mom's garden parties had a baby with the one you threw after that track meet."

"I can do that." He turns to Larena. "Let's talk right after this meeting."

Larena looks like she's sucking on a lemon, but she says, "Yes, of course."

One less thing to worry about.

The doors open again, and this time several people walk inside. Edam pointedly ignores Noah and circles the table to sit right next to me. Balthasar takes the seat on my other side. Frederick stands by the door like he's here as a door guard. Inara trails in after the boys and sits directly across from me. Marselle waltzes through the door and takes a seat on the end of the table near Noah. Franco takes the seat on Inara's right, adjusting his already immaculate, bright red tie, and brushing the lapels of his suit before sitting down. Maxmillian is wearing a suit that looks exactly like Franco's, but his tie is sky blue and has a matching pocket square.

Now that everyone's here, I stand up. That might be unnecessary, but Mom used to stand.

"If you're here," I say, "it's because I trust you. For some of you, this is a promotion. For some of you, it may feel like a demotion." I glance at Balthasar, and he closes his eyes and shakes his head slightly. Good, he's not angry. "But I need each and every one of you. At my coronation tomorrow I'll announce your names officially, but the real work is already starting. No one is operating under any delusions here that I'm perfectly prepared. I'm not. Mom left things in disarray when she passed, so we have a lot of clean up to do. But Alamecha is the first family for a reason, and we will rise even stronger for this period of chaos."

"This is your final Council?" Maxmillian glances around doubtfully, his eyes lingering on Noah.

"I'm sure I'll be adjusting things with time," I say, "but for now, yes."

"A human and a half-human?" Maxmillian asks. "What kind of message will that send?"

I expected someone to complain, but I didn't expect it to be Lark's uncle. "Angel is gone. We don't know the circumstances yet, but it doesn't look promising. I'm delighted that Lark is willing to step in as my new Food Services Director, even without a lot of experience. As I'm sure you'll understand, I need someone I trust absolutely." His niece may not be fully evian, but I trust her more than anyone else.

"What about your pet human?" Franco pins Noah with a glare.

"He's my new Human Relations Liaison."

"That's not even a position," Franco protests.

"Change is always hard." I pause to let that sink in. "And while I have nothing but respect for Mom's reign, I am not Enora the second. I am Chancery Divinity Alamecha, and I disagree fundamentally with many of Mom's policies and laws."

"Your mother didn't create those laws alone," Franco says. "All evian rulers worldwide agreed on many them."

"They had their reasons when they established most of

them." I meet Franco's eyes. I will not flinch, and I will not back down. "And I have mine now. You all know Alamecha's motto. *Accept the world as it is, or do something to change it.*" I spread my hands wide. "It's my turn to do something, and I won't shy away from what needs to be done, no matter how unpopular."

"What exactly are you planning to change?" Balthasar asks.

"I'll be changing a lot, but I will stagger some of it."

"Over decades?" Franco asks.

I shake my head. Sometimes I forget how old they all are. Decades. It's hard, but I don't roll my eyes. "No, over several weeks."

Inara, Larena, Balthasar, Franco, and Maxmillian look grim. Noah and Edam and Marselle, bless them, remain entirely calm. Frederick is behaving like he's not part of my Council.

"Freddy, come sit at the table. I value your opinion. You're not here to guard my door."

His eyes dart from Balthasar to Edam and then back to me. "I'm not clear on what my role is."

"You were my mom's head guard. You're mine. I'm simply adding that position to my Council, because I value your opinion beyond protection of my physical body."

"What's my position?" Edam asks.

"I apologize," I say. "I forgot that I hadn't already announced your formal positions. Larena, can you take these down?"

She pulls a pen from her pocket and nods.

"Balthasar will be my Warlord, Edam will be my Chief Security Officer, and Larena will remain Chamberlain. Inara will be my Steward, and also my interim Political Advisor." I was hoping to name Alora to that, if she agreed to move back to Ni'ihau. Now I'm not sure who to ask. "Lark will be my Chef, and Maxmillian my Operations Manager. Franco will be Head of Governance, and Marselle will be my Chief Intelligence Officer, but her official title will be Chief Technology Officer. And I already mentioned that Noah will be my Human Liaison."

"A bold and diverse cast for your Council," Inara says, "and an interesting mix of Mother's advisors and your own. Now that you've explained, would you care to enlighten us on your other plans?"

"This is a working list, but to start, I'll be providing humans with the same complement of rights as evians."

Franco leaps from his seat. "The vast majority of humans don't even know about us. Are you proposing we change that?"

"I haven't decided yet, but we will set up a rigorous list of protections for humans. They aren't disposable, and it's wrong to treat them that way. Our purpose has always been to preserve the world and its resources, but we lost sight of the obligation we have to all our subjects, especially humans."

Complete silence.

"Most of you haven't spent much time around them," I say, "which is a shame."

"I've spent more than enough," Franco says. "They're untrustworthy, greedy, self-aggrandizing without support, violent, and duplicitous."

"I'm sorry, are you describing evians? Or humans?" I raise my eyebrows. "We are human, you know. And they are evian. We descended from the exact same place."

Inara's eyes widen. "Are you saying we're *equal*?"

"That is exactly what I'm saying."

"You're wrong," Balthasar says. "Respectfully, this is an untenable position to advocate. You're only seventeen, and while you're bright and show a lot of promise, you have less experience with humans than any of the rest of us. Watching their entertainment has not given you a realistic view of how they will behave or who they are at their core."

I slam my hands down on the table. "I welcome intercourse, but I will not be patronized. I will not have you tell me my core beliefs are wrong. Argue implementation, argue timing. Do not tell me that humans are dogs. Do not compare them to cannon fodder or pawns on a chess board. Our great grandparents are all the same. It's not their fault if they've suffered some genetic deletions, and it doesn't mean they have no value!"

I realize I'm shouting and moderate my voice. "I do welcome your input. But I will not budge on this point. Noah is here so that you can interact with a human and see that they are just like us."

Balthasar, Inara, Franco and Maxmillian look at Noah as though I've deposited a bag of refuse at the table.

"Lest you think the human rubric is the only major change, let me tell you that evian society is corrupted in other ways, and I intend to course correct on all fronts. To that end, there will be no more sales of royal sons, period, full stop."

Edam maintains a completely blank expression, but his eyes sparkle with joy.

Inara clears her throat. "We can certainly enforce that for our family. Mother wasn't obligated to sell her children, or to buy others. She chose to participate, but her reasons remain. When you give birth to a female heir, how exactly will she choose a Consort?"

"My heir, should I be lucky enough to have one, will marry whomever she chooses, just as I intend to, without regard for what family trained them."

"What if she falls for a human?" Inara asks.

"Oh." I scan the table slowly, meeting each Council

member's eyes. "Like my sister Alora?" I try to moderate my voice, but it doesn't work. "I understand and respect the purpose of the requirement that an empress be the youngest daughter, to provide as much consistency in leadership as possible. I understand the value in preserving the bloodline. My Heir will be required to marry someone suitable, someone close to seventh or eight generation. But should she choose to abdicate and marry a human, I'll throw her the most beautiful wedding you've ever seen. Because becoming the ruler of a vast expanse of subjects should be *chosen*, not forced."

"And half-humans?" Lark asks.

"They will be welcome in my service, and welcome in this family. Always."

"What about one quarter evian?" Maxmillian asks. "What about one-eighth?" He grunts. "You'll degrade the line with this nonsense. Alamecha will be corrupted within a century."

"Exactly what he said," Franco says. "These changes will spell the doom of Alamecha as we know it."

I can't quite help my grin. "Funny you should mention that, but here's where you went wrong. You're saying that as though it's a bad thing." I gesture around the entire room. "Alamecha is rotting with selfishness, greed, and manipulation. So if I doom the Alamecha we know, that's fine with me. The world we create will be so much more, and we will figure things out as we go."

"You won't announce anything today, right?" Inara asks.

"I won't, not until after the inauguration."

Cue the chorus of relieved sighs, since everyone here plans to try and talk me out of these changes before I make them official.

I hold up my hand. "I welcome your feedback in the confines of this room. In fact, I demand that you share with me what's on your mind. Absolute honesty is what I want from my Council. But when we're in public, you will not question me. Speaking against any of these changes will be grounds for immediate removal. And if you don't stop, I'll consider it treason. Is that clear?"

Mouths click shut and heads bob all around me.

"Will you be naming a Consort?" Larena asks. "Because I'll need to prepare the Consort's chambers."

I shake my head. "No Consort, not yet."

"With Judica gone," Inara says, "your heir is Melina."

Shoot. I hadn't considered that.

"She's not . . . strictly reliable." Inara shifts in her chair. "It would be wise to name a Consort soon."

"Duly noted," I say.

"What do we plan to do about Judica?" Franco asks.

I let her go after failing to kill her, and then she disappeared. I have no idea whether she fled, or was taken, whether she's alive, or dead. I don't know whether to send out search parties, or prepare for attack.

"I ask for honesty, and I'll give it in return," I say. "I probably made a mistake in sparing her life, and I certainly made a mistake in not detaining her in a holding cell. But what's done is done. I'll be spending quite a lot of time with Edam to discuss our next steps, and Balthasar to discuss our military assets in anticipation of a retaliation by my sister."

"You admit that you've opened us up to war with that rash, ill-conceived decision?" Franco asks. "And yet, you have no intention of altering course from other, far worse, decisions?"

Edam scowls, clearly ready to jump in and protect me. But I don't need his protection from my own Council.

"We've been at risk for war from the moment my mom was murdered. Didn't you see the other families licking their chops, salivating over Alamecha like a wolf circling an injured gazelle?"

Franco drops his gaze.

"I'm only seventeen, and I'm not perfect. None of us are. I'm going to do my very best, and you'll tell me when you think I'm making the wrong call. Then I'll decide, and we will all live with it."

"Since you aren't naming a Consort," Marselle says softly, "you should prepare yourself for the other families to be unbelievably annoying, thrusting their eligible sons at you until you name one."

"Yes, the ambassadors at court are about to get much younger and better looking," Inara says. "Thanks for that, at least."

I lift one eyebrow. "Hardly. They've sold all their sons."

Inara tuts. "Not quite. The empresses sell their sons, mostly, but many of their siblings haven't. So there will be quite a few sons of other royal members of the family who would be excellent matches. If you haven't made your choice yet, be prepared for the parade of man-meat."

I hope she's exaggerating.

"I think we've covered enough ground for today. You should all begin sussing out what needs to be done in your particular sections, and tomorrow morning, we'll meet again to prepare for the inauguration. Seven a.m. sharp."

When I stand up, Duchess hops to her feet too. Edam follows us out the door, the two guards at the door following us at a distance of ten feet. "You handled that exceptionally well."

"You think so?"

"Absolutely," he says. "You didn't get rattled, and you've begun establishing a level of trust. Excellent initial foray."

"That's good to hear, because I have no idea what I'm doing, and now I'm panicked that my changes will crumple

Alamecha like a house of cards." I reach the door to Mom's room and freeze in front of it.

"You're brilliant, and brave, and merciful," he says, "and you'll figure out how to make these things work without breaking what your mother created. I know you will."

I swallow. "I hope your faith is not misplaced."

"It's not." Edam reaches for my hand and then drops his back at his side. "Are you going inside?"

"Mhmm."

"Okay." Edam leans against the door. "Well, if we're hanging outside for a bit, may as well take care of some housekeeping."

I meet his eye. "About what?"

"If Frederick is head of your guard, but I'm in charge of security for the island, am I able to add guards to your detail?"

I roll my eyes. "Freddy will do fine."

Edam's eyes burn into mine. "Fine isn't good enough."

"You two are cut from the same fabric." I glance at the guards behind us and lower my voice. "He wants to beef up the guard and double the number on duty at all times. He's been analyzing the lists of guards to make sure the two on duty dislike one another heartily. He thinks it will increase their motivation and vigilance."

Edam bobs his head. "I agree. I'm happy to coordinate with him and pass off some of the better men on my force to help with that."

"Oh come on. I don't need two of you."

"Clearly you feel safe, standing in the hallway, too nervous to go inside your mother's room."

I close my eyes and see her body on the floor, blood streaming from her nose and mouth to form a puddle around her. And then a barrage of memories flood my brain from the other side of this door. Choosing clothing, eating snacks on her bed while we watch human television programs. Training together in our private courtyard.

"I'm sorry I said anything," Edam says.

"It's not about feeling safe from outside threats," I whisper. "I miss her so much that going into her room hurts."

"Take your time," Edam says. "I'm not going anywhere."

"You have work to do," I say.

"You're higher priority than all of that." He takes my hand in his and we stand together, in front of Mom's door for several minutes.

Finally, I'm calm enough to push the door open and walk through. The door to her records sanctum in the corner looms larger than I remember. It's larger than her closet, and the stainless steel door beckons me. I have what I need to enter, but I've been putting it off.

"Thank you Edam. I needed the support."

"Anytime, anywhere, against anyone," he says.

"But I have to do this alone." I walk across the room to the huge door.

"I'll be out here, making sure you aren't bothered."

"Thanks." I press my hand on the bio scanner and a panel emerges from the wall. I press Mom's staridium ring into it. Then I key in Mom's code. *Divinity*.

The locks tumble and then come to rest. I twist the huge four pronged wheel and open the door. I glance back at Edam, and he smiles at me. "You've got this."

More than seeing mother dead, or fighting and defeating my sister, or finding Mom's ring, walking into the records room feels so final. Mom will never come back. She will never train or teach or tutor me again. I blink as I enter the room. I'm prepared for it to be dark, windowless and lead lined. Mom told me about some of the precautions, but the lights that run up either side of the space are bright, harsh almost. Thousands and thousands of volumes of books and journals line the walls from the wood floors to the top of the ten foot ceiling.

I would have put this task off for weeks and weeks, but we have no real leads for Mom's killer. Zero. Which means my best hope for a clue is right here, in Mom's own records and letters and notes. With her funeral tomorrow, followed by my inauguration, I've got an excellent opportunity to confront many of those who were here for her birthday party. I need to know where to apply pressure.

I sit in her leather wing chair and open the journal sitting on the center of her desk. She records a surprisingly high level of detail about each day, but I spend a particular amount of time on her feelings, her plans, and her hopes. I stop reading periodically to close my eyes and imagine her face. My memories, combined with her notes, bring her to life in a way she hasn't been for me since she passed away. Then one passage catches my attention.

I suspect that I'm being poisoned.

I drop the book like it burned me. She knew. Of course she knew. But, why didn't she do anything about it? I force myself to pick it up again.

I can't be sure, of course. Job has run his standard blood panel on me recently and found nothing, but I feel. . . suboptimal. My appetite is declining along with my energy level. I've spent quite some time reading mother's, grandmother's and great-grandother's accounts of their last few years. Most of my symptoms are also symptoms of age, but I'm not yet nine-hundred. If I'm already aging, that doesn't spell good things for Alamecha's bloodline.

The next day is dated ten days prior to her death.

I'm not being poisoned after all. My fatigue, my appetite shifts and my body aches have an explanation. A happy one, in fact. Against all odds, something strange and wonderful has happened.

I'm pregnant.

I want to tell the father, but I don't know how he'll take it, and then I'll have to explain so many other things. I might be better off letting him assume it isn't his. I can't even quite bring myself to write his name. I'll examine my reticence about this later. But for now, I'm more optimistic than I've been for a long time.

It sounds terrible, but I'm most excited about this baby for the hope that it might heal things between Judica and Chancery. Their anger and inability to get along pains me deeper than any other wound of my long life. I would give almost anything to repair their relationship. A new Heir would free them both and clean up the fallout from my refusal to spare Chancery.

If it's a girl, I'm going to name her Sotiris, because she will be their salvation.

The next twenty pages have been torn out. I search for loose pages all over her desk and in drawers with no luck. Why would she tear out the rest? It had to be mother who did it, since she's the only one who had access to this room.

I don't find the missing sheets, but I stop in front of a framed papyrus scroll. The prophecy.

In time of great peril, when the lives of women and men shall fail, the Eldest shall survive certain death to unite the families. She comes in a time of blood and horror, in a world overrun with plague and warfare. She shall command the stone of the mountain, be it small or large. Its power shall destroy the vast hosts arrayed against it. With the might and power of God, the Eldest shall destroy all in her path and unite my children as one. Only through her blood can the stone be restored to the mountain. Together, with the strength of her strongest supporter, she shall open the Garden of Eden, that the miracle of God shall go unto all the Earth to save my children from utter destruction.

Utter destruction. I close my eyes. I want nothing to do with this. Why couldn't Judica have been born before me? I don't want to be the Eldest, and I definitely don't want to destroy anything in my path. But I fear I've already fulfilled the first prong. Or at least, everyone seemed to think that fighting Judica would lead to my certain death, and yet, here I am. Maybe the destruction was simply the bomb I stopped from hitting China. Wouldn't that be nice?

Somehow, I doubt it.

Or maybe this entire thing was some whacked out delusion that people fixated on wrongly. That would be nice. Perhaps my rule will be uneventful and peaceful. Of course, if it's not true, then my drastic, sweeping social and political changes might all fail. They might be a tremendous mistake, if I'm not the Eldest like Mom thought.

How old is this prophecy, exactly? Without thinking about it, I take the frame off the wall and carry it over to the desk.

Before I can set it down to look at it closer, something flutters to the ground from the back. A white envelope.

I lean down to pick it up, but my hand stops, hovering over the words scrawled across the front in my mom's hand.

Chancery Divinity Alamecha

If you liked that sample, grab Disillusioned today!

ACKNOWLEDGMENTS

First and foremost, my husband is AMAZING. He cheers, mourns, grumbles and shoves me forward in turn, whatever I need. He has the patience of a saint, and every time I wonder whether I'm a fraud, he reassures me I'm not.

My son Eli and my daughter Dora have been tireless fans, reading everything I write and getting excited long before these stories are even out. They make jokes about them and generally make me feel like they care. It helps me to feel like what I'm doing isn't a waste of time.

My mom (and dad!) have been unfailingly supportive. They will drop everything to lend a hand when life happens so I can meet deadlines and finish things up.

My editors, Peter and Mattie, are AMAZING. Thank you! I could not put out the product or the blurbs that I do without their help.

My cover artist Christian is just phenomenal. I mean, really. The covers for this series make me smile every time I see them.

And speaking of covers, my sister Linsey, just WOW. What a talented photographer. Of course in this instance, it helps that our model, Alyssa, is a KNOCKOUT. You have all worked your magic, and I truly appreciate it.

And to my friend Esther, who always lends an ear, support, friendship, thank you! To Tamie, Victorine, Shauna, Amy, and countless others, you guys keep me going when I am struggling. You are SO very appreciated.

And last but not least, my ARC team—I love you guys! You have grace in helping me spot those pernicious typos I missed. You give me feedback when I'm fragile and anxious, and most of all, you give of your time to help my books succeed. Thank you all!!

ABOUT THE AUTHOR

Bridget won her first writing contest in first grade with a story about a day in the life of a little spot of air. (Who says you need a good hook?)

She hasn't stopped writing (or talking) since then, although she was briefly derailed by her pursuit of a legal career. Ultimately, boring words, well, bored her. She quit her job to spend less time counting gobs of ill gotten gains, and more time writing stories.

She loves her husband and all five of her kids (most days). She has a yappy dog, two goofy horses, backyard chickens and two demanding cats. Every day is a battle between playing with kids, riding her horse Splash, and writing. If her publication speed has slowed down, you can blame the kids and the horse.

She makes cookies all the time, and thinks they should have their own food group. In a possibly misguided attempt at balancing the scales between overconsumption and exertion, she kickboxes every day. So if you don't like her kids, her cookies, or her books, maybe don't tell her in person.